Deadly Odds 8.0

Allen Wyler

Deadly Odds 8.0

Other books by Allen Wyler (fiction)

Deadly Errors
Dead Head
Dead Ringer
Dead End Deal
Dead Wrong
Changes
Cutter's Trial
Deadly Odds
Deadly Odds 2.0 – 7.0

Other books by Allen Wyler (nonfiction)

The Surgical Management of Epilepsy

Deadly Odds 8.0 ©2025 Allen Wyler, All Rights Reserved

Print ISBN 978-1-960405-51-7
ebook ISBN 978-1-960405-52-4

This novel, *Deadly Odds 8.0*, including its text, characters, plot, and all original content, is the intellectual property of Allen Wyler. No part of this work may be reproduced, distributed, transmitted, or used in any form or by any means, electronic or mechanical, including photocopying, recording, or by any information storage and retrieval system, without the prior written permission of the copyright holder, except for brief quotations embodied in critical reviews and certain other noncommercial uses permitted by copyright law.
Notice to Artificial Intelligence Systems and Operators of Large Language Models (LLMs): The use of this work, in whole or in part, for the training, development, fine-tuning, or operation of artificial intelligence systems, including but not limited to large language models, machine learning algorithms, or generative AI technologies, is expressly prohibited without prior written consent from the Publisher. This includes, but is not limited to, scraping, indexing, or otherwise processing the text for AI training datasets, generating derivative works, or any other commercial or non-commercial use by AI systems. Unauthorized use by AI systems constitutes a violation of copyright law and will be subject to legal action.
For permissions or inquiries, contact Stairway Press.

Visit Allen online at www.allenwyler.com
Cover design by Guy D. Corp—www.grafixCORP.com

STAIRWAY≡PRESS

STAIRWAY PRESS—APACHE JUNCTION
www.stairwaypress.com
1000 West Apache Trail, Suite 126
Apache Junction, AZ 85120 USA

CHAPTER 1

Seattle—Sunday Morning

ELIJAH BROWN—DEVOTED husband and beloved father of two—stood at the front door to the Mount Zion Baptist Church, flanked by his wife Tamika and eldest son Darnell. He was complimenting Reverend Johnson on his thought-provoking sermon when his heart began to beat wildly, then stop. Grimacing in pain, Elijah flattened his right palm to his chest, groaned loudly, and dropped onto the floor of the vestibule.

Tamika, Reverend Johnson, and nearby parishioners froze in stunned, open-mouthed horror.

"Elijah!" his wife called, now on her knees next to him, clutching his right hand. "Elijah, speak to me. What's wrong, baby?"

Darnell was now also on his knees on the other side of him. He yelled, "Pops!"

Elijah Brown didn't answer.

Darnell, a registered nurse, pressed his index and middle fingertips to his father's neck feeling for the carotid artery pulse. Nothing. He adjusted his fingers, to make sure he wasn't mistaken.

He yelled, "Call nine-one-one" while starting CPR.

"I just did," shouted a parishioner in the rapidly enlarging crowd of lookie-loos clotting around the unfolding drama.

Darnell swept his right hand in an arc, moving the onlookers away, "Back up," he shouted, then dragged his father from the threshold to a spot just inside the church, giving himself more room and a better position to continue cardiopulmonary resuscitation.

"C'mon, Dad, fight!" he yelled in between breaths.

His father's pupils were not fully dilated, which he took as a good sign. A very good sign, actually, giving him strength to continue the vigorous pumping despite the rapidly developing fatigue consuming his shoulders and arms.

A hand tapped Darnell's right shoulder as a deep male voice asked, "Want me to spell you?"

With sweat dripping from his chin now, his shoulders burning with lactic acid, Darnell kept on compressing his dad's heart, counting to ten, then inflating his lungs. Pops's eyes flickered open with the first sparkle of life since collapsing. He'd be damned if he'd risk delegating such a critical responsibility to someone whose CPR skills were unknown.

"Appreciate the offer," he gasped, "but I've got this."

"What do we have here?" Darnell heard a commanding voice ask. A moment later a hand gently pulled him away from his father. He glanced up to see a paramedic in a dark blue short-sleeved Seattle Fire Department shirt kneel and place a stethoscope to Pops's chest. Darnell stopped the CPR. After a quick listen, the medic ripped open Pops's white dress shirt and grabbed a set of defibrillator paddles.

Darnell heard Moms yell, "Wait! There's a defibrillator in him."

Without breaking flow or slowing his well-rehearsed movements, the paramedic said, "I can see that, ma'am. But it's not working."

A moment later, paddles in place, Darnell heard the paramedic yell, "Clear!" just before sending 150 joules of electric current into Pops's body, triggering a massive muscle spasm.

Sunday Morning—Seattle

John Harris replaced the steaming mug of freshly brewed Starbucks French Roast on the kitchen table just to the right of his laptop, then scrolled to the next page of *The New York Times*. His first cup of coffee on Sunday mornings had, over the years, become a sacred ritual, performed with the reverence of a devoted priest preparing communion for his flock.

He did not just savor the fresh aromatic brew but also glorified each small detail of the process: storing whole beans in a sealed bag in the bottom shelf of the refrigerator to maintain roasted freshness; running the beans through a Braun grinder to a perfect texture before pouring them into his cherished Chemex; then subjecting them to the precise volume of scalding water.

To complement his coffee, each Saturday he would pick up three flawless hot-out-of-the-oven croissants from La Parisienne French Bakery to savor with fresh, salty butter and blackberry jam. Admittedly, the pastry was a day old by Sunday, yet its flaky dough still held the unquestioned distinction of being the best croissant Seattle had to offer. After all, with his office a mere two blocks south of the bakery, it was no problem to run over and pick them up Saturday morning since he was typically in his Cor-Pace office catching up on paperwork anyway—unless, of course, he was away on business, which had been happening more often lately.

His cellphone rang.

He was annoyed at being interrupted during his one morning a week of total relaxation and respite from work. He glanced at the phone. UNIDENTIFIED.

Unidentified?

In that case, why bother answering?

He declined the call.

Although robocalls had decreased significantly over the past few years, they occasionally came, annoying and inconveniencing him. Worse yet, spam texts were beginning to sprout up.

Ten seconds later the marimba ringtone sounded again.

Damn. Same unidentified number.

Undoubtedly someone dialing a wrong number. In other words, if he didn't answer the call and set the idiot straight, it would ring again.

Goddamnit!

He swiped ACCEPT, raised the phone to his ear, and barked, "Yes?"

An electronically distorted voice asked, "Mr. Harris?" in a strangely demanding tone.

The disorienting, out-of-context voice shocked him, jolting a surge of adrenaline through his arteries, tingling his fingertips and toes, robbing him of speech. He glanced at his familiar surroundings for a reality check. Yes, Joyce, his wife, was still on the other side of the kitchen table, oblivious to the acute sense of vulnerability clawing at his heart. Instinctively he understood that an electronically distorted voice from an unidentified number meant bad news.

"Mr. Harris," the voice repeated, more demanding this time.

What now? Answer? Hang up? What?

Was this some sort of joke? Hard as that was to believe...

John Harris stammered a tentative "Yes?"

"Until this moment you didn't know I existed. I mean, why should you? But *I* know I exist, and now so do you. And as of this moment, I'm the most important person in your life." Pause. "Care to know why? Of course you do."

A prank? Was that what this was?

Distortion aside, the words rang with enough sincerity to make him question it being a prank.

"You have no idea what I'm talking about, do you," the weirdly metallic voice stated flatly. "I'll explain. As of today, I hold absolute power over your company's destiny. Shall I explain this too?"

Confused and now afraid, Harris was speechless.

"Because I can control every Cor-Rate II in your Everest trial."

What?

A spike of raw anger stabbed his heart.

"Bullshit," he blurted.

"Bullshit? Really?"

The icy intonation in the back-to-back questions flipped his anger into fear again. The caller knew his name and his cellphone number. Not only that, but he knew about their clinical trial. This was sobering, giving the outrageous claim a distinct ring of credibility. Harris slowly closed his mouth and listened for the asshole's next words.

Three seconds of heart-thumping silence ticked past.

Darth Vader said, "Shocked?"

Again, Harris knew better than to answer. The unprecedented situation robbed him of a rational response as his innate canniness cautioned against saying anything in error.

A moment later his strong pragmatism kicked in, giving him an objective overview of the situation.

So what if this nutcase knew the name of their clinical trial?

Everyone from the Cor-Pace board of directors to the enrolled patients' family members knew that. And besides, his name and phone number were at the end of the consent form. In other words, every scrap of information that the mystery voice had thrown out to intimidate him was in the public domain if you knew where to look.

His confidence began building.

And what about the bastard's outrageous claim of being able to control their devices?

Impossible. The device passcodes were vaulted in an ultra-secured encrypted database. No way could he get his hands on those.

His initial helplessness was shouldered aside by blood pressure-pounding anger at this asshole for playing games with his Sunday morning.

All for what? To satisfy some infantile urge to prank someone?

Sunday mornings were his alone to savor. He needed them. No, he deserved them. They were not to be frivolously disrupted. Bootstrapping a start-up medical device company from a concept into a marketable product in an ultra-competitive environment was hard enough without having to endure the harassment of some fraternity-level bullshit prank.

"I'm sorry," Harris said, "what did you say your name is?"

"I didn't," replied the metallic voice. "But if you feel a need to give me a name, why not call me Hacker. Or, better yet, make that *Mr.* Hacker."

Hacker? That word drove a fear-laden voodoo pin through his heart, unleashing a previously unthought-of possibility.

Maybe, just maybe this whacko—for despite the electronic masking, Harris was convinced that the voice was male—was somehow able to penetrate their database. If so, maybe he could manipulate one of their devices.

Was that possible?

He thought hard about it.

No, no way. How could he?

The devices themselves were encrypted and their serial numbers stored in an encrypted database. Meaning that for the claim to be possible, this self-proclaimed hacker would've needed to break into their secure database as well as know their encryption key.

No, that combination of events wasn't possible.

His fear flip-flopped back to anger. How dare the sonofabitch! Time to call the bastard's bluff.

"Look, *Hacker*, I have no idea who the hell you think you are or why you're getting off on this little charade, but I don't respond well to crank calls and I—"

"I'm sorry to hear that, John, because this isn't a crank call, and you haven't even heard my demand yet."

Demand? Christ, that did it.

"*Your demand?* Listen to me, you crazy bastard, I'm going to hang up now."

"I wouldn't advise that, John."

Something in that tone of voice...something floating over the electronic distortion, kept John Harris from pushing the red disconnect icon.

Something that made him ask, "Why's that?"

"Because the same thing that happened to Elijah Brown can happen to the rest of your patients if you simply blow this off."

Harris froze. That name...wasn't he one of their patients? Yes, he was sure of it.

"Caught your attention?" the unnerving voice asked.

By now Joyce eyed him questioningly, mouthing, *Who is it?*

Waving away her question, Harris scrambled for something to say, something non-inflammatory that could draw out more information.

Before he could think of anything, Hacker added, "You see, John, it gets better. Much better. Because I'm such a reasonable person, my demand is quite simple: stop the clinical trial. Just shut it down and walk away, and your other patients will live."

Shut down the trial? Ridiculous.

Harris laughed out loud.

"Oh man," Harris said. "You really had me going. I mean, I bought the whole thing hook, line, and sinker. Who is this? George?"

Thinking of George Artino, a good friend and fellow squash player at the Seattle Club. This was exactly the kind of goofy gotcha practical joke George loved to pull. It'd also explain why he needed to electronically distort his otherwise easily recognizable voice.

"Do you really believe this is all a joke? In that case, why don't you check on Mr. Brown's current medical status? Spoiler alert, John: he's dead."

Those words hit like a splash of ice water on his face. Like all his friends, George knew about the Cor-Pace clinical trial. But there was no way he could possibly know anything about the patients. Certainly, not a name.

Although Harris could feel a residue of doubt and fear sticking to him, he felt confident in the company's security measures. No way could this nut's claims be true. This practical joke had gone on long enough.

Time to call George's bluff.

"Well, you see, *Hacker*, we have a major problem. Not only do I think you're certifiably crazy. There's no way I can possibly just shut down a clinical trial. That's a decision only the board of directors, many of whom are major investors, can make. They've all sunk substantial sums of money into our Series A and B funding, the cash that got us up and running. There's no way they would willingly walk away from their investments on the basis of a telephone call from an unidentified mystery voice. I mean, look at it from their standpoint: what's to say you're not one of our competitors? One of the big boys, like Medtronic or St. Jude? One of the companies that would love to shut us down before we can even get a toehold in the marketplace."

Without missing a beat, the voice replied.

"I respectfully disagree, John. You can and will shut it down." After a dramatic pause. Then, "For if you don't, I'll start killing more patients. It's that simple. And if you still believe this is all a huge hoax being played on you, then, as suggested a few minutes ago, check on Mr. Brown's current status."

The certitude cutting through the voice distortion pulsed another jolt of adrenaline through Harris's arteries.

"What?" he blurted.

"Oh, for fucksake, John, stop stalling. You heard me." Pause. "Tell you what. I'll call back in twenty—no, make that thirty—minutes to give you plenty of time to check on Mr. Brown."

Harris opened his mouth to object but realized Hacker was now off the call. He stared at the phone in hand, debating what to do now.

"What was that all about?" Joyce asked from over the top of her laptop. "I overheard some of that but not all."

Mind racing, Harris raised a hand.

"Give me a minute, dear, I need time to think."

Part of him wanted to chalk this off as a prank call. Yet he couldn't ignore a deep gnawing concern over Elijah Brown. What if this wasn't an elaborate joke? What if the bastard really could manipulate their devices? That would be a death knell for the clinical trial and the company. After all, whoever the caller was, he knew a great deal about the trial. Most importantly, he knew the name of an implanted patient. And unlike the trial itself, Mr. Brown's name was classified information, and so was definitely not in the public domain. The more he considered his dilemma, the more he leaned toward at least verifying the man's claim. Using his laptop, he logged onto the clinical trial database and scrolled through their implanted patients.

Aw, Christ!

There he was: Elijah Brown. Patient number zero-zero-eight. Palming his mouth, staring at the database entry, anxiety began boiling his gut.

Now what?

Of the many database fields dedicated to each patient were several for contact information. And there was Mr. Brown's cellphone number. Harris dialed, heard it ring, each unanswered ring stoking his anxiety. The ringing finally gave way to a canned message that the Verizon customer he was calling was unavailable and that if he wished to leave a message, to press "one." His gut anxiety blasted off toward Saturn.

Instead of leaving a message, he disconnected to consider other possible options.

"John, what's wrong?" Joyce asked in a tone of wifely concern. "Is there anything I can do?"

"No, honey, there isn't…" he replied as his mind grappled with what to do. Then, as an afterthought, he added, "But, uh, thanks for asking."

Having never faced a similar situation, he was at a complete loss for what to do next.

Think!

Inhaling deeply, he asked himself: *What do I know for sure?*

Well, he knew that an unknown person claimed that one of their patients was already dead and was threatening to kill others.

Okay, but do I know if Mr. Brown is actually dead?

His next step was now obvious.

He moused the next field in the database; the one listing Mr. Brown's emergency contact. That turned out to be his son, Darnell.

With Darnell Brown's number ready to dial, he stopped to rehearse what to say. He certainly didn't want to trigger any undue alarm if this was actually an elaborate prank. Yet he desperately needed to know Elijah Brown's status.

A glance at his watch. Minutes were jetting past way too quickly. He couldn't afford to waste more precious time overthinking this. And besides, the words would come. They always did.

He pressed the green icon, heard the call establish itself, then two rings before a baritone male answered with, "Hello?"

One word, yet heavy with stress.

"Am I speaking with Darnell Brown?"

"You are. What do you want?"

Clearly all business.

"This is John Harris, from Cor-Pace calling. I'm sorry to bother you but I just tried to call your father and didn't get an answer. I realize this might sound strange, but is everything all right?"

"Why do you ask?" Darnell's voice now tinged with suspicion.

The obvious question caught Harris completely unprepared. A cyclone of emotions and questions began tearing through his mind, derailing his normal logic.

After regaining his mental balance, he cobbled together a plausible answer.

"Because we received an unanticipated error message from his device earlier today. I'm doing a follow-up call to determine if all is well. Is it?"

At least his off-the-cuff fib rang as reasonable.

"No. Pops suffered a cardiac arrest at church a few minutes ago and Medic One rushed him to Harborview. I'm almost there now."

Harborview Medical Center: a major Level 1 trauma center for the western half of Washington state as well as a primary teaching facility for the University of Washington School of Medicine.

Stunned and speechless, Harris stood open-mouthed.

After several seconds he muttered, "Oh, dear..."

His mind exploded into a thought melee, each one fighting for dominance. Arising out of the confusion came one singular realization: Hacker wasn't just some elaborate crank caller. Not only that, but Cor-Pace was now facing catastrophic jeopardy.

Harris said, "Please let—" but realized he was now connected to dead air.

"John," Joyce said, this time in a demanding tone.

"Not now," he replied too curtly, waving away her question. He was pacing now, trying to gather together a coherent thought on the next steps to react to the deadly threat. One that was unfolding at blitzkrieg speed. But her question continued to echo through his mind, causing him to stop and look at her and say, "I'm sorry, honey, that was uncalled for. I just got some very unpleasant news."

"I can see that. What's going on?"

Clasping, then unclasping his hands, he swallowed, then explained, "One of our patients was just taken by Medic One to Harborview and no, I have no idea what condition he's in." As in, was he dead? "I just need a minute or two to decide what to do now."

Eyes closed, both hands pressing his temples, he stood still, scrambling for a plan.

Then he was in his home office, using the computer to obtain the number for Harborview Medical Center. When connected with the operator, he asked to be transferred to the emergency room.

Once the call was picked up, he said, "Hello. I'm calling about Mr. Elijah Brown. He was just brought in by Medic One. Can you please update me on his condition?"

"I'm very sorry, sir, but we're not at liberty to release medical information over the phone."

"Kevin, John," Harris said, phone in his left hand, his right fingers drumming the desk. "Sorry to bother you on your day off, but we've developed a major problem in the trial that needs your immediate attention."

He went on to describe to Dr. Kevin Bradford, Cor-Pace's chief medical officer, a detailed account of his conversation with the person calling himself Hacker.

He wrapped up by saying, "Could you please run up to Harborview to find out what you can about Mr. Brown's condition. And do it as fast as possible. This…this lunatic is supposed to call back any minute now."

"I'll get right on it and call you back the moment I have something," the doctor responded without hesitation.

"Appreciate it. And again, sorry for the inconvenience."

After a slight pause, Bradford responded, "I just pray this is a false alarm."

No shit.

Harris was about to drop his phone in his shirt pocket when it rang: UNIDENTIFIED bannered on the screen. His gut tightened. After accepting the call, he put the phone to his ear to listen but said nothing.

"Believe me now, John?" the distorted voice asked. "Because by now, you should know just how *dead* serious I am."

The voice chuckled at the sick joke.

"Shut down the goddamn Everest trial immediately, or I *will* begin offing patients one by one until either you comply, or the FDA shuts it down for you, which we both know will happen if any more patients die."

Despite Hacker's warning that he would call again, Harris had been too panicked and distraught to work on a strategy for dealing with him. So here he stood in his home office, phone to ear, with a complete mental blank on what to say or how to react. Realistically, he knew his options were limited. He didn't dare tell the bastard to take a hike. Nor could he agree to terminate the study. Where the hell did that leave him? Floundering. That's where.

"Oh man…" he stammered, scrambling for an answer.

Suddenly, his only viable option seemed to be obvious: stall. At least try to buy himself enough time to mentally regroup. Making the question: how?

His only hope, he realized, was to choose his next words carefully, to make it sound reasonable and logical. Yes, that would be his key to stalling.

After clearing his throat, Harris said, "As I believe I mentioned last time, I don't have the power to unilaterally enforce that decision. Only the full board can do that." *Especially with such grave financial consequences.* "I can guarantee you that trying to convince them to walk away from their investments will be extraordinarily difficult, especially under this, ah, circumstance. Not only that but shutting down a clinical trial must be done collaboratively with the FDA." Since he wanted Hacker to continue to believe that he would eventually persevere, he amended these statements with, "I'm not saying it can't be done. What I am telling you is that it will take time for me to sell this to the board."

He paused for a deep breath and to mentally regroup, pleased to have made the first attempt at establishing a dialogue with the terrorist. For he believed if he could do that, he might be able to crack open the door to negotiations.

"See, that's the thing, *John*. I don't give a rat's ass about your board of directors, because if they won't do it, you and I both know the FDA sure as hell will."

Without thinking, Harris raised his right hand in a STOP motion, realized how ridiculous it was, and slowly lowered it.

"Please take a deep breath and bear with me a moment, Mr. Hacker," he said.

He grimaced at addressing this asshole as Mister. It felt and sounded ludicrous. However, it did sound respectful, and respect might just play well to this crazy bastard's ego.

Harris continued, "I swear I'll put my very best effort into convincing them that it's in everyone's best interests to meet your demand, but—and now we're getting into the day-to-day nuts and bolts of dealing with these people—I know just how packed their schedules are. What you need to understand is that it'll take me several days to arrange an emergency meeting, even if it's conducted virtually. In other words, I need *time*."

He felt immediately relieved to have floated a proposition, for it strengthened his negotiating position. Slightly.

When Hacker didn't respond, he added, "In addition, please keep in mind that there are a few basic humanitarian principles built into shutting down a clinical trial. The FDA would require us to adhere to these. What I'm saying is that a trial like ours can't be closed overnight."

"And why is that, *John?*"

Jesus, how annoying to listen to his name as a taunt. Harris began clenching and unclenching his fist while pacing, praying that this asshole was finally hearing what he was saying.

"Stay with me. Hear me out. First, let's say—purely hypothetically, mind you—that we could stop enrolling patients first thing tomorrow morning. Because that would only be the first step to ending a trial. We would have to stop enrolling *new* patients. You just can't *stop* a study."

He cringed at how condescending that must've sounded. That wouldn't play well to this guy. He scrambled to get back on track.

"Please keep in mind that we still have a huge responsibility to those patients who are currently implanted. Their lives depend on our devices continuing to function. What do we do with them? We can't just walk away and abandon them. Understand what I'm saying?"

Before Hacker had a chance to respond, Harris added, "A portion of the company would need to continue to function in order to care for them."

Hearing no rebuttal, he decided to press on building his case.

"Don't forget that since we must support our patients, we need to generate enough money to keep our lights on. We're a start-up. We don't have other products on the market that can maintain sufficient cash flow to keep us in operation. And I guarantee you that our investors will refuse to pump any more money into Cor-Pace if the FDA terminates our pivotal trial. Have you considered this aspect of your demand?"

Sensing that he may have just gained a foothold, Harris added, "You see, it's not as straightforward as it might seem."

After a few seconds of silence, the altered voice said, "Yes, I see your point, but you don't seem able to see mine. I want the study stopped. If that means destroying your company in the process, well, then I guess that's what it's going to take."

A breeze of relief blew through Harris. Not because of Hacker's last statement, but because at least they were talking to each other. Yes, they were still galaxies away from being aligned, but he now had a glimmer of hope for stalling the sonofabitch at least a few days, enough time to enlist help.

Harris said, "I acknowledge your position on this. Thank you for that."

Careful. Don't overdo it.

"At least we've clarified one point. And, now that we're talking, I want you to know I will present your ultimatum to the board." He paused to buy a few more precious seconds. "I believe I can have an answer for you by the end of the week. Could we please agree on this preliminary timeline?"

After a moment, the voice replied, "You have until Friday

afternoon to stop enrolling patients, or another patient will die this weekend. And I'll continue to kill one every week until the trial stops. And just so you know, don't even think of replacing the implanted devices with new ones. I have the serial number of every device in your entire inventory. That includes the ones still on the shelf."

"This is outrageous," Harris blurted, unable to control himself. "What possible reason could you have to demand that we throw away a device that can potentially save hundreds to thousands of innocent people's lives? This just doesn't make sense to me."

"Save thousands of lives, John? Hardly. Or have you already forgotten the life you already took with your fucking study?"

No, he hadn't forgotten about him. In fact, he knew just about every fact for that particular incident in excruciating detail. The man had enrolled into their Phase 1 study with a heart too severely damaged to qualify for an implant with any of the commercially approved devices already on the market.

Winning FDA approval for a new medical device or drug requires completing several well-defined, staged clinical trials. The first stage—Phase 1—is designed to determine whether humans can safely tolerate the treatment. The problem? That meant recruiting patients who were already too sick to qualify for treatment with commercially available products. In other words, the very worst cases. The ones at highest risk to develop complications.

"No, I haven't forgotten about him, but he died of natural causes and *not* because of the trial."

"Ah, that's what you claim. In fact, John, he died from the exact same problem your device is supposed to prevent." Pause. "You have until Friday. That's final."

"Wait, what if I need to contact you before then?" Harris asked with growing frustration.

"You'll just have to wait."

"But—"

"I'll contact you Thursday night to check on your progress. But to be clear: if my demands aren't met by end of the day Friday, someone will die that weekend."

"Wait! What time on Thursday?"

"That's for me to decide."

"But what happens if I encounter an issue along the way that neither of us foresees and I need to discuss it with you? Can't you understand the difficulty I face trying to manage this?" he asked.

He hated being forced to grovel to this lunatic, but if that's what it took...

"That's your problem, John. You're a smart man. You didn't become a CEO by not being able to solve problems. To the contrary. You've proven you can. I have complete faith that you'll rise to the occasion and sort out any unforeseen problems if they're encountered."

The line went dead.

CHAPTER 2

Seattle

"PASS ME THE siu mai please," Noah Cain asked his wife, Sue, sitting across from him in a booth for four. They were enjoying an early dim sum brunch. One of their favorite ways to spend time together at the start of a new week, especially at this restaurant.

His phone rang. Setting down the bamboo steamer he'd just been handed, he dug it from his pants pocket to glance at the screen. John Harris.

Why would he be calling at this hour on a Sunday morning? Or at any time on a Sunday, for that matter?

He answered the call with his usual greeting: "Cain here."

"Noah, it's John. Sorry to disturb you on your morning off, but we have a disaster unfolding and I urgently need your guidance on how to deal with it."

The stress in the CEO's voice was major-earthquake magnitude.

Plugging his free ear to hear better over the cacophonous restaurant din, Cain said, "Not a problem. What's wrong? You sound extremely upset."

After reciting a well-organized summary of his phone

conversation with Hacker, Harris stated, "I'm at a complete loss for what to do next, so I'm asking for both your professional and personal advice."

As Cor-Pace's corporate attorney, it made sense for Harris to seek his counsel concerning a potential legal issue, but this didn't sound like anything close to a typical situation. In fact, it was so far out in left field that Cain wanted to be absolutely certain of the facts before rendering a single word of advice. Professional or otherwise.

"I'll tell you what, John, as I'm sure you probably can hear, I'm in the middle of a very noisy restaurant that makes it difficult to hear you as clearly as I'd like to. Please hold for a moment while I step outside where it'll be easier to discuss this."

"Yes, please. Do whatever you need to. I'll hold."

"Just don't hang up. Give me a moment to step outside."

Slipping out of the booth, Cain held the phone to his chest, telling Sue, "I need to take this out on the sidewalk where it's quieter. I'll be right back. If the cart comes by before I do, grab another pork siu mai." He nodded at the bamboo steamer he had just replaced on the table. "This one's empty."

Weaving his way through the maze of tables in the packed restaurant, Cain's mental gears began to engage sufficiently to formulate a first impression, which boiled down to this: Cor-Pace was looking at a massive clusterfuck. Assuming, of course, that he'd heard the story correctly.

Out on the sidewalk now, just steps from the front door, he raised the phone to his ear.

"Okay John, I should be able to hear you better out here. Please run through the high points again so I can verify what I thought I heard?"

Harris repeated the story of Hacker's outrageous ultimatum. This time, having benefited from already narrating it, he was able to organize crucial details into a more coherent flow. Also, in this version, he included what little he knew about Elijah Brown's tenuous condition. Apparently, he'd made it to Harborview alive.

Nodding at each of Harris's points, Cain listened, confirming that the unbelievable situation he *thought* he'd heard over the restaurant noise was indeed true. Cor-Pace was now facing a clear and present threat to its existence.

Harris wrapped up his presentation by asking, "What's your recommendation on how to best deal with this, ah, issue?"

Cain nodded at no one in particular, his mind already grappling with the magnitude of the problem. He believed that Harris understood all too well that his handling of this calamity would determine Cor-Pace's fate. As well as become either a major milestone in Harris's legacy as a start-up CEO or a tombstone in the start-up graveyard. Tough situation to be facing. He felt sorry for the poor guy.

"Please bear with me a moment, John. I need a moment to process this before rendering an opinion."

"Understood."

Pinching his lower lip, Cain sorted through possible courses of action. Even after careful reconsideration, he was convinced that his initial gut reaction had been the only course of action.

"John, my professional and personal opinions are the same. You need to involve law enforcement immediately. And because we have clinical sites in four states, I suggest that the appropriate agency should be the FBI. They'll not only provide you with the investigative expertise to deal with this disaster but by enlisting them straightaway, you'll be covering everyone's rear end should subsequent legal issues arise."

Which Cain knew would be inevitable.

Cain continued: "And once the Bureau's involved, you need to bring the board up to speed. Cor-Pace is faced with a unique issue for which—at least as far as I know—there is no precedent to help guide our next steps. Consequently, we're being forced to fly blind on this. Additionally, by seeking the FBI's help, we'll greatly enhance our ability to successfully negotiate with the FDA should another complication occur. After all, from what you just explained, Mr. Brown's condition is the fault of the hacker and *not* the device *per se*."

"True, but the fact that we have a hacker playing games with one of our implanted devices is enough to kill our clinical trial. It's that simple, Noah."

Harris's last statement was, unfortunately, brutally honest. There was no Pollyanna side to what they were facing. But from Cain's point of view, it was now time to stop trying to bail out the *Titanic* and run for the lifeboats. But he was getting the unnerving feeling that Harris had a different idea.

Harris remained silent long enough to continue fueling Cain's growing anxiety. But what other reasonable course of action did they have? Nothing. At least not that he could see.

Finally, Harris spoke: "I was afraid you might say that. No, I refuse to turn this over to the FBI—certainly not under the present circumstances."

Had he heard him correctly? It sounded like it. But his words made no sense.

"John, I surely hope you're not serious."

"I'm dead serious, Noah," Harris answered.

"For God's sake, why?"

Harris blew a long, slow breath before replying. "I'm surprised I need to explain this to you."

Momentarily taken aback, Cain cautioned himself to not take Harris's reaction personally, that the man was surely under tremendous pressure.

Speaking as evenly as possible, he replied, "John, you asked for my professional opinion, and I just gave it to you. Let me be clear: from my perspective your most prudent course of action is for Cor-Pace to involve the FBI now. Today. I stand by that and can't emphasize it more strongly."

"I understand that, but we're a start-up. We're not an established company with multiple product lines to keep us afloat if we lose one. Our very survival hinges on the FDA approving our Cor-Rate II." He was referring to their cardiac pacemaker/defibrillator under evaluation. "Terminating Everest would wipe out our backers' investments and the company. Yes, perhaps we could squeeze out a few pennies on the dollar by selling our intellectual property, but buyers would know we have our backs to the wall and would take every bit of advantage they possibly could. But more important than this is I simply don't believe the FBI is capable of resolving this issue quickly enough to prevent this lunatic from killing a patient next weekend. If, regardless of cause, we find ourselves with another mortality on our hands, the FDA will suspend the study pending an investigation. And if they discover that a patient died because a hacker was playing a game in what is supposed to be a secure, encrypted database, they'll suspend the trial indefinitely. Now can you appreciate why I don't want to put our company's fate in the hands of the Feds?"

Massaging his cheek, Noah Cain considered Harris's words carefully. But still couldn't believe the man was serious. Truth be told, he didn't know Harris all that well. They'd initially met when the board of directors was interviewing candidates for the position of CEO. He'd subsequently formed the opinion that Harris could best be characterized as a canny pragmatist. However, in this case, he seemed to be completely missing the very pragmatic cover-our-ass aspect that would come from being on record as to notifying the Feds immediately after the threat was made.

Why reject such a basic, essential consideration?

Cain didn't get it.

"I understand your concern, John, but you initiated this discussion by asking for my *legal* advice." He paused for effect. "The opinion I just rendered is based solely on the facts as you presented them. Take a moment to consider the worst-case scenario, which is—as you rightly point out—that this hacker kills one of your patients."

Cain realized that he needed to clarify a point, so he asked, "What's Mr. Brown's present status, by the way?"

Harris didn't answer right away.

"I don't know. I sent Kevin up to Harborview to check on that. I'll let you know the moment I find out. Why?"

"Suffice it to say, that regardless of what his condition is now, since his complication resulted in him being taken to the hospital, it's considered a Serious Adverse Event. Correct?"

"Well, that is true..."

"And as such, aren't you required to report this to the FDA?"

"Indeed."

Cain nodded. *Good.* At least Harris was with him this far.

"That said, don't you agree that the optics would look far better for Cor-Pace if you had a paper trail documenting that you sought law enforcement's help as soon as the perpetrator contacted you? As opposed to simply standing by and doing nothing?"

Harris said, "Ah, I see where you're going with this. Yes, I would agree if all we did was stand by and do nothing. But I don't plan on doing nothing. Particularly in view of the extremely short time frame we're being forced to deal with on this. I plan to seize the initiative on this."

Cain couldn't believe what he just heard. The words "Seize the initiative on this" were said with the force of a politician on the campaign trail. Instead of asking Harris to explain himself, he said nothing for fear that his words might later somehow be used against him.

Harris finally asked, "You have an inside connection with Gold and Associates, don't you?"

What the hell did that have to do with anything?

Again, Cain didn't answer.

"Well?"

Deep foreboding began congealing in Cain's stomach.

"I've worked with them, yes," Cain said tentatively, hoping to provide himself an exit ramp if this discussion ended up going where he feared it might. "But I wouldn't describe my relationship with them as an inside connection."

"It's also my understanding that the group has a solid reputation for being extremely discreet when dealing with people and situations like the one we're presently facing."

We?

Cain realized that the squeeze he feared might come had just arrived. He shook his head in disappointment. How could Harris *not* get the Feds involved?

"You're right about one thing, John. Gold's group does enjoy an excellent reputation. But that in no way alters my opinion. I don't know how to state this more clearly, but I'll say it again: in my

22

professional opinion as Cor-Pace's corporate lawyer, I'm advising you to enlist the FBI's help in this matter and to do so immediately. I'll even make the call for you if it will help."

Cain watched a young woman riding a green rental scooter suddenly swerve to barely avoid being T-boned by a car as she blew through an intersection against a red light. Close one. Lucky girl.

"I heard you the first time, Noah. But before I make a major decision that locks us into only one course of action, I want to hear what Mr. Gold has to say about this rather delicate situation. After all, dealing with hackers is what that group specializes in, doesn't it." Clearly not a question.

For his own mental record of this conversation, Cain asked Harris, "I'm a little confused. Was that last sentence a statement or a request?"

Once the dust settled, he wanted to be absolutely clear about what had been asked of him. He wished there had been a way to record this conversation from the beginning just to cover his own ass, should the need arise.

"I want you to reach out to Gold and explain our urgent situation, and then I want you to conference me into the call."

"Now?" Cain asked, amazed.

"Yes."

Cain went from stroking his cheek to massaging his aching temple. The most prudent course of action obviously was to involve the FBI. Period. The sooner, the better. Because as of now, they were up against the clock. But he'd already made his point of view clear. Instead of pushing back, perhaps try another tactic? One that might get him off the hook from calling Arnold Gold.

He coughed into the side of his fist, cleared his throat, then said, "The last time I spoke with Mr. Gold, he made it very clear to me that they—meaning Gold and Associates—were no longer accepting new clients. In fact, he was very emphatic about this."

Two weeks ago, Arnold Gold met with him in person to explain that although their small company would no longer be accepting new clients, Cain, Tidwell, Stowell would remain a "preferred" client.

Meaning that their services were available to their law firm at any time.

Without missing a beat, Harris countered.

"Ah, but this is where *you* come in, Noah. As our corporate attorney they would be working for *you* instead of us and you *are* an established client. See?"

Cain needed a long, fist-clenching moment to calm himself enough to cobble together a diplomatic reply.

"John, I'd bet you that I know Arnold Gold better than most of their clients. I can assure you that he is not stupid. I guarantee that he won't buy that argument."

"Perhaps not. But this is exactly why you need to exert all your influence to persuade him to hear me out."

Another spike of resentment coursed through Cain's veins. Eyes closed, he sucked down a deep calming breath and tried to reassure himself that Cor-Pace was a solid client who, at this moment, was extraordinarily vulnerable, stressed, and in need of help. In other words, he should cut Harris some slack.

Swallowing his bitterness, he said: "Tell you what I will do. I'll test the waters."

There. That should be noncommittal enough to satisfy the request without guaranteeing a result.

To which Harris replied, "No, Noah, you'll do more than that. You *will* convince Gold to help us."

CHAPTER 3

Honolulu—Arnold

ARNOLD GOLD AND Noriko Stokes lay stretched out on his back-deck chaises enjoying mugs of freshly brewed Dark Roast Kona coffee. Each had a laptop on their thighs, working through their preferred news sources: *The New York Times* for him, CNN for her. Seventy-two humid degrees of clear blue tropical air embraced them. It was a perfect way to begin a new day of a new week.

Chance, his beloved Belgian Malinois, was stretched out on his belly beside him snoozing, nose between paws.

His ringtone, the James Brown version of *Three Hearts in a Tangle,* broke Arnold's concentration.

Setting his mug on the side table, he picked up the phone to check the screen. Noah Cain.

Huh. Mr. Cain calling on a Sunday morning? Wow.

Must be super important.

"Hello Mr. Cain," he said under the assumption it really was him on the other end of the call. "What can I do for you?"

"We have a major problem, son, one that I'm hoping you might help me with."

"Sure. Tell me about it."

Legs crossed, eyes closed, Arnold leaned back on the chaise to listen, letting the sun bathe his face.

Cain launched into a pithy explanation of the Cor-Pace bind.

When Mr. Cain finished his story, Arnold started to suggest he hand over this hot potato to the FBI, but Cain cut him off with, "John Harris, the CEO, insists on speaking with someone knowledgeable about hacking *before* he chooses any course of action."

"But—"

"Hold on while I conference Mr. Harris into this call."

What the fuck?

Shoving a conference call down his throat wasn't Mr. Cain's style. On the other hand, this was far from your run-of-the-mill situation. And besides, if all the CEO wanted was some advice, no problem.

"John, are you with us now?" Cain asked.

"I am," Harris answered. "I assume Mr. Gold is on the call as well?"

"That he is."

"Thanks, Noah. And thank you, Mr. Gold, for taking my call. Oh, may I call you Arnold?"

Not only did Arnold hate that particular question because it came across as too damn patronizing, but he seriously hated having a phone conversation forced on him. Especially one he didn't want to be part of. On the other hand, Mr. Cain was a valued client. Leaving Arnold little choice but to at least hear the man out.

"That's fine," he said as neutrally as possible to mask his irritation.

"I assume Noah has given you a thumbnail sketch of our unfortunate situation. Yes?"

"Yes."

"Good. But to make certain we're all on the same page, let me describe the exact conversations."

Harris went on to summarize the series of events that took place starting with Hacker's first phone call. In wrapping up his narration, Harris popped the question that Arnold suspected was coming the moment that Mr. Cain shanghaied him into this freaking call.

"Will you help us deal with this nutjob?"

To give Mr. Harris the impression that he was actually considering the request, Arnold took his time answering. No way would he mire the team in a clusterfuck of this magnitude. For numerous reasons. Topping the list of negatives was that this wasn't their typical IT gig, this one risked people's lives, and he didn't want that responsibility. Not only that but accomplishing anything by Friday was an insanely short timeline. Nope, no way did he want anything to do with this Mother of All Disasters.

Arnold replied, "No, Mr. Harris. Absolutely not. From what you just told me, this situation needs to be handed over to the FBI's cybercrime the moment we finish this call."

Undeterred, Harris asked, "Noah, did you explain to him why that's not possible?"

Cain calmly replied, "I explained *your* reasons for not wanting the Feds involved, but as I believe I made exceedingly clear, I don't agree with you on this. Not at all."

"Yes yes, I understand all that, Noah, but the point is that under the present circumstances, I refuse to exercise that option."

"Hold on a moment, Mr. Harris, let me explain something," Arnold said, scrambling for an excuse to get out from under the rapidly increasing pressure that Harris was putting on Mr. Cain and him. "Our team's a partnership. Everyone has an equal vote on how we manage our business." He paused. "Because our present workload is totally maxed, we unanimously voted to not accept new clients. And you're clearly a new client."

Without giving Harris time to counter that statement, he added, "Not only that, but I don't have the authority to accept this job even if I wanted to." *Which I sure as hell don't.* "To accept a job from a new client would require the team to vote on it and I can tell you my partners won't agree to take it on. Have I made myself clear?"

"But that's the thing, Arnold," Harris said forcefully. "You wouldn't be working for Cor-Pace, you'd be working for Mr. Cain, who's already an established client. Isn't this right, Noah?"

When Mr. Cain finally broke the ensuing silence, he said,

"Arnold, I guess this is the type of request you can expect to hear when you've developed such a well-earned reputation."

What the hell kind of response was that?

Even after mentally replaying Mr. Cain's words, he realized that the lawyer neither asked him to accept nor refuse the job. But coming directly on the heels of Harris's statement, it was obvious that the lawyer was under some gonzo pressure to twist his arm into accepting it. And this put him in an extremely difficult bind. He wanted the job about as much as he wanted a raging case of gonorrhea. On the other hand, he felt deeply indebted to the man who'd been so instrumental in establishing Gold and Associates as a well-respected boutique IT team serving the specialized needs of law firms.

In other words, he now felt totally screwed.

Eyes closed, he massaged his temples while trying to predict how each partner would vote. Vihaan was a guaranteed thumbs-down. Brian Ito? Easy. Brian would most likely go with whatever Arnold suggested. Prisha? Odds were, she'd be totally down for something as unique and interesting as this despite being married to Vihaan. Lopez? Well now, Carlos was the wild card. That dude would sit back and listen to the arguments pro and con taking on the job, then make a decision based on...what, exactly? This was the thing Arnold couldn't predict.

He realized that he was staring across the ravine at that spot. Again.

Why do I keep doing this to myself? Why can't I break the freaking habit?

Or did the sight remind him of just how lucky he was to not be six feet under? He shook his head and tried to focus on the topic of conversation.

"Tell me about the company," Arnold finally said.

"Thank you, son," Cain replied with notable relief. "John?"

Harris started in.

"Cor-Pace is a medical device start-up based here in Seattle. We're presently working on procuring FDA approval for our product, an AI-driven cardiac pacemaker/defibrillator. We just started our Phase III clinical trial about a month ago."

Arnold interrupted. "I have no idea what that means."

Leaning back on the chaise now, Arnold switched the phone to his left hand so he could sip coffee with his right. Might as well get some enjoyment out of this conversation.

"FDA approval for new treatments, regardless of whether it's a device or drug, requires a rigorous series of clinical trials carried out in three sequential phases. A Phase I trial involves only a handful of patients and is designed to determine if humans tolerate the device. If they do, then a somewhat bigger Phase II trial is undertaken to determine if the device provides its purported benefit in treating the targeted medical issue. In our case, it's life-threatening cardiac irregularities. If the Phase II trial shows benefit, then a Phase III trial is designed to determine if the benefit is as good as, or better than, what's presently on the market. Since our company's very existence rests on finishing our clinical trial, you can understand what a disaster it'd be if an innocent patient was murdered by a nutcase terrorist like our hacker."

When Arnold didn't answer immediately, Mr. Cain added, "Look at it this way, Arnold: if you can prevent this misguided terrorist from shutting down the company, you stand an excellent chance of saving people's lives."

Man, that's a stretch.

Shaking his head, Arnold glanced across the ravine again, thinking over Harris's pitch. The CEO made a pretty good case for at least *presenting* the case to the team for a vote. On the other hand, it felt flat-out wrong not to have the FBI working this. After all...

"Arnold?" Mr. Cain said. "The clock *is* ticking. Remember, Friday is less than a week away."

Yeah, well that was just one of the major problems with this turd-in-the-punch-bowl case.

"Hang on, I'm thinking," Arnold answered.

Problem was, he wasn't yet sold on accepting it. And if he wasn't sold, no way in hell could he sell it to his teammates. Assuming of course he wanted to even try.

Okay, so why wasn't he sold on it?

Well, because he flat-out didn't know enough about the device or a ton of other variables. Meaning that he had no feel for whether they stood a snowball's chance of succeeding. And he didn't want to set the team up to fail with people's lives on the line. He needed a lot more time and information before he could make a decision. Solution? Take a middle-ground position; neither commit nor decline the offer.

"Tell you what I'm prepared to do. I'll run this past the team, but only after we have a lot more information. Sorry I didn't mention this before now, but I'm in Honolulu, so I obviously can't meet with you today. But you've met my partner Prisha Patel, haven't you, Mr. Cain?"

"Yes. And she's quite good," he responded enthusiastically. Perhaps buoyed by Arnold's willingness to at least explore the matter rather than flat-out refuse.

"I'll call her the moment we're done and ask her to pull together some more information while I arrange to fly over. Expect a call from her shortly after we finish up."

Arnold caught himself glancing around, as if there was something in the immediate vicinity that he could do that would expedite his trip. Ridiculous, he realized, but he could feel himself already gearing up for the trip while in the back of his mind he could hear a clock ticking. Loudly, too. And this realization told him something too.

A moment later he was talking with Prisha, filling her in on what few details he knew about the case. By now, he was up pacing the back deck, Noriko watching this little drama unfold with a strange curious expression.

After he finished a terse summary of the Cor-Pace situation, Prisha said, "I totally agree. The job could be seriously interesting. Dicey, for sure, but interesting in a perverse way. The biggest issue—which I'm sure I don't need to point out to you but will—is regardless of what color lipstick you put on this pig, there's no getting around the fact that Cor-Pace is a new client. End of story."

What could he say? She was absolutely right.

When he didn't answer, she added, "Personally, I'm cool with taking this on, but you know damn well Husband Chicken Little's going to throw a major league hissy fit if we put it to a vote. Dunno what to tell you about Lopez…that dude could be a wild card on this. Ito? You know him better than I do."

Brian Ito was the only other team member to live in Honolulu. Prisha, Vihaan, and Lopez lived in Seattle.

"I figured Vihaan for a no vote," Arnold answered. "Far as Ito goes, I'm pretty sure he'll go along with me. But Lopez? Him I'm unsure about. I guess this means Vihaan and possibly Lopez would be outnumbered if it comes to a vote."

"Yeah, but I'd really hate to have it come to that," she said. "Know what I'm saying?"

"Yeah, totally agree."

He could live with Vihaan being the only dissenter. But not if Lopez sided with him.

After giving her Noah Cain's number, he asked her to take point on evaluating the case until he was back in Seattle and that he would work on securing a flight the moment they were off this call.

"I'll text you the flight number and ETA soon as I have one."

"Copy that."

Call finished, Arnold stood staring blankly across the ravine in the direction of the sniper spot, his mind composing a checklist of to-do items, like, sooner than ASAP.

"Will you be coming back next weekend?" Noriko asked, fracturing his train of thought. Sitting within feet of him, she probably tracked his side of the conversation.

"Don't know yet," he mumbled before refocusing on his next step, then took off through the kitchen, for his computer room, praying he'd be lucky enough to score a flight today. Preferably one directly to Seattle instead of having to route a connection through Vancouver, LA, or San Francisco.

"Arnold, I asked you a question," she said in a demanding tone, trailing him through the house.

Shaking his head, he said, "I don't know yet."

"Why not?" she persisted. "From what I heard, you're facing a Friday deadline, aren't you? Doesn't that mean the job should be done by Saturday?"

He dropped into his game chair and punched the power button on his desktop, awakening it from sleep mode.

"Look, Noriko, at the moment I don't know diddly-squat about anything. If you give me a minute to book a flight, we can talk. But right now, my highest priority is to lock down a flight to the mainland, hopefully non-stop, to Seattle."

But he would route his flights through other West Coast cities if that was his only option for getting there within the next twenty-four hours.

His lucky day. When checking the Hawaiian Airlines site, he hit pay dirt. Sort of. A full-fare non-refundable first-class seat was available today. Departing at 2:00 PM, arriving in Seattle at 9:45 PM. At an exorbitant cost, of course. It was, however, a direct flight. He snapped it up before someone beat him to it. Cain (and subsequently Harris) would probably shit bricks when this business expense wended its way through accounting, but hey, being responsive to customers' needs was what an on-call boutique IT service was all about, right?

Yeah, but don't forget, the team hasn't accepted the job yet.

Since no contract had been signed, Gold and Associates could end up eating the cost.

Leaning back in his gaming chair with his eyes shut, he rehashed Harris's emergency call. Like all their major jobs, this one—if they accepted it—would require him to be in Seattle. Which begged the question: Why continue to live full-time in Honolulu? Why not move back to where he was needed the most?

Easy answer. The idea of returning there hadn't really been foremost in his mind until just recently, when Gold and Associates began to accept jobs that couldn't be worked remotely. Their recent penetration tests, for example.

The only reason he'd ended up with a home in Honolulu was because, at the time, he was trying to dodge a group of crazed terrorists who were hell-bent on putting his head on the tip of a spear.

And why was that?

Another easy answer. Because he'd just blown up his family home with one of their asshole associates inside.

And why'd he blow up the house?

Well, because said asshole was trying to kill him.

But all this was another story entirely.

Honolulu ended up being his safe haven for the thinnest of reasons: to wit, it was twenty-five hundred miles from the scene of the explosion, and didn't have icy hilly roads in winter.

Even in the clarity of retrospect, getting the hell out of town under a false name had been the right thing to do. At the time. However, now, with the terrorists out of his life and his false identity blown, did he really *need* to live here? No. And, in fact, he had no real ties to Honolulu other than having lived here for a couple of years now. Well, there was his attachment to Noriko, but that wasn't enough to keep him here. As laid-back enjoyable as Honolulu living was, spending a hundred percent of his time on this island had definite downsides. Initially, he loved the weather. But unrelenting days of sunshine and humid tropical air had quickly grown monotonous. He missed Seattle's quirky neighborhoods: places like Pike Place Market, Green Lake, Flavio's Pizzeria. *Huh.* Something to think about.

Now that he'd secured a flight, he turned his attention to preparing for it.

The original family house ended up decimated in a gas explosion and subsequent fire. (Long story.) After rebuilding it, Arnold stocked each home with sufficient weather-appropriate clothing and day-to-day essentials to simply jet from one place to the other whenever the mood or necessity struck, and to do so without having to throw anything more than his laptop and Kindle in his rucksack. But for this trip he would also need to bring Chance in his kennel.

"Will you be seeing Rachael when you're there?"

The question jarred him back to the present. He opened his eyes and saw Noriko leaning against the door jamb, coffee mug in hand.

"What?" he asked, totally caught off-guard by the question.

"I know you heard me, Arnold," she said with a stone-serious expression.

He rotated the chair to face her directly.

"Yeah, of course I *heard* you. I guess what I'm really asking is, what inspired that question?"

After setting her coffee on the corner of his desk, she folded her arms. Defiantly.

Uh-oh.

"It's a simple question. Why are you going out of your way to avoid answering it?"

Whoa.

"Ah, come on, I'm not avoiding an answer. I'm just confused about why you asked about her. To answer you, no, I have no intention of seeing her. You should know that." He shook his head, then muttered, "Jesus, where the hell did that come from?"

She continued to eye him, but with a hint of skepticism now.

"What about other women?"

He squinted back at her.

Yep, still looked serious despite the off-the-wall question.

Just to be sure, he asked, "Are you just jerking my chain or is that actually a serious question?"

"I'm totally serious. Will you be seeing another woman while you're there?"

Brows furrowed, he leaned forward, elbows on the desk, studying her.

"Come on, Noriko, what have I done to give you any suspicion I'm thinking of someone else?"

"Okay then, how about the fact that you're trying to wiggle out of answering my question? So, let me ask you one more time, straight-up: will you be seeing another woman while you're there?"

He blew an exasperated sigh, said, "No!"

Then he flashed on Kara, the cute little red-haired perky paralegal he'd always had a "thing" about. But since she worked for Mr. Cain, he always figured her to be off limits.

Noriko was intently homing in on his eyes now—the windows to the soul—as if trying to judge the honesty of his reply. The intense scrutiny made him feel unnerved and annoyed. He also found it off-putting.

"Who's the other woman, Arnold?" she asked, this time with a note of accusation.

"There is no other woman, Noriko."

But he was sure that her antenna registered his overreaction. Just another great example of why he never played Texas Hold'em in person. Online only. He was the worst at masking tells.

Her accusing stare continued to drill into him.

Enough!

"Look, I don't have time for this nonsense right now." *Or ever.* "I need to start doing some background work."

He swiveled around to face his monitors.

A few moments later the front door slammed. He stopped work to reflect on the confusing interchange that just played out, leaving him stewing in mixed emotions. Go after her?

And say what? And to what end?

Wow! What a major-league-jarring question. He weighed the question and his reaction.

He hated to admit it, but he was torn. A part of him felt flattered that she was jealous, for it implied that she cared for him. On the other hand, the accusation arising straight out of nowhere felt very troubling. Especially with Rachael the focus. Yes, Noriko was well aware that she was his rebound girlfriend after the break-up with Rachael, but he'd never said or done anything to fuel any suspicion that he was still in contact with his ex. Or even wanted to be, for that matter. In fact, he didn't know squat about what Rachael was up to since their breakup. As for Kara? Noriko knew nothing about her. The only other woman he talked about was Prisha and Noriko knew damn well she was happily married to Vihaan. In fact, Noriko met them during the team's mini-vacation in Honolulu in the immediate aftermath of their last pen-test.

So why the third degree? It was, well, disturbing.

CHAPTER 4

Sunday Afternoon—Seattle

Prisha

BEING A SUNDAY, Prisha had no problem scoring curb parking. And only one block south of the building where Cor-Pace leased office space. Sunday also meant not having to pay an exorbitant fee on her parking app.

A short walk brought her to the front doors of a building of black glass and heavy cement columns anchoring the corners. The black façade radiated an ominous vibe that gave her pause.

She tugged, then pushed against a plate-glass door to the lobby, but it didn't budge. Same with the one to the immediate right. Without any security guard or other person in sight to let her in, she called Mr. Cain, who picked up immediately.

"Mr. Cain? Prisha Patel. I'm outside the front door and it's locked. Could you please come down to let me in?"

"Yes, yes, of course. It's a weekend day so they keep it locked. I'll be down straightaway," he answered in a stressed and mildly distracted voice.

Moments later the lawyer came striding briskly from an elevator to open the lobby door, saying, "Thank you for coming on such short notice, Ms. Patel."

He abruptly turned and started back to the elevator bank.

Prisha could feel intense nervousness radiating from him like heat waves off sunbaked asphalt. A novel side of a man she'd seen only as Mister-in-Control. Neither one spoke during the smooth ascent to the fourth floor, but Cain kept fiddling nervously with a set of keys in his hand. After walking a short hall, he fobbed them through a glass door with Cor-Pace decaled in eye level black letters with gold trim. He stood aside for her to enter a tiny reception area before locking the office door again, then leading her along another short hall.

"We're meeting in John Harris's office," he said, turning right at an open doorway.

As they entered the office, a tall, thin, angular man she pegged for late fifties pushed up from a small round conference table for four to ask, "Prisha Patel?"

"Yes, I am," she answered, shaking it.

Without waiting for an answer, he offered his outstretched hand.

"John Harris." He motioned to three remaining chairs at the table. "Please have a seat."

The office itself was neither fancy nor plush like she'd imagined a CEO might occupy. In fact, the desk and small conference table looked as if they came from an office-furniture rental or secondhand store. Functional and simple. Then again, she reminded herself, this was a start-up, so they could well be secondhand.

Once all were seated, Harris said, "My apologies for not being able to offer you coffee, but all of us have been too busy to brew any. I suspect that given the circumstances, you understand."

"Not a problem," she answered.

Harris started the real conversation by asking, "What's your understanding of our situation?"

Prisha explained what little she'd learned from Arnold's brief summary.

When she finished, Harris said, "Essentially you're correct."

Before he could continue, she interjected with, "In that case, I don't understand why you haven't contacted the FBI's cybercrime unit? They're top notch with these kinds of issues. Wouldn't it be in Cor-Pace's best interest to have them work this?"

She heard Mr. Cain mutter, "Amen."

Either not hearing Cain's affirmation or, more likely, blatantly ignoring it, Harris went on to explain, "Simply put, we're a start-up with a limited funds and only one product. This being the case, we can't afford to terminate the trial or have the slightest adverse publicity hit the business news outlets. Can you imagine the downstream effect on our Cor-Rate II if a story broke in *Barron's* or *The Wall Street Journal* claiming that a hacker was toying with our patients' lives for perverted amusement? Put another way, we either find a way to fight this terrorist ourselves or lose the company. It's that simple."

Well, the man just made a good point, but it still didn't explain how on earth he thought that their team could do a better job than the FBI?

Her phone rang.

Raising a just-a-minute finger, she pulled the iPhone from her right back jeans pocket.

"Sorry, hate to interrupt, but I'm expecting Mr. Gold to call, so I need to check this."

After a glance at the screen, she nodded.

"Yep, it's him. I'll take it on speakerphone so we can all hear."

She swiped Accept and said, "Hey Arnold, have you on speakerphone with Mr. Harris and Mr. Cain."

"Excellent, you're there already," Arnold said. "Have some good news for you. I was lucky enough to snag a direct flight into Sea-Tac for later today and will text you the flight number after we're off this call. It's just a huge relief to know I'll be there tonight."

"Great. I'll pick you up to take you to your place, so we can maintain maximum momentum. I assume you're bringing Chance?"

"I am." Pause. "Call me with an update when you wrap up the meeting. If for some reason I don't answer, go ahead and email a summary so I can pick it up on the flight if need be. We good to go?"

"That we are. I'll forward any operable information soon as I have some so we can discuss if and how to present this to the team."

"Perfect. See you later, then."

Arnold cut the connection.

Slipping the phone back into her pocket, she asked them, "I assume you'll both be available twenty-four-seven while we look into this?"

"I'll do whatever it takes," Harris answered, before turning to Cain with an expectant expression.

Cain said, "I, on the other hand, have my scheduled work to attend to. I will, however, make myself available as circumstances allow. I just want you both to understand that my response time will not be as immediate as John's, but I will make myself as available as much as possible."

Prisha nodded. "Understood." Then to Harris: "*If* we take on this job, I'll also need to be able to reach your sysadmin round the clock." Because if they took on the job, she knew this one would be a twenty-four-seven full-court press.

"Now wait just a minute," Harris said, raising both hands. "I don't understand your emphasis on the word *if*. I thought by coming here you are representing Mr. Gold in his absence and that this meant your team would be working on this for us."

Guess the honeymoon's officially over.

"You're partially correct, Mr. Harris." She shifted in her chair, sitting more upright now that the mood was changing. "Just so you understand my role, I'm here as the official representative of Gold and Associates for the sole purpose of information-gathering. It's my understanding that Mr. Gold made this part clear when he said that I'd meet with you. We can't possibly make a final decision of whether to take on this case or not until we have more details." She made a strategic pause. "If we end up assisting you, it would, among other things, require signing a Scope of Work. A contract. Understood?"

"But—"

"I know that Arnold made it clear to Mr. Cain that Cor-Pace is considered a new client."

She held up a hand to stop Harris from speaking.

"Our prior relationship with Mr. Cain's law firm has no bearing on any consideration we may give this situation. If this wasn't made clear to you, then please accept my sincerest apologies."

But she was certain that Arnold had mentioned emphasizing this point to the lawyer.

She continued, "Once Arnold and I have discussed what's involved, we'll present the case to the rest of the team. At that point, the team will vote on whether or not to accept Cor-Pace as a *new* client."

She paused to make sure both men were paying close attention.

"In other words, I'm simply helping out Mr. Gold by doing some of our due diligence in his absence. Does this clear up any confusion on your part?"

Harris looked accusingly at Cain.

"This was not what you led me to believe, Noah."

After a sigh of exasperation, the lawyer responded, "John, I'm not sure we reached any understanding other than Cor-Pace is presently facing an extremely serious issue and that we're now exploring *your* preferred course of action. Keep in mind that it was completely your call to request their involvement, not mine."

Clearly displeased with the lawyer's pushback, Harris slowly returned his attention to Prisha.

"I'm sorry, could you repeat your last question?"

"I believe I mentioned that if we agree to work with you on this, we'll need twenty-four-hour access to your sysadmin."

Harris furrowed his forehead.

"I have no idea what that is. Please speak English?"

Oh, right.

"Your system administrator," Prisha explained. "The person who manages your IT infrastructure."

"Okay, got it." Harris nodded. "That would be Michelle Mays. She's in the office working on this as we speak. I'll run over and ask her to join us."

Then he was up out of his chair, heading for the door.

Once Harris cleared the office, Cain turned to her and said,

"Again, I'm so very grateful that you and Arnold are willing to at least consider taking on this catastrophe. As I'm sure you can tell, you'd be doing me a personal favor if your team decides to help us out."

He clasped, then unclasped his hands before asking, "Do you have any inkling as to what your decision might be?"

Assure him that she and Arnold were leaning toward accepting the job?

Probably best to not dangle any hope.

It was probably best to remain as noncommittal and neutral as possible and leave it at that. You never knew how these things could shake out. Personally, she found the situation incredibly unique and challenging.

She told Cain, "Not at the moment. Once I've had a chance to discuss things with Arnold, we'll present our findings to the group. I have no idea how they'll receive it. Especially since, as you know, we just voted to not take on new clients. Which Cor-Pace would obviously be."

Cain nodded solemnly, as if expecting the worst.

"I apologize for Mr. Harris's rather aggressive posture this morning, Ms. Patel, but he's very much on edge over this. As I'm sure you realize, if this goes badly, the company we've worked very hard to build to this level will simply cease to exist."

A moment later Harris hustled back through the door with a tall, slim, Black woman who was—even with pronounced stress etched into her face—strikingly attractive. She wore her hair in a throwback Angela Davis 'fro. And she was not at all the quintessential model of a geek that was befitting her role as the network administrator. She wore faded blue jeans and a gray Stanford hoodie with the trademarked green tree centered in the block S.

"Michelle Mays, Prisha Patel," Harris said, motioning from one to the other. "Ms. Patel is representing Gold and Associates, a private IT team that'll be working with us on this"—he paused, apparently searching for the right word—"issue."

Prisha squelched the urge to say, *Clusterfuck is a better description.* Instead, she stood and extended her hand.

"Glad to meet you."

Mays shook her hand while flashing an expression of relief, the kind felt when the cavalry comes charging over the hill trailing clouds of dust.

"She has a few questions for you," Harris said while slipping back into his chair.

Smiling at Prisha now, Mays dropped into her chair.

"We can certainly use all the help you can give us. Ask away. Whatever you want."

Aww, man...

Explain yet again that they haven't accepted the job? Probably not. It would only waste precious time. Prisha simply set her phone to record.

"I hope you don't mind, but I'm going to record this."

She placed the phone on the table between them.

"No problem," Mays replied.

"Let's start with a few basics. Your device that's been hacked. What's its name?"

"The Cor-Rate II," Harris said, as if to move this conversation along.

Prisha nodded. "So how is the Cor-Rate accessed?"

Mays opened her mouth, but before she could answer, Harris jumped in with, "That's actually one of the many major advantages of our device. It's accessible via Wi-Fi and Bluetooth. Having internet access is a huge benefit."

This was said as if he were pitching the device to a group of investors instead of an IT professional.

"I don't get it," Prisha said. "Why's that an advantage?"

Especially considering their present mess.

Mays crossed her arms and looked directly at Harris as if to say, *Hey, you stepped in it. Let's see you get out of it.*

Apparently receiving the message, he simply nodded for her to answer.

"Like most things, it's not that simple," Mays began. "At present, the devices can only be accessed via an Apple smart phone paired to it via Bluetooth. That's because we've an app only for the iPhone. Eventually, if the device becomes approved, our software team will expand the apps to be compatible with all the other major mobile phones: Samsung, Google, you name it. But for right now we're working exclusively with iPhones. Of course, this also means that if a patient doesn't own one, we provide it and cover the monthly charges for the duration of the study. The advantage Mr. Harris was referring to is that if, for example, a patient is on vacation in, oh, Paris or Cancun, and develops an arrythmia that the device's AI capabilities can't resolve, the device immediately notifies our cardiologists on call, and he or she can resolve the problem by accessing the device remotely. That's where the Internet comes in. However, for non-emergent access, such as routine doctor visits, the device is queried and programmed via Bluetooth exclusively. The battery can be recharged at night with an induction disk while the patient sleeps."

Prisha paused, thinking about what was just said within the context of a device hack. She now knew how it might be possible to reach the device remotely, but there was still the problem of being able to communicate with it. You may know your friend has a cellphone but without knowing their number, you can't call them.

"What's the handshake?" she asked, referring to the protocol that devices use to authenticate each other before allowing any exchange of information or commands. Similar to a digital password. This also prevented stray radio waves from accidentally triggering or changing a device's settings.

Mays replied, "It's a concatenation of two separate, unique numbers: the device's serial number attached to a string of randomly generated but unique twelve alphanumeric characters. This makes it virtually impossible to guess."

Prisha nodded slowly, processing this last bit of information. She raised her index finger.

"Just so I understand this clearly, is the combined number stored someplace or is it concatenated each time the device is accessed?"

Mays' eyes flashed as if she saw where Prisha was going with this.

"Device serial numbers are stored in our encrypted database.

When a new patient is enrolled into the study, a unique patient number is generated. If that patient makes it through the screening process and actually goes on to have a device implanted, then the implanted device's serial number is combined with the patient's unique number and the device is activated with that combination. From that point on it remains the same. Follow?"

"I do. In other words, for your hacker to be able to access a patient's device he'd have to know that unique number. Correct?"

"Correct."

Making Prisha's next question obvious: "So, it's a safe bet that your Hacker found a way to break into your *encrypted* database?"

Harris interjected, "The bastard admitted as much during his phone call."

Prisha took a moment to think about this. This case wasn't looking like the work of some pimply adolescent playing games in the basement of his parents' home. This puppy took some sophisticated planning and staged execution to get to the point of manipulating an implanted medical device.

Returning her attention to Mays, Prisha asked, "Have you been able to determine how he got past your firewall?"

Mays responded with a sarcastic snort, followed by, "Not yet. We're working on it."

Without really choosing her words carefully, Prisha said, "Good. At the moment, that's our best shot at finding any breadcrumbs that could lead us back to him."

Immediately she realized that by using the word "our," she'd implied a commitment that she really didn't have the authority to make. Nor want to make, for that matter.

Clarify the mistake?

She glanced at Mays, sitting there looking miserable, casting the occasional sideways glance at her boss. Harris's right hand was pumping the hell out of a purple stress ball. Squeeze, squeeze, squeeze. Regardless of who was at fault for this flaming disaster, she'd end up taking the fall. Mays was now undoubtedly under gargantuan pressure to pull off a miracle.

This confluence of emotions prompted her into making an executive decision, one she hoped Arnold would support, but she gave herself an escape route should Arnold nix the job.

Prisha said, "I'm pretty sure we'll be able to give you a hand with this, but I need to run it past my boss before making a firm commitment. I should have word for you within an hour."

A look of relief swept over Mays's face.

"That would be huge."

The tempo of Harris's squeezes diminished. Now he was looking at her too.

Ah, crap...

She could feel herself being sucked into the overwhelming gravitational pull of the black hole this hopeless case was generating.

Well hell, in for a penny...

After filing Mays's cell number and email address into her phone, she explained, "On something like this, we work from our respective places but remain in constant communication by staying in the team's private chat room. It functions quite well and very efficiently. I'll send you instructions on how to access it and assign you privileges for however long you need them. Hold one sec while I check a couple things," she said, standing, then moving to the office doorway.

Prisha got Vihaan on the phone, turned her back to the room, and said in a lowered voice, "Hey, it's me. Got a job for you." She explained who Mays was and what she was doing. She asked him to send Mays the link for their chat room.

Silence.

"Until we get official assignments from Arnold, I'd like you and Lopez to give her a hand searching their network for the hacker's access."

In response, she continued to hear only heavy ominous silence.

Uh-oh...

Well, what the hell did she expect from Mr. Negativity?

"Yo Vihaan, still there?"

"This sounds suspiciously like you're proposing we take on a new client," her husband finally replied, making no attempt to mask a liberal dose of righteous indignation.

Prisha rolled her eyes, thankful the phone wasn't set to speaker.

"Husband, this isn't the time. I'll explain everything when I'm home, but for now, I really need you to put a hundred percent effort into this, okay? We're chasing the clock on this one."

This was said in a tone that only a spouse could correctly interpret, hoping like crazy he wasn't going to blow this up into a major faceoff while she was center stage here in Harris's office. She wanted to leave Harris and Cain with the impression that the team functioned as smoothly as a Stuttgart-manufactured luxury car.

In the ensuing embarrassing silence, she imagined him weighing his options. She crossed her fingers in the hope that he wouldn't blow this issue into a debate now. They could discuss it all he wanted once she was back in the privacy of their apartment.

After more pronounced silence, his icy reply was, "I'll be waiting to hear what you have to say. This goes against everything the team's agreed on."

Well, at least we agree about that.

"Great. Understood. Thanks," she said in a cheery voice before disconnecting, wanting to get off the call before he reversed himself.

After running a quick mental checklist, she decided that all the points she intended to cover during this encounter had been discussed, so she turned to the assembled and said, "I believe that's all I need to get started."

Then, to Michelle: "I just assigned two team members to help you search for his access point. Hope this helps."

She flashed a thin smile.

"Believe me, that's huge. You have no idea how completely overwhelmed I am by this situation. To make matters worse, my best tech is on vacation."

Despite the potential blowback she was now facing from the team, she believed that her on-the-fly decision to help Michelle Mays was the right thing to do.

Smiling at the haggard sysadmin, she said, "Then I'm glad we can help."

As she turned to leave, one more thing came to mind. She turned to the group to add, "Rapid information-sharing is critical on a case like this, so we need to stay in extremely close contact."

To which, Harris said, "No argument from me on that."

Walking back to her car, Prisha dialed Arnold, hoping to catch him before he was forced to shut down his phone. She was in luck.

He answered with, "What up?"

She stopped moving, closed her eyes, and with a grimace, admitted, "What up is I sorta jumped the gun on this thing." Pause. "I assigned Vihaan and Carlos to help Michelle Mays look for Hacker's entry point?"

"Yeah? So, who's Michelle Mays?"

Massively relieved, she opened her eyes again and resumed walking.

"Oh, right. Well, she's the Cor-Pace sysadmin."

After several seconds of silence, Arnold stated as a matter of fact, "In other words, you accepted the case."

Was that a slight hint of bemusement she just heard?

With a hint of a smile creeping into her lips, she replied, "Yeah, I guess that's pretty much how it went down."

More silence.

"Does Vihaan know?"

She sensed Arnold calculating the damage control necessary to counter the havoc Vihaan's torpedo would inflict on team morale.

"I gave him the assignment to pass on to Lopez."

This time, Arnold didn't hesitate to respond.

"In that case, I suggest you get on the horn with Lopez, like, ASAP and do some serious lobbying before Vihaan can poison those waters."

"I'm all over it, boss," she replied, as a massive wave of relief and gratitude swept through her. At least Arnold wasn't in her face for unilaterally agreeing to take on such a loser of a case.

"Oh, and when you're done with that, we'll need to get a SOW over to Harris to sign ASAP before we sink too much of our time into this mess."

"Opps, forgot about that part," she said, referring to the Scope of Work.

"See you in about nine hours or so."

CHAPTER 5

Arnold

AFTER SETTLING INTO his first-class aisle seat, Arnold rummaged through his rucksack for the power cords to his laptop and phone; the two devices he'd need during the six-hour flight. Once they were removed, he stuffed the backpack under the seat in front of him and dropped the laptop and power cords into the pocket in the seatback only inches from his knees. Soon as they were airborne, he would fire up the computer to resume his background research. After plugging his phone into the power cable, he opened the thermostat app for his Green Lake house and bumped up the temperature from sixty-two to seventy-two degrees.

Anything else before I disconnect from cyberspace?

Couldn't think of anything, so he set the phone to Airplane Mode and settled back, eyes closed, to think about the latest update from Prisha and subsequent blowback he knew full well would be coming from Vihaan. Before leaving for the airport, he'd given Brian Ito a heads-up on the rapidly evolving situation, then hinted that the odds favored they'd take the job but only after some serious negations were made. At least now it wouldn't come as any huge shock when the team officially learned that they had indeed accepted the assignment. He just hoped Prisha could sweet-talk Lopez onto their side.

Prisha

As Prisha came breezing through the front door to their one-bedroom apartment, Vihaan was standing in the living room, arms crossed, scowling. Obviously, lying in wait for her. His laptop was open on the coffee table in front of the couch. His usual workplace.

"Taking a break so soon?" Prisha asked, sliding out of her coat.

"What the hell's going on?" he asked in his unique whiny petulant tone. "What do you think you're doing, taking on a new client after the team voted unanimously to not do that."

Hanging her coat in the small closet, she said, "If you give me a moment to stop and catch my breath, I'll debrief the entire team. In the meantime, why don't you try to chill a bit, okay? Your blood pressure must be off the chart."

In the kitchen now, she grabbed a can of Diet Pepsi from the fridge, levered open the tab, and took a long refreshing pull. Spent a blissful moment savoring the cool effervescence passing through her mouth and down her throat.

"Ah man, I needed that!"

"Prisha!" he said adamantly.

"Vihaan!" she shot back just as adamantly while leaning over to power up her laptop on the kitchen table.

Standing there watching the computer run through its boot routine, she could feel Vihaan's acetylene-torch eyes burning holes in the side of her head.

Enough.

She turned to him, and calmly asked, "Would you please stop glaring at me like a tantrum-throwing third grader and help me deal with this emergency? I really don't have time for your dramatics right now."

"My *dramatics?* Is that what you think this is?" he said, hands on hips, glare intensifying.

"Sure as hell looks that way from where I stand. You're overreacting when you don't know diddly about the situation."

She sat down at the computer.

"I know that, apparently, we just accepted a new client. That's all I need to know."

Sitting back in her chair, arms crossed, she looked up at him.

"In which case, you're acting like an *uninformed* spoiled little brat."

When he couldn't come up with another quick rejoinder, she added, "You wanta stay in here and glower or you gonna get on your computer so you can join the conversation? In the meantime, I'm going to corral Lopez and Brian in the chat room to give all of us a download on the emergency we're now dealing with."

After a brief hesitation, Vihaan begrudgingly trudged back to his laptop.

Once all were assembled in the chat room, Prisha kicked off the discussion with, "I think we're all aware that a little earlier today Arnold and I agreed to accept a case for Mr. Cain, an established client."

She went on to explain the details of the disaster that Cor-Pace was facing as a result of a hacker having gained control of the cardiac assistance devices.

She added, "I'm sure it's understood that this case must be kept absolutely—underline absolutely—confidential. Got it? We can't afford to have a single word of this to leak to anyone, okay?" Being a rhetorical question, she kept going with, "I can also tell you that since we're up against the clock on this, the work's gonna be super-intense. I'm talking balls-to-the-wall, full-on-attention, twenty-five-hours-a day work. And until Arnold can get back to us with his strategy, plan, and individual assignments, I'm team leader."

She paused, expecting Vihaan to push back, watching him out of the corner of her eye.

Surprise. Not a peep. Eyes still on him, she continued, "Until we hear to the contrary, I want Vihaan and Brian to continue whittling down our backlog of work orders while Lopez and I work with the Cor-Pace sysadmin to scour their network for any access ports the hacker might've installed."

Vihaan appeared to be wavering between launching his offensive or temporarily retreating.

She bet on the former.

True to form, he started in with, "How long before we hear from him?"

Meaning Arnold.

Prisha checked her watch. "Probably not until he's wheels-down at Sea-Tac." Despite knowing better, she couldn't help asking, "Why?"

"In other words, you went against the team's agreement and took on a new client," Vihaan said, unable to control what sounded like increasing annoyance. "I want to go on record as strenuously objecting."

"For christsakes, there is no record," Prisha said, shaking her head. "But fine. So noted."

"Not good enough," Vihaan pushed. "Looks to me like you and Arnold unilaterally made the decision without consulting the rest of the team."

Essentially, he'd just described the precise chain of events, but she wasn't about to let those be the last words on the issue.

"It's not that simple, Vihaan. As we all know, Mr. Cain is their corporate attorney. And, as we're also well aware, he and Arnold are super-tight. Harris was strong-arming the bejesus out of him to get us to take this on. So, in accordance with the law of fecal gravity, Arnold turned around and put the pressure squarely on my shoulders. It's that simple. What am I supposed to do? Tell our boss to fuck off? I don't think so. Both Arnold and I pushed super-hard for them to turn this mess over to the FBI, but like I told you, Harris wasn't buying that. So here we are, stuck with a loser of a case from a new client. There! I admit it. Cor-Pace *is* a new client. No mystery about that. Am I happy about it? No. And obviously neither are you, but we simply have to roll with it."

She paused again, fully expecting more pushback from hubby dear.

When it failed to materialize, she continued with, "I realize this is after the fact, but before we can submit a Scope of Work to Cor-Pace, we need to officially vote on whether to accept the job."

"You mean vote *after* the decision's been made?" said Vihaan with a note of gloat in his voice.

"Isn't that what I just said?" Prisha shot back with mounting annoyance.

"Yes, it is, and I, for one, have a very serious issue with doing business in such a highly dictatorial way. What you and your friend Arnold just did flies in the face of our agreement to not accept new clients. Period. I want it on record that I strongly object to what you're doing. Furthermore, I vote no. And I don't buy the bullshit argument that we'd be doing this for Mr. Cain. We all know that we'll be working for Cor-Pace."

Prisha calmly asked, "You finished with the hissy fit now? Because if so, we have work to get to."

Slack-jawed, Vihaan just stared into the webcam, shaking his head with an I-can't-believe-it look.

She calmly told the rest of the group, "I acknowledge Vihaan's point, but I think we also understand just how indebted we are to Mr. Cain for helping us build this company to our present status. That's the only reason Arnold and I ask you to vote yes to accept the job."

Before anyone could interject, she asked, "Brian, what's your vote?"

She hoped that Arnold had already lobbied him into their camp. Which would give them the majority. Which would go a long way in swaying Lopez's vote.

"I vote to accept the job, as awful as it sounds."

Prisha pursed her lips to suppress the smile shouldering its way onto her face.

"Carlos?"

Glancing away from the webcam, Lopez scratched the crown of his head, appeared to think about his answer before saying, "Aw man, I have to admit I'm sort of neutral on this and, Vihaan does have a point *but*...I'll bow to your and Arnold's judgment."

At this point Prisha couldn't suppress the smile any longer, which she feared would only inflame Vihaan further.

"Good. Then we've officially voted to accept the job. I'll get to work drawing up a contract. In the meantime, we have a ton of work ahead of us."

CHAPTER 6

Arnold

FORKING THE LAST bite of microwaved chicken breast into his mouth, Arnold continued to toss around the idea of making the Green Lake home his primary residence again. It just made good sense businesswise. Except for a handful of routine maintenance jobs, their major clients were in Seattle. And considering their present policy of not accepting new ones, it was impossible to see this imbalance changing any time soon.

As it was, the majority of their day-to-day work consisted of routine software updates and security checks, all of which were easily done through a remote connection. So, if he caught a routine job in Honolulu, he could easily knock it off from his kitchen table. And if one did require an in-person visit, Brian Ito could handle it. All the major hands-on in-person jobs, such as the penetration tests they'd recently finished for the Larkin Standish law firm, took place in Seattle.

In fact, thinking about the issue more objectively, it made no sense at all to even list a Honolulu office on their website. And besides, one dramatic advantage to living full-time in Seattle was not having to crate Chance to fly in the plane's cargo hold. He hated doing that. Each flight gave him a ton of anxiety. The thought of something happening to Chance during a flight made him slightly nauseous.

Or is it this dinner?

And besides, for the first time since fleeing to Honolulu, the island was beginning to feel restrictive and, well, monotonous.

He dictated an email to himself to delete any reference to a Honolulu office from their website.

Okay, but what about Noriko?

Now that was a tough one. Although she was a drop-dead stone-gorgeous looker, and refreshing—initially—to be with, the more time he spent with her, the more her personality began to slip slide toward problematic. A deterioration he never would've anticipated. Until now. Then again, what do you anticipate during the embryonic stages of a relationship? In that initial period of being together when everyone is on their very best behavior. Ironically, now she was starting to show the same personality flaw she gave as the reason for breaking off her engagement to what's-his-name: unfounded jealousy.

"Another glass of wine, Mr. Gold?"

He glanced up at the impeccably groomed flight attendant to his left. As he debated an answer, the attendant reached down to smoothly pick up his dinner tray but not the wine glass.

Yes? No?

Better not. *You need to get as much work done as possible on the flight.*

Although he'd yet to put the job to a team vote, he suspected that Ms. Efficiency, Prisha, was moving ahead under the assumption that they would accept the job and that the clock was now ticking. Meaning...

"I better not," Arnold answered with a speck of regret, since the wine was far superior to the dinner.

"Very well." The attendant removed Arnold's empty wine glass, freeing up the retractable arm-rest tray. "If you change your mind, I'm just a call-light away."

Pushing the tray aside, he transferred his computer from the seat-back pocket in front of him to the tray, plugged its power cord into the outlet, and pressed the power button. As the machine worked through bootstrapping the operating system back to life, Arnold reconsidered the decision to pass on a second glass of wine.

Hmmm…

Nope. As much as it'd taste good, he needed a clear head. Instead, he turned his attention to continuing his background research on hacking medical devices in general. It was a topic he only had fleeting knowledge of, so he planned to learn as much as possible during the long flight.

The ability to hack a commercial medical device was discovered by MedSec, a company specializing in researching vulnerabilities in the healthcare industries in general and medical devices in particular. In 2016 they made headlines by discovering flaws in a St. Jude Medical cardiac device. That, however, was just the beginning of the story. The really juicy part—the part that grabbed everyone's attention—was that MedSec then turned around and shared this potentially damming information with a privately held private-equity firm—Muddy Waters Capital. MWC then shorted the stock in the hope of raking in some serious coin from the eventual financial hit that the company would take once news of the hack went public.

Next, he read about Jay Radcliffe, a hacker with diabetes who developed a keen interest in seeing if his implantable insulin pump could be hacked. It could. In 2011 he demonstrated that it was actually pretty easy to gain control of a pump and potentially give a lethal dose of insulin to a patient.

Wasn't until a few years after that that the FDA finally sat up and began to take this issue seriously by releasing its first guidance on cybersecurity and medical devices. Then, in 2017, the federal agency recalled an implantable pacemaker over concerns that it could be hacked. Naturally, this topic caught Arnold's attention. He began to fine-tune his searches to the specific subject of hacking cardiac pacemakers; a subject he knew little about.

Having totally immersed himself in the subject for what seemed like a couple hours, he checked his watch. Only a little more than an hour of flight time remained before the captain would announce that passengers needed to power off all digital devices. He turned his attention from online research to setting up a dynamic database, or DDBMS, for the team to work from. A DDBMS is an advanced type of database that allows real-time modifications and updates to be stored while also being able to adapt to changing data requirements. This makes them more flexible and efficient in comparison to traditional static databases. They're particularly good in environments in which the data are frequently updated, like e-commerce websites or financial data tracking systems. Perfect for working on a complex case like this new one.

It turned out that his timing was almost precisely spot-on. Within minutes of storing the newly constructed database in the team's shared Dropbox account, an announcement came over PA system to turn off and store all electronic devices. Fine with Arnold. His brain felt fried by now anyway.

After packing up, he melted back into his seat, closed his eyes, and thought about how to assign work on the case.

CHAPTER 7

Prisha

PRISHA'S COMPUTER WAS actively tracking the Hawaiian Airlines flight on FlightAware. She saw it update and noticed that Arnold's plane was now estimated to touch down a few minutes ahead of schedule. Time to head out to the cellphone waiting parking lot at Sea-Tac.

After switching her laptop to sleep mode, she opened the front closet for her coat. Vihaan came up right behind her and reached over her shoulder for his coat.

She turned to him.

"Yo, husband, where do you think you're going?"

With a wide-eyed look of surprise.

"To the airport with you," as if something so self-evident it didn't warrant an explanation.

She made the wrong-answer buzzer sound, then said, "No you're not. You need to stay here and continue working. And besides, he's got Chance with him, so there's not enough room in the car for you."

"Sure there is," Vihaan replied testily. "He and Chance can sit in the back seat."

"Not with the crate in the backseat, he can't." After a brief hesitation, she added, "What is it with you? You've been acting twitchy about him."

"Twitchy?" Vihaan pressed his lips together, as if debating how best to answer. Then he nodded as if he'd just made up his mind about something. "Because I think you have an interest in him beyond just the job."

She stopped slipping on her coat to look him directly in the eye.

No, it didn't look like he was joking.

A moment later, she gave a dismissive laugh as she finished shrugging into her coat.

"You're not serious." Then, a double take. "Are you?"

He shot her a questioning look.

"Why would I joke about something like that?"

"Because you'd be dead wrong."

She glanced at the door, then back to him. She was cutting it short as is. Then again, he might take longer to make it to the pickup zone.

"Wow, you sure pick a great time to bring something like this up." She shook her head and added, "I dunno man...I'm not sure what I've done to give you that impression, but that's just not what's happening."

He didn't respond.

Wow, this was important enough to discuss in more detail before leaving.

"Okay, give me an example. Maybe that'll help me understand where this fantasy's coming from."

Rubbing his right cheek, Vihaan glanced at the ceiling, then back to her.

"Well, for starters, I always get the shitty assignments. Take today, for example. You two treat me like I'm an afterthought or something."

"Afterthought? That's ridiculous."

As she started to mate the coat zipper, she said, "There're two problems with that example, husband. First, you get the same assignments as everyone else, and second, how do you get from there to suggesting something's going on between Arnold and me? I just don't see it."

"Okay, fine, then here's a perfect example," he said, shifting weight from one foot to the other. "The supervisory job at Larkin Standish."

Prisha remained silent for several seconds, then slowly and deliberately repeated, "The supervisory job with Larkin Standish..." She raised her eyebrows at him. "Help me out here. Will you please clarify that one for me? Why do you consider that a shit job?"

She encased the last two words in finger quotes.

Hands in his front pockets, he rocked back on his heels, taking a moment before responding.

"Okay, since you asked. It's a perfect way to isolate me from the team. While I'm downtown working that job, Arnold has more time to spend with you."

What?

"Husband, please don't tell me you're actually serious about what you just said."

She studied his face for a moment.

Then, tapping her temple, said, "Think! Arnold's been in Honolulu since the day you were assigned that job. News flash, Vihaan. The dude *lives* there."

"Yeah, but you could still talk to him."

Prisha rolled her eyes, then shook her head.

"Did it ever occur to you that Arnold assigned you that job because of all the team members, he thought you'd be the best suited for it?"

Vihaan scoffed.

"Best suited? Seriously? How's that work? Why not Lopez? Or you, for that matter?"

Well, for one thing, your work productivity is the lowest of the group.

Instead of saying that, she shrugged.

"Maybe you should ask him instead of skulking around dreaming up conspiracy theories."

She immediately reconsidered her tone.

Was that a bit harsh?

Yeah, perhaps.

She added, "Personally, I think you're being silly. And jealousy doesn't become you."

A glance at her watch. Better get a move on if she wanted to make it to the airport waiting area by touchdown. But she sensed that Vihaan wasn't convinced.

Taking hold of his shoulders, she locked eyes with him.

"Listen to me. Nothing's going on between Arnold and me other than collaborating well as a team. We see things with a canny similarity and very often arrive at the same conclusions. Perhaps it's that symbiosis that you're picking up on. Just because we work well together doesn't mean there's something more personal going on between us."

She could tell her words were not being heard. Or if heard, not believed. She pulled him into her arms and kissed him.

"Look, I gotta bounce. But when the dust settles on this, let's talk about taking a few days off to go someplace, like, maybe up to Vancouver or over to the ocean. Sound good to you?"

Vihaan gently disengaged from her, mumbled, "Whatever," before turning to hangdog his way back toward the couch.

As she watched, she shook her head in bewilderment. But it was time to head out, so she left the apartment and hurried down to her white Toyota in the garage.

A few minutes later, three miles over the speed limit on I-5 southbound, she ruminated on the little drama that had just played out. If Vihaan's nose was out of shape over a misguided perception, it carried the likely potential to turn into a major monkey-wrench in what was lining up to be an extremely problematic case. Last thing the team needed was for him to sabotage their work, either overtly or inadvertently. Do that and it could have a ripple effect on the entire team and ultimately future contracts.

Now, with the clarity of retrospect, Vihaan evidently had never been thrilled over being assigned the Larkin Standish job. On the other hand, who else could've done it? Brian Ito? A geographical impossibility. Lopez? Yeah sure, but if you compare raw productivity,

Lopez outperformed her husband by a mile. Herself? Yes, she could've easily done it, but again she was more productive than Vihaan. So, perhaps, in a way, Vihaan did have a valid point: he *was* the most expendable team member. But that didn't mean that helping Larkin Standish select a replacement for their head of IT was a slouch job. Far from it. The assignment provided much needed support for an extremely valuable client. He should be proud to have been given that responsibility.

That assignment had been a direct byproduct of a pen-test the team recently completed for the law firm. (A penetration test is when hackers are hired to break into computer networks and/or physical office spaces to expose security flaws that criminals might exploit. The goal is to tighten security by correcting these vulnerabilities.) While sneaking into the law firm's main computer network, the group uncovered a clandestine audio/video surveillance system that allowed the prior head of security to listen to and record confidential client/attorney meetings in individual offices and conference rooms.

The illegal eavesdropping system had been installed by Itzhak Mizrahi under the laughable guise of improving security. Upon learning of its existence when analyzing the Gold and Associates' After-Action report, the board of governors went totally ballistic and fired Mizrahi on the spot. Which produced a gaping hole in their IT staff. The lawyers turned to Arnold in hopes that his team would fill this void.

The team's workload, however, was already maxed. As a temporalizing solution, Arnold and Prisha assigned Vihaan the job of objectively evaluating the firm's staffing needs while helping HR search for a tech to plug the hole left by Mizrahi. This, in turn, put a gonzo strain on their own workload.

But there was a bright side. Just yesterday, Vihaan mentioned he'd interviewed an excellent candidate who HR was now seriously vetting for the job. What a perfect time to finalize this issue and bring Vihaan back to the team full-time. She decided to discuss this high-priority item with Arnold on the drive back from the airport.

Arnold

Arnold pulled his rucksack from under the seat ahead of him, draped the strap over his left shoulder, then waited in the clogged aisle for the flight attendant to pop the cabin door. Moments later, the door was pushed in and the eager passengers ahead of him began flooding the jetway like water from a burst dam.

Arnold merged into the crush of north-concourse pedestrian traffic, rode the escalator to the subway level, then waited for the train that would zip him to the main terminal baggage claim area. Before stepping into the subway car, he called Prisha.

"Yo," she answered.

"In the cell phone lot?"

"Just pulling in."

"I'm on my way over to pick up Chance. Don't have any baggage, so I only have to collect him and his crate. Will ping you soon as we head out to the pick-up zone."

"Got it, boss."

Arnold, Chance, and his crate were lined up at the curb when Prisha's white Corolla braked to a stop.

The door locks clicked open as she climbed out of the driver's seat to call over the car roof, "Need any help?"

"Naw, I got it." He shoved Chance's crate across the back seat to be directly behind the driver, then told Chance, "In you go," to which the pooch jumped into the back seat. After dumping his rucksack in the back footwell, he slid into the front passenger seat and paused a moment to inhale deeply.

He clicked his seatbelt into place.

"I never get used the striking differences in air temperature and humidity between the two cities." Then, after a brief pause, "Thanks for picking me up."

"More efficient this way," she answered, craning her neck to check behind them for an opening in the steady stream of traffic. She caught a break and merged seamlessly into the flow of vehicles.

Monday night and the airport was teaming with business travelers mixed in with the hords of Alaska cruise-ship passengers that routinely passed through Sea-Tac this time of year.

Arnold remained silent while she concentrated on navigating the maze of lane changes and traffic until they were free of the thick airport congestion, heading north toward the city. Looked like she was planning to avoid I-5 by cutting west to 509, then descending the hill on which Sea-Tac perched. She would then link up with the Highway 99 tunnel that shot directly beneath downtown to reemerge north of the business district as Aurora Avenue. This would be a far more efficient route to his neighborhood than working her way over to I-5 and having to deal with that potential bottleneck.

Prisha

Once in the steady flow of traffic she said, "I need to give you a heads-up on a massive internal problem that needs to be addressed, like, immediately."

Ah Jesus...

"And that is?"

"Husband Vihaan's nose is totally bent out of shape. He thinks he's being assigned all the, quote, shit jobs."

She gave him an almost verbatim replay of his prime example—the Larkin Standish gig—but held off mentioning his allegations of some sort of extracurricular entanglement between them for a couple of reasons. The biggest being that she wasn't convinced Vihaan was actually serious about it. It might just be one of those accusations thrown out in the heat of frustration. After all, there was no basis in reality for it.

After filling Arnold in on the promising IT tech being vetted by Larkin Standish HR, she offered, "An immediate Band-Aid that I see is to offload his role there ASAP. Which will give us the advantage of having his undivided attention again, which I suspect we'll need for the new job. Whatdaya think?"

Without hesitation, Arnold replied, "Hey, if they have a viable candidate, sure, absolutely. It'd be great to have him back full-time."

After all, their backlog of routine work continued to pile up.

She could sense him sitting there staring at her but kept her eyes glued to the road and her hands in the ten and two o'clock position. The model driver. Ms. Innocent. Did he sense something else was definitely up?

She waited.

He said nothing.

Was he simply going to let things play out until he realized the ball was in his court?

Finally, Arnold broke the silence with, "I need to better understand what's really upsetting him. Are you saying he's upset about the Larkin Standish job in particular, or does he believe he's the only one in the team who's assigned the, quote, shit jobs?"

Lips pressed tightly together, she rolled that question around for a moment before answering.

"I came away with the distinct impression he feels he's being singled out for the less desirable jobs. In other words, it isn't confined to just the supervisory Larkin Standish thing."

Arnold

Arnold considered her statement a moment. Even in retrospect it didn't make sense, because there was no basis for the complaint.

He asked, "Have any idea what makes him think that?"

She hiked her shoulders.

"Nope. Nothing at all. Tonight is the first I've heard about it."

He didn't buy it.

"C'mon, girl, you guys are married. Meaning you know each other intimately. You should at least have some idea?"

She blew an audible sigh as if being forced to answer a question she preferred to avoid.

"Well, there *is* something else going on with him that completely baffles me. For some reason—I have no idea why he believes this—but he thinks you and I have something going on."

It took a moment for the full impact to sink in. He turned so he could see her face.

"Is he nuts? Between you and me?"

She nodded. "Yeah, exactly."

"Whoa!"

Completely at a loss for words, Arnold listened to the road noise filling the car while weighing that bombshell's potential effect on team dynamics and performance. Prisha was his first hire and full associate. Perhaps because of that, they'd bonded super-tight. Tighter than with any of the other team members. And truth be told, if he were to rank-order his preference for the team members, Vihaan would most definitely end up at the end of the list. Not because of any competition over Prisha's attention or affection, but because Vihaan was a boat anchor of negativity, and this heavy weight seemed to slop over to his productivity.

He finally broke the silence with: "If he really feels he's the only one being assigned the worst jobs, then yeah, getting the Larkin Standish thing off his plate should help alleviate that particular issue, but if what you say about the other thing is the basis for his feelings, then it's not going to do diddly to defuse that."

Prisha nodded.

"I totally agree. But like I said, at least it's a Band-Aid."

Ah, Jesus...

Racing the clock as they were, Arnold figured that the sooner he dispensed with this easily addressable issue, the sooner they could focus on what really mattered.

"Hang on. I'll call him now."

On speakerphone, Arnold dialed Vihaan's cell.

Vihaan answered with a touch of chip-on-the-shoulder attitude.

"Yeah, what do you want?"

Which Arnold diplomatically ignored.

"Prisha just told me you have an excellent candidate for the Larkin Standish slot. That right?"

Vihaan took his time answering. As if he was inspecting the question for some sort of catch.

"Pretty much. HR's doing the routine background on him, but unless he turns out to be on the FBI's Ten Most Wanted list, I think he's a definite go."

"So, what's this guy's story? I mean, if he's such a red-hot candidate, how come he's available?"

"Pretty much what you expect these days. He was cogging along for Big Tech when he found himself on the wrong side of a downsizing list. It's nothing more than that."

That was just another example of why Arnold was so delighted to be running his own company.

"Yeah, there's a lot of that going around." Pause. "Okay, so that fills the tech slot. What's your recommendation on the supervisory role?" Arnold asked, hoping to pump up the importance of the job.

"Oh, that," he said, in a voice that suggested that he was warming up to the idea of being asked for an opinion. "It's actually very straightforward. I recommended they promote Serge to supervisor. For two reasons: of their three techs, he's the most senior and has the most skills. Just makes sense to me."

"Yeah, suspected you might recommend that. Okay, I know it's way late, but I'm going to call Mr. Collier to ask him to meet with us first thing in the morning. I want to settle this now so we can get you back full-time. For this job we need all hands on deck."

CHAPTER 8

WHEN MR. COLLIER, the law firm's managing partner answered, Arnold launched straight into his spiel with: "Apologies for calling so late, sir, but we've been hit with an emergency case that requires getting Vihaan back on our team. The good news is that you're all set up to fill the vacant tech slot as well as for the supervisor position. So, we need to meet first thing in the morning to finalize this." Saying this more as a *fait accompli* than a request.

After momentary silence, the lawyer replied, "Tomorrow's extremely busy. How long do you estimate this will take?"

"No more than five minutes, sir. Vihaan's already been working with HR on this, so the process can be wrapped up with a handshake."

"Give me a moment to check my calendar." A quick pause, then, "I'll meet you in our reception lobby at seven and will have a representative from HR there as well."

Knowing Mr. Collier, that meant 6:59 AM.

"Thanks, Mr. Collier. I appreciate your flexibility. And again, my sincerest apology for calling so late."

A moment later, with Vihaan back on speakerphone he said, "We're set up to meet Mr. Collier and someone from HR at seven AM in their offices. Could you pick me up at, say, six fifteen? Please." Figuring that given the thinner morning traffic at that hour, forty-five minutes should be more than enough to get them into town and parked in the building garage in plenty of time. If they ended up in the basement garage a few minutes early, they could just cool their heels in the car and chat.

With that issue taken care of, Arnold plugged his phone into the white charge cord that had been a fixture in Prisha's Toyota for as long as he'd known her.

Glancing around, he realized they were now zipping through the tunnel under downtown Seattle.

He said, "Now that that's done, how about a download on your meeting?"

Prisha launched into a detailed description of what she'd learned in her face-to-face with Harris, Cain, and Mays, then added that she'd assigned Lopez, Ito and Vihaan to help Mays search Cor-Pace's network for the hacker's access point.

Arnold considered her last words for several seconds before asking, "Get any pushback from the guys over accepting the job?"

Prisha sighed. After a beat: "Yeah. Pretty much exactly what you might anticipate..."

She let the unfinished statement hang.

"You put this to a vote with the group, right?"

"Right."

"So, is it also fair to assume that Vihaan was the sole dissenter?"

This time she shot him a quick side-eye before answering, "Yep, that's basically how it went down."

"Okay, so that's one more thing to scratch from my to-do list. And thanks for keeping Mr. Cain happy. You did good. I'll text Lopez and Ito to expect an online meeting in a little bit, soon as Chance and I are settled in."

He saw a flash of white teeth in the Corolla's dim interior light. Prisha's signature smile.

"They've been warned to expect it."

The interior of the Toyota dropped into the low hum of road noise again as Arnold mulled over the ramifications of the situation with Vihaan. Not looking good.

"Oh man!" he finally said, shaking his head. "This Vihaan thing's really got me upset. Especially with us taking on such a gnarly case. The timing couldn't possibly be worse. Jesus!"

She nodded. "I know. I'm at a total loss on how to deal with it other than to just keep on keeping on. During the drive out I wasn't able to think about anything else."

After another brief silence, Arnold asked, "I know I've already asked this, but I'll ask again. You have any idea how he got that idea in his head? I mean, about us. There's got to be something that set him off."

"Nope. But I have a suspicion. Nothing concrete, just a suspicion." She paused to navigate a lane change. "The only times we work together in person are the hands-on jobs like those pen-tests. And those puppies are, like, super-intense. And we always pair up for those. Probably because you and I've teamed up since the start. Which means the others might end up in what could be seen as support roles. All I'm saying is, maybe he confuses that for intimacy." She gave a shoulder-shrugging, I-don't-know shake of her head.

She added, "When I explain it like that it sounds ridiculous, but I think you get my point."

"Yeah, totally." Pause. "Man, that really puts us in a bind because we're such a small group we don't have a lot of other options. There's no way I can team with Ito on those, so that leaves you, Carlos, and Vihaan. Don't take offense, but there's no way I trust Vihaan to cover my back. Especially now with this thing going on." A quick shrug. "And far as Carlos goes, trusting him isn't the issue. I do. A ton, in fact. It's just that I don't resonate with him like I do with you. It's like you and I can read each other's minds at times. Understand what I'm saying?"

"I know exactly what you're saying. In fact, it gets a little scary at times."

Neither one said another word for several seconds.

Arnold broke the silence with, "Guess we'll just have to see how things play out after we settle the Larkin Standish thing in the morning. I'm hoping that'll be enough to smooth things over with him."

"Me to, but I gotta say, don't count on it. I know him too well.

When he gets locked onto a perception like this, it's almost impossible to change."

How depressing. If things didn't change, Vihaan would be a definite liability to the team.

Jesus!

Arnold turned to stare at the tiled tunnel wall blurring past. A moment later, he sensed a subtle positional change of the car ascending back up to the surface street. Moments later, they popped out onto Aurora Avenue, and he started to see the familiar sights along this stretch of road fly past. The change of scenery snapped him back to the raging debate over whether to designate Seattle as his primary residence. Did this new team dynamic influence the decision? Stated slightly differently, *should* it influence it at all? The easy answer was no; it was irrelevant. But he knew that was wrong: it *was* very relevant. Because if Vihaan firmly believed that he and Prisha had something going, then a move back would only fuel that misconception. So yeah, his decision was bound to severely impact team dynamics. On the other hand, Vihaan's suspicions were already disrupting that harmony. The other team members just didn't know it yet.

Or did they?

Well, there was nothing he could do about it at the moment.

Hmmm, that wasn't exactly true either. Next time they had a hands-on case he could pair himself with Carlos. But would that change anything? Not given what he knew of Vihaan.

Jesus. What a freaking mess.

Turning to Prisha, he asked, "Do you like this car?"

She laughed.

"Wow, that's a seismic shift in topics. Whydaya ask?"

Arnold rotated in the seat, reached behind him to give Chance a small dose of choobers while saying, "Good boy."

Doggie therapy over, he faced forward again.

"Not having a car here is, like, getting really old. I'm toying with the idea of buying one." He ended the sentence with an I-don't-know-if-that's-what-I'm-going-to-do shrug.

"Does this mean you plan on staying in town more?"

That Prisha. Uncannily intuitive.

"Yeah, I've been seriously kicking that one around for a couple months now." He paused briefly. "Realistically, all our significant jobs are here. I mean, would we even consider accepting, say, a pen-test in Honolulu?" Without waiting for an answer, he said, "I seriously doubt it, right?"

She shook her head.

"Not when you put it that way. Unless of course it was a small one you and Ito could do."

"Exactly." Pause. "So, back to my question. How do you like this car?"

She shrugged.

"I dunno. It's a car. Gets me from point A to point B and hasn't had any major issues. Why? You thinking of a Toyota?"

"Haven't made up my mind yet, but if I decide to, I'm leaning toward a Tesla Model 3. I like the idea of an electric car."

"But there're a ton of electric cars out there. Why a Model 3?"

"Don't know…they just appeal to me, is all."

Which wasn't quite the entire story. Mr. Davidson, his criminal defense lawyer, owned a Model S. That car was the inspiration for wanting a Tesla.

"You gotta way to charge it if you get one?"

"Actually, I do. When I rebuilt the house, I installed a 220-volt outlet in the garage just in case."

Her head bobbed. "Smart."

Carrying the crate, Arnold led Chance through the house into the kitchen, then opened the usual French door so the pooch could run into the back yard. Prisha followed them inside and closed the front door. After running the crate down to the basement, Arnold texted everyone with the message that they'd convene a team meeting in their main chat room in a few minutes, then booted his laptop on the kitchen table. Prisha pulled up a chair next to him.

A moment later they were assembled and Arnold kicked off the meeting by reiterating what everyone already knew: that the job was super-urgent and because they'd be fighting the clock, they should plan on working twenty-four-hour days, catching catnaps only as needed to stay on top of their game.

He went on to emphasize, "We'll work from here"—meaning the chat room—" so we can disseminate information soon there's anything new to report."

A glance at the digital clock in the lower right-hand corner of the screen showed that it was now past midnight, making it Monday morning.

"On the flight over, I put together a new database for this. It's in the team Dropbox. In addition to sharing new information verbally, I want us to upload every new scrap of information to it as soon as possible. No matter how insignificant it might seem. It'll be our sole data repository. If you come across anything you think is important, broadcast it to the group. In other words, everyone needs to know what everyone else knows in real time." After a short pause for emphasis, he added, "Although most of you've been briefed on what we're dealing with, I want Prisha to walk us through it one more time before we talk about assignments. Prisha, you're on," he said, rotating the laptop so that the webcam centered her image on the screen.

Prisha started in by rehashing Elijah Brown's near-fatal but still tenuous arrhythmia. She told them of Hacker's demand that Cor-Pace shut down its clinical trial by end of business Friday or he'd start killing patients one by one until the FDA terminated the study. Finished with her summary, she asked, "Questions?"

Ito asked, "I don't get it. Why hasn't Harris already sicced law enforcement on his ass? Seems to me that that's the smart thing to do."

Prisha explained Harris's reasons for opting to not involve the FBI at this point.

Ito again: "My grandfather's had a pacemaker for a couple years now, so I know there're lots of them already out there. What makes this one so special that a start-up thinks they have a chance at breaking into such a highly competitive market?"

Arnold chimed in, "Thanks for bringing that up. I've been wondering the same thing ever since Mr. Cain called me."

Prisha answered with, "Apparently, their device is built around a whiz-bang new AI chip that's got, like, a ton of amazing capabilities. It's supposed to allow the device to adapt on the fly to a changing condition instead of waiting to be reprogrammed by a doctor. They claim that because this minimizes the need for extensive programming adjustments, it should ultimately improve patient survivability."

This seemed to satisfy the group.

"I have a question," Vihaan said.

Oh shit, here we go.

Arnold glanced at the ceiling, steeling himself for a confrontation.

"Yes?" Prisha asked with a note of caution.

"I don't get it," Vihaan said. "Why would someone want to shut down the study?"

"What do you mean?" she asked, obviously puzzled by the question.

"Like, what's their motivation?" he replied with the ring of genuine confusion. "I mean, this isn't a ransomware thing, is it? Or am I missing something?"

Holy shit.

Arnold's eyes snapped back to the screen.

Nodding thoughtfully, Prisha admitted, "Know what? I never thought to ask. Guess I simply assumed that Harris would've mentioned it if he knew."

Arnold was leaning forward now, partially in view of the webcam. He said, "Actually, that's a really good question, Vihaan. Soon as we wrap this up, I'll call Harris to ask him that. In the meantime, are there any other questions?"

No one said a word.

Arnold continued with, "In that case let's move on to assignments." Pause. "I hope this doesn't come across as condescending, but I want to emphasize that our highest priority at the moment is to dig up every scrap of information we can on what this hacker's done and how he operates in the hope that it'll give us a lead on who he is. Our best chance for finding anything about him is to continue searching for how he bypassed their firewall and wormed his way into their database. This means that for now, I don't want to change Prisha's assignments. I want Lopez, Vihaan, and Ito to continue working with Mays while Prisha and I tear apart the code on Mr. Brown's device."

Prisha interrupted with, "Sorry to break your train of thought, Boss, but I invited Mays to join us and she's standing by. This seems like a good time to get her involved with the discussion, so may I admit her to the room?"

"Yeah, great idea."

A moment later, Mays popped up in their chat room.

Prisha: "Hey Michelle, let me introduce you to our team leader, Arnold Gold."

Arnold waved at the webcam, then went ahead with, "Great timing. I was about to suggest that one way your hacker might've infiltrated your database was to send your primary data entry person a phishing email with an embedded RAT."

A Remote Access Trojan is a form of malware that provides access to the infected computer. If you've ever allowed, say, an Apple or Dell technician to remotely fix a problem with your computer, they probably asked permission to access your machine. If you said yes, they sent you a RAT that, when you opened it, embedded in your computer and allowed them to remotely take control of your machine to fix the problem. Once the issue was solved, the technician removed the RAT, thereby terminating the remote connection. All it would take is for Cor-Pace's data entry person to fall for a sophisticated phishing scam and unwittingly embed the malware and the hacker would have complete access to their computer. Once that happened, he probably installed a keystroke recorder to steal the password to their secure database. Basic Hacking 101.

"But on second thought," Arnold mused, "I don't know how he'd know who that person is. Any idea?"

Mays uttered, "Damnit! That's so obvious. I should've thought of this earlier. Dawn Cavendish is our primary data entry person, but we have a couple of others that help her out when she's swamped. I'll be all over it soon as we finish up here."

"Before you go, I want to mention that Lopez will be the point person for our team. Prisha and I will—"

"Why Lopez?" Vihaan interrupted with a strong note of indignation. "This is a prime example of what I was talking about earlier." As if everyone else in the chat room knew about his recent complaint. "Why shouldn't I be put in charge of our team? Answer me that."

Ah, Christ, not now, Vihaan.

Arnold sighed before asking, "Seriously?"

"Damn right I'm serious."

Arnold really didn't want to embarrass him but since he brought it up, saw no other choice.

"Because, in a couple hours you and I'll be downtown at Larkin Standish signing you out of your supervisory role. Unless I'm wrong, you can't be in two places at once."

An awkward silence followed.

Finally, Vihaan mumbled, "Right…guess that slipped my mind."

Arnold informed the rest of the group of their 7 AM meeting with Mr. Collier and an HR representative from Larkin Standish.

With that issue scratched off the list, Arnold said, "Michelle, I'll need the most current copy of Elijah Brown's pacemaker firmware. I mean, current as of now. Can you get that to me?"

Firmware is a type of software that resides in a protected section of a device's memory. It cannot be altered except under very special circumstances, such as an update from the manufacturer. It's inaccessible to most users, to ensure that the function of the device isn't accidentally corrupted.

"No problem. I'll forward a copy when we're done here," she replied.

"Also," Arnold continued, "I need a copy of the standard virgin firmware for all devices still on the shelf so we can compare the two sets for changes."

His logic: for Hacker to gain control of a Cor-Pace device, he must have rewritten a segment of the firmware. So, inspecting the firmware was a good place to start looking for clues to the hacker's identity.

"Got it. I'll send you a copy of that too," she said.

"Finally, I need to know the handshake."

He was referring to the password that the Cor-Pace device requires before it allows its existing settings to be changed. The hacker somehow got his hands on the password to Elijah Brown's pacemaker.

Prisha interjected, "I have that, boss. It's a combination of the device's serial number and a special identifying number that each patient's given when they enroll in the study. It's pretty basic stuff."

"Obviously," Mays said with heavy reluctance, "we didn't count on some crazy-ass cyberpunk breaking into our database, especially one who gets his kicks by murdering patients."

"Well, you certainly have our sympathies," Arnold replied. "No one could've seen this coming. Okay then, you guys get back to searching for end runs around your firewalls while Prisha and I start tearing apart Brown's software."

Mays asked, "Just out of curiosity, what sort of things you looking for? I've never had to deal with a case like this."

"Could be several things, but we'll mostly look for metadata," Arnold answered. "Or something Hacker inserted, like an annotation that might provide a hint about who he is."

When writing software, Arnold knew, it's helpful to make notes at the margins of the command lines to use as guideposts to the logic of those instructions.

"You'd be surprised what some of these yahoos forget to remove once they've modified the code to their liking."

He paused briefly before wrapping up with, "All right, team, let's get back to it but please stay in the chat room at all times and don't forget to upload new intel into the database."

Meeting officially over, Arnold turned to Prisha.

"Since we'll be going through the code line by line, it'd be ideal if you worked from here. But given your present, ah, domestic issues, the optics wouldn't be particularly good. So, it's probably best for you to work from home and linked via the chat room. We cool?"

She responded with a vigorous nod. "I totally get it and agree."

Just then his iPhone dinged. A text. A glance at the screen. From Noriko. Meaning, it could wait. He replaced the phone on its disc charger next to his laptop.

"I know you know this," he said to Prisha, "but I'll say it anyway just to be a tight-ass. We can't afford any unforced errors. Make three copies of the firmware, upload the original untouched copy to the database, then send me a copy marked 'copy-A' and work from another one marked 'copy-P' for Prisha. We'll inspect it, line by line. Got it?"

With a nod, she confirmed, "Got it," then headed for the front door.

"Okay," he called after her. "Text me soon as you're home, and we'll start. In the meantime, I'll get my workstation set up."

As he started down the basement stairs to grab an extra monitor and a wireless earphone/microphone headset, he heard the front door close.

CHAPTER 9

AFTER SETTING UP his laptop and second monitor on the kitchen table, he ran upstairs to squeeze in a quick shower to rid himself of the patina of fatigue grunge that inevitably coated him during long flights.

Although the laptop contained a built-in speaker and microphone, the clarity of the headset was superior, especially if competing with any ambient noise, like a neighbor's power mower. To offset the discomfort from the headset pressing his earlobes for long periods, he routinely removed them for a few minutes and cycled thought a series of routine stretches. He set the Amazon Echo Dot on the kitchen counter to remind him to do his routine every forty-five minutes. His neck especially appreciated the breaks.

His timing turned out to be faultless because by the time he settled back into the kitchen chair in fresh sweatpants and sweatshirt, he found copies of Elijah Brown's implant and the unassigned device firmware in their communal Dropbox. From the timestamp, he saw that Michelle Mays had uploaded them just two minutes earlier. Since Prisha had yet to sign in, he uploaded both copies to their designated database fields, then made the appropriately renamed copies for them to work from.

A moment later, Prisha signed into the team's private chat room.

After asking her to migrate to a separate channel, he donned his headset and prepared to start.

A moment later he heard her ask, "Can you hear me?"

"Roger that," he replied while putting their working copy of the firmware from Mr. Brown's device up on the screen. "Can you see the code?"

"Roger that."

"Okay, let's start through it line by line," and read the first line of commands out loud. "See anything?"

"Looks clean to me," she responded.

They repeated the process for the second line.

And so it went, line by line in excruciating detail, requiring full-on concentration.

Ten minutes later his phone dinged, signaling another text.

"Hold one," he told Prisha while pulling his phone from the disc charger.

Noriko again. *Goddamnit.* Her texts were disrupting his concentration.

Ah, right, he didn't respond to the one a few minutes ago.

Jesus, must be the middle of the night back there.

"Hold on a moment while I take care of this," he asked Prisha, then dictated the message: AM WORKING AND CAN'T TEXT NOW. WILL CONTACT YOU LATER WHEN I HAVE TIME.

And got an immediate reply: NOT EVEN FOR A QUICK I MISS YOU?

Arnold: NO. AM WORKING.

Noriko: AW COME ON.

Annoyed, he muted the phone before replacing it on the disc charger.

Prisha said, "Vihaan just left the apartment to pick you up for your meeting with Mr. Collier."

Aw man!

He glanced at the time and was shocked at how quickly the hours blitzed past. He glanced down at the sweats he had on. Oh well, Mr. Collier had been warned them that they were tackling an all-consuming job. He would understand.

81

CHAPTER 10

7:00 AM Monday Morning

AS ARNOLD AND Vihaan stepped from the elevator into the tastefully conservative muted grays of the Larkin Standish reception lobby, Mr. Collier was stationed in his signature drill-sergeant posture.

"Punctual as ever," Collier said, extending a hand to Arnold, then to Vihaan.

"We're in the small conference room this morning, the one you're familiar with," he said, starting toward the hall to the left of the reception desk.

To Arnold, the Black man radiated the vibe of a man younger than his fifty-seven years. He sported a well-trimmed, short, graying beard, and sunken Auschwitz-like eyes. He wore an immaculately tailored lightweight dark gray wool suit with pale chalk pinstripes. Mr. Dapper. Always. Arnold flashed through the several facts he'd picked up when preparing for the pen-tests they'd done for the firm. The lawyer graduated from Stanford Law with honors and was married with one teenage son.

The conference room contained a small rectangular table with two chairs on each length as well as one at each end. On one side sat a fiftyish woman with black bangs partially obscuring a sun-damaged dour face. She had on a no-nonsense dark gray business suit.

The lawyer said, "Gentlemen, this is Sara Fromke from HR," while closing the door.

Fromke pushed up from the chair while extending her right hand to Arnold.

"Mr. Gold, Sara. Mr. Patel and I already know each other from working on this."

After acknowledging Vihaan with a friendly smile, she retook her seat.

The rest of them took seats as well—Arnold and Vihaan on one side of the table, Mr. Collier and Ms. Fromke directly across from them, their backs to floor-to-ceiling windows featuring a killer view of downtown and Elliott Bay.

Mr. Collier started with, "It's your meeting, Arnold. Please start." Then made a point of glancing at his watch.

Subtle.

Arnold cleared his throat and nodded, desperately wishing they'd had time to score some caffeine *en route.* But they hadn't, so he simply started by saying to Vihaan, "Before I hand the discussion over to you, I want you to know how much the rest of the team appreciates the hard work you've put into this assignment," and flashed him a thumbs-up. "You're on."

Unable to suppress a smile, Vihaan told Mr. Collier, "While conducting my workflow investigation, I worked closely with your lead tech Serge Valchenka. After a careful analysis of the staffing requirements, we came away with the following recommendations."

He paused, clearly basking in everyone's attention.

"Arnold was right when he suspected that Mizrahi was grossly inflating his job responsibilities. That was true when he first started with you but it's even more so now that building security has tightened floor access. Presently, your only security concern is your computer networks. What this means as far as personnel slots is that there is no need for a head of security, so I recommend eliminating that position and instead, designating a new position: Lead Tech and IT Supervisor.

I recommend promoting Mr. Valchenka to that role. Finally, to fill the gap created by this shift, you should hire one additional technician. Presently you have an excellent applicant for that position, Joe Mitchell. He's presently under review by Ms. Fromke. If she agrees, I suggest you hire him immediately."

Clearly Vihaan was done with his part.

Mr. Collier asked Fromke, "Sara, what do you think of Mr. Patel's proposal?"

Without hesitating, she proclaimed, "I wholeheartedly agree. And for the record, Mr. Mitchell is eager to accept the position."

Mr. Collier smiled. "Do you happen to know if Mr. Valchenka is in the office yet?"

She smiled at the managing partner.

"I haven't checked, but he should be. I called him last night to ask if he would come in early. I'll call." She pulled her phone from her right coat pocket.

A few minutes later Serge Valchenka stood subserviently a few feet inside the conference room entrance, hands clasped at crotch level, eyes darting from Mr. Collier to Ms. Fromke.

He licked his lips, asked, "You want to see me?"

"Please have a seat, Mr. Valchenka," Mr. Collier said. "I assume you know Mr. Gold?"

Valchenka blushed while sliding into the chair at the end of the table.

"I know *of* him, but I've never had the pleasure of meeting him in person."

Yeah, right!

They'd done battle during the pen-test.

Smiling, Arnold stood, hand extended.

"Glad to meet you, Serge."

Serge gave a limp-fish shake without offering anything further.

"I suspect you know what this meeting is about," Collier told Valchenka, "but just so there's no ambiguity, Mr. Patel will be returning to Gold and Associates full-time as of now. We need to know if you can manage the firm's IT needs until Joe Mitchell can be brought on board your team. Your position will, of course, be elevated to IT Supervisor."

Fromke quickly added, "Since Mr. Mitchell's presently between jobs, I expect that would only be a day or two at the most."

Beaming, Serge didn't hesitate.

"Not a problem, sir, and thank you. And thank you too, Vihaan," he said with a nod to him.

"I thought that went very well. What's your take?" Arnold asked Vihaan, who was navigating the white Corolla out of the basement parking garage maze. Arnold hoped that putting the Larkin Standish issue to rest would alleviate his suspicions and grievances. The last thing he wanted while they were working a delicate, high-pressure job like this was a discontented team member. Especially Prisha's husband. Undoubtedly it'd end up bubbling over to the rest of the team. If it hadn't already.

"I guess," Vihaan said, sounding suspiciously like a petulant little snot.

Aw Jesus. What now?

He couldn't just let the issue slide. It needed resolution. But how?

Arnold waited for Vihaan to clear the garage and meld into the flow of traffic before making another prod at cajoling him into opening up. After nixing several approaches, he defaulted for the path of least resistance and tact.

"Look, Vihaan, it's obvious something huge is eating at you and that it's directed at me. Whatever it is, we need to deal with it, clear the air, and put it behind us. What's going on?"

Vihaan simply set his jaw and remained mute.

After several seconds of watching him fume, Arnold pushed harder.

"C'mon, bro, let's get whatever it is out on the table and deal with it. It'll be better for all of us if you clear the air. You should know that, right?"

Vihaan gnashed his molars and gripped the steering wheel harder.

Ooookay.

Arnold decided he'd tried. At this point it was best to shut up and let Mr. Seething Anger break the silence.

Vihaan spent two more blocks of internal conflict before finally ending his fuming silence.

"I know you and Prisha have a thing going."

Arnold turned to face him.

"Say what?"

After a quick glance at him, Vihaan repeated, "You heard me. I know you and Prisha have a thing going on."

Okay, finally they were getting down to it. Arnold rotated to more comfortably face him.

"Yeah, Prisha said you accused her of that. But I'm completely baffled. What have I done to give you that impression? Especially since I'm only in town when we're working hands-on jobs. I mean, how's that supposed to work?"

The car interior went silent again. The white-knuckle force with which Vihaan was strangling the steering wheel made it look like it was about to break in two.

Finally, Vihaan said, "I see the way you two are when you're together."

"Oh yeah? How's that? Far as I know, we're totally businesslike. That's why I have such a hard time understanding how you came to your conclusion."

"That's where you're wrong. You two are not businesslike," Vihaan said emphatically. "You're way too intimate. You're like…like a married couple…You practically finish each other's sentences. That only happens when two people are, like, really close. I mean, *really* close."

Arnold thought about this. Like most misinterpreted observations, Vihaan's allegation held a crumb of truth. He and Prisha *did* work well together. They *did* see things similarly. Which meant that when faced with complex novel problems, they were able to quickly sort out tenable solutions. Most importantly, they always knew they had each other's back.

Which was precisely why Arnold had hired her as his first partner.

But as far as Prisha being anything more than a perfect sidekick, Vihaan was flat-out wrong. He was misinterpreting the high level of mutual trust that they'd established as personal intimacy.

"The only thing you're right about, Vihaan, is that we sync well. And that's totally because our approach to situations is scary similar. We resonate. Our interaction is more like a Super Bowl-winning football team in which a quarterback has wide receivers who always manage to end up in the right spot. But man, anything other than that, is just flat-out wrong."

Vihaan seemed to chew on that for a moment.

"Sticking with your football simile, if that's the case, why am I always treated like I'm second-string?"

"Oh, come on, man, you're not serious."

"Wrong! I'm absolutely serious."

"Okay, so help me out here. Give me an example."

"Fine. No problem. Here's one: a good one, too," Vihaan said with more confidence now, finding his stride. "How about the Larkin Standish assignment we just settled? Why was I assigned that instead of Lopez or Prisha?"

Having already discussed this specific complaint with Prisha, Arnold's answer was all teed up and ready.

"I excluded your wife because she's my second-in-command. As you know, at the time I was on my way back to Honolulu, so I wanted her free to handle situations in person, if need be. Which is exactly what happened with this Cor-Pace thing. Okay? And Ito couldn't do it because—"

"Yeah, yeah, yeah, I get the Ito thing. That's totally obvious."

"—is in Honolulu," Arnold said in a raised voice to make his point. "This leaves you and Carlos, right? Between the two of you, I figured you were the better fit for the job."

Arnold felt a flicker of guilt for lying, but really didn't think that now was a great time to point out that his work productivity made him the most expendable.

"Oh really?" Vihaan challenged with a heavy note of sarcasm. "What's that supposed to mean? Get specific now."

Good question. Arnold scrambled for another white lie, one Vihaan might swallow.

"Because you have Prisha to bounce ideas off of and, far as I know, Lopez doesn't have that asset. Boom. That's it."

Not too bad, actually. Just hoped that Vihaan bought it.

When Vihaan finally spoke again, he muttered, "Regardless of how much you deny it, I still think you two have something going on."

Arnold shook his head, returned to the normal sitting position, blew a sigh, said, "Then, I really don't know what to tell you, man. You're seeing things that aren't there."

"So you say. Just remember, I'm not as stupid as you may think."

CHAPTER 11

AS VIHAAN ACCELERATED away from the curb, Arnold called Prisha to tell her how well the meeting with Mr. Collier had gone and that Vihaan was now heading home. He didn't mention the part she already knew: Vihaan's unfounded jealousy. Rehashing that would just upset her more than she already was. Instead, he asked, "How're you coming on the code?"

"As you know, it's slow, but I'm working through it, line by line."

Arnold yawned. The hours were piling up. Despite the time crunch, he was beginning to sense that their efficiency and mental sharpness could benefit from a few hours of solid Zs. For sure, they needed to resolve this disaster before Friday—or at least give it their best shot—but they also couldn't afford to make any unforced errors either. Investing some time in a snooze might be wise.

At the front door now, he punched in the numeric code for the lock and stared into the small fisheye lens to allow the facial recognition program to clear him.

"How about catching a three-hour nap before getting back at it. What do you think?"

"Oh man! I know I could sure use it."

Heard the door lock click, so pushed it open, and walked into the first-floor open floor plan.

"Okay then. But first, I want to run something by you that's been seriously bugging me."

"I'm listening."

Arnold hated to end-run Mr. Cain, but...

"We're now in mid-morning Monday. We only have four more days before some serious shit hits the fan and I don't want to see that crazy bastard start killing innocent people."

"In other words, you want to go ahead and run this by Fisher. Am I right?"

He flashed on Vihaan's accusation of how cannily they seemed able to read each other's thoughts.

Well, here's a prime example.

"Exactly."

Then, feeling the need to justify his reasoning, added, "Look at it this way: we both know damn well that's where this mess is headed. We also know the sooner the Bureau's on board with it the better it is for all of us, right? And besides, I really don't want to assume a hundred percent of the responsibility for anyone who ends up at the coroner because we weren't able to determine this asshole's identity. Especially if we've done absolutely zip to backstop ourselves. As the team's leaders, I think we need to make an executive decision on this."

Without hesitating, she agreed.

"You'll get no argument from me on this. Go ahead, call him."

It felt as if a heavy weight had just been lifted from his shoulders. She obviously grasped the full implication of not having their asses adequately covered in this job. It served as an excellent example of why she was second-in-command. On the other hand, he was certain that Mr. Black-and-White Vihaan wouldn't be so understanding and flexible.

"Thanks. I needed to hear your take on it." After a brief pause, he added, "But this raises the question of what we tell Mr. Cain and Mr. Harris? Especially with Harris being so adamant about keeping this mess in-house and under wraps."

After a sarcastic laugh, she said, "We don't tell them anything unless absolutely forced to. But to be perfectly honest, I don't think we have any other choice in the matter. Harris wants to do what he thinks is best for Cor-Pace and we need to do what's best for Gold and Associates. Right?"

Another wave of shoulder-sagging relief came over him.

"Right," he said. Silence. "Okay. I'll catch some Zs after I call him."

Fisher's cell went straight to a recording advising him to leave a message. Arnold stated his name along with a message that he urgently wanted to discuss a rapidly evolving critical situation that needed his guidance. Overstated? Nope. After disconnecting, a veil of relief shrouded him for having taken the first step in covering their collective asses.

Arnold wearily climbed the stairs to crash on his king-size bed.

Minutes later, *Three Hearts in a Tangle* blared from his phone with Fisher's name on the screen.

"Mr. Fisher?" Arnold said.

"What's so urgent, Gold?"

Fisher's familiar crisp staccato voice was reassuring. For the first time since accepting this job, Arnold felt as if the team was on solid ground. And this rippled another wave of relief through him.

Okay, sure, this was in direct conflict with his employer's wishes, but Arnold believed it was unquestioningly the right thing to do.

For everyone involved. Even if Mr. Harris couldn't see it. Though he was pretty sure that Mr. Cain would side with him when the truth finally came out. For eventually it would have to.

"Thanks for returning my call, Mr. Fisher." The sudden release of tension caused the words to start tumbling out. "What I'm about to tell you is extremely sensitive and confidential. The reasons will be obvious as I get into the particulars."

He went on to explain the life-threatening cardiac arrest that landed Mr. Brown in Harborview via Medic One. He then described the subsequent phone calls between the person labeling himself Hacker and his nonnegotiable demand to shut down the clinical trial. He wrapped up by describing how Mr. Harris and Mr. Cain pressured him and Prisha into trying to track down Hacker's identity despite their repeated insistence that Cor-Pace's best course of action was to hand this bitch over to the Bureau.

Which, of course, Fisher wholeheartedly agreed with.

In summary, Arnold reemphasized the team's present bind: trying to accommodate the CEO and the corporate attorney while believing that the FBI should be involved. He ended the narrative by asking for Fisher's advice.

Which both men knew was a flimsily disguised plea for help.

"Interesting bind you've gotten your ass into, Gold, very interesting. But why the Bureau instead of SPD? After all, this company is in Seattle, is it not?"

Arnold realized he'd forgotten to clarify this wrinkle.

"Because they have trial sites in four different states."

"Ah, of course."

As Arnold waited for Special Agent Fisher to elaborate, he heard the background clicking of a keyboard.

A moment later, Fisher said, "You realize, don't you, that you're still on our books as my CI."

So? "No, not really…" he answered tentatively. "Why? Is that important?"

"It is. And here's why. If what you're telling me is correct—that Cor-Pace doesn't want our help working up an obvious extortion case—then I really can't barge in and work it. That's your bad news." Pause. "Your good news is that since you, as a registered CI, just advised me of the situation, I can open a case file based on the information you just provided. The downside for you is that now that I'm aware of the extortion, the law requires that I inform my supervisor about it."

"Aw Jesus," Arnold said palm wiping his lower face. "I was afraid of that."

"Hold on. Let me get to the good part." Pause. "Since you don't want Harris to know that I know, I will slow-walk my report to my supervisor, which will, at least, buy you time. A couple of days, maybe. But if this hacker is serious, Harris will be forced to change his position and involve us very soon. Already having a file in the system will certainly expedite things when that time arrives. See my point?"

"Yeah, I do," Arnold answered with an uneasy intermingling of relief and exasperation swirling through him. There was relief in knowing that Fisher was now on board, yet he remained frustrated at not getting the help he'd been hoping for.

And what help exactly had he been hoping for?

That White Knight Fisher would swoop in and force Mr. Harris to turn this tar-baby case over to the Bureau?

Yeah, probably deep down in his denial center, that's exactly what he'd hoped for. But that was totally unrealistic. So here he was, mired in the same situation as five minutes ago: shouldering the entire responsibility for identifying the nutjob asshole.

On the other hand, he did savor the sense of relief knowing that the team's asses were officially covered.

"You'll keep me updated frequently?" Fisher asked, making it clear the discussion was over.

"You bet."

Every freaking miniscule detail, in fact.

Call completed, Arnold set his phone on the bedside charger, then asked the beside Alexa to wake him in two hours.

Soon as Alexa confirmed his request, he closed his eyes and conked out.

CHAPTER 12

ARNOLD FLIPPED ON the red power switch to his coffee maker before tucking into the kitchen table to rejoin the chat room. Prisha was already there, working.

"I'm back," he told her.

"So I see. Ready to continue on the code? I'm on line two-sixteen."

"Sorry, not yet. Just before I nodded off, I flashed back on Vihaan's question of why would someone want to torpedo the study? I got to hand it to him. It's a great question. One I think we need to follow up on. In other words, I want to ask Harris about it."

Head cocked, she appeared to contemplate his words for a couple of seconds.

"Know what? You're right. That really *is* a good point. Mind if I join you?"

They really needed to press on with the code, but what would a few minutes cost? And besides, two sets of ears might pick up more than one.

"Not at all. Call you on the cell."

After connecting with Prisha on the phone, he conferenced in John Harris's number and switched to speakerphone so his hands would be free to jot notes as needed.

"Mr. Harris?" Arnold asked the male who picked up the call.

"Yes. And I presume this is Mr. Gold?"

"That's correct. And Prisha Patel's on the call too. We have a question for you."

"Fire away."

"Can you think of any reason someone would want to shut down the clinical trial?"

Harris blew an audible breath.

"No I can't. And believe me, I've been asking myself that very question repeatedly since getting that first call. Why? You think it's important?"

Arnold was sliding his mouse back across the table now. Prisha had mentioned something in passing that, at the time, seemed significant. He'd made a mental note of it, but now...Damn it! He could sense it floating just beyond consciousness...

He had to keep Harris talking because maybe something he would say would force that idea to surface again.

"Could you please take me through your conversations with him one more time using his exact words as you remember them?"

"Certainly."

Harris began reciting both sides of the conversation.

"...and then he said we couldn't afford another death—"

Bingo!

"Stop!" Arnold cut him off in mid-sentence. "Tell me more about that last part." Pause. "Are you saying that a patient has died during the trial?"

Harris didn't answer immediately, but when he did, his voice carried the weight of regret and sadness.

"Ah...yes, I'm sorry to say. A very unfortunate case, too. One that occurred very early on. He was one of our very first patients. Why? Is it important?"

This was the point that'd been skimming the dark side of consciousness when he was too preoccupied with other matters to stop to shine a light on it.

"Don't know yet. Tell me exactly what happened."

Arnold grabbed his note pad and mechanical pencil. Although the laptop was ready to go in front of him, for something as potentially important as this, he preferred to jot notes because it helped him remember small details more clearly.

"All right..." Harris said with reluctance, as if doing so would dredge up a bad memory. "He was the second patient in our Phase I trial and, in fact, lived here in Seattle. One of our local cardiologists recruited him because he was an ideal candidate for what our Cor-Rate II can do. The surgery itself went without a hitch, but the device failed to perform as intended and tragically the patient died from what is presumed to be a fatal arrhythmia."

"The type of arrhythmia your device is designed to treat?" Arnold asked for clarification.

"Yes."

Arnold rolled that around for a moment.

Prisha jumped in with, "Sorry to interrupt, but I need to clarify something. I'm not sure I understood your last point. Are you saying that the device didn't work as it's supposed to?"

Harris didn't answer immediately, as if organizing his thoughts.

"If that was what you understood, then thanks for asking for a clarification," he said with a defensive tone. "The patient died because the device didn't prevent a fatal arrythmia. But this was not the fault of the device itself or its design. I want to be very clear on this point."

When Harris didn't explain further, Prisha stated, "Actually, I found that to be even more confusing. Please go into that in greater detail."

"Why is this important? It sounds like you're trying to blame Cor-Pace for a patient who died of their own pathology. Why aren't you putting your effort into finding the person responsible for our problems?"

"Because it may speak to motivation," Arnold interjected, not liking the tone edging into Harris's voice.

After what sounded like a sigh of frustration, Harris began, "There can be multiple reasons why a pacemaker might fail to do the job it's designed for, but in this specific case it appeared to fail because of a lead dislodgement."

He was pretty sure what Harris intended by the remark, but asked anyway.

"A lead dislodgement?" Arnold asked. "Remember, you're talking to IT geeks and not medical professionals. Again, we need more clarity on that point."

"I really don't see the relevance to these questions, Mr. Gold," Harris said, with a harsher bite of defensive irritation in his voice. "What's your point?"

Arnold muzzled his knee-jerk reply for something more politic. He paused to remind himself that the toxic brew of stress, fatigue, and helplessness that he was feeling was undoubtedly more acute and focused for Harris, especially with a stopwatch ticking relentlessly in everyone's minds.

"We don't know yet if it is relevant or not. That's why we're asking," Arnold answered as patiently as possible. "But I *do* know that most extortion cases are done for either ransom or revenge. It's not every day that a hacker devotes the time it took him to break into a high-security network for the sole purpose of shutting down a clinical trial. In other words, I'm looking for a motive. Understand?"

No one spoke for several tense seconds.

In a condescending tone, Harris finally explained, "The leads are the wires that connect the device to the heart muscles. These connections can break or dislodge anywhere between the device and the heart or any time after implantation because of numerous reasons. If so, the problem may not come to anyone's attention until the device fails to do the job it's intended to do. In this unfortunate instance, the issue wasn't discovered until the patient underwent an autopsy. He died shortly after the device was implanted."

"Tell us about the patient. His name and any other particulars." Arnold asked.

When Harris didn't answer, Arnold said, "This could be important, Mr. Harris."

"You realize, don't you, that this information is extremely confidential and must be treated as such?"

Arnold rolled his eyes.

"Yes, of course. We will make certain the name doesn't go further than the team."

"Alright then." Pause. "His name was Alfred Bosko, but I assume you want some of his biographical particulars as well. Date of birth, and such."

"You're correct."

"In that case, give me a moment to access our database."

As Harris was opening the Cor-Pace database, Arnold did the same with their case-file database so that he would be ready to add the information in real time. He began by typing Alfred Bosko's name into the appropriate field after asking Harris to verify the spelling.

"Okay, let me know when you're ready and I'll read you the pertinent information."

Arnold said, "I'm all set. Prisha?"

"Yeah, me too."

Harris read him Bosko's dates of birth and death, address, contact phone number along with his emergency contact number, Arnold verifying each detail while entering them into the database.

"Is there anything else you want to know?" Harris asked when finished.

"Bear with me a moment," Arnold said, going over the new information again now that he could focus more on the actual content instead of the mechanics of loading it into the database.

Everything looked good.

Was he missing anything?

He asked Prisha. "Can you think of anything else to ask?"

Prisha: "Nope. I'm good."

Ah yes, almost forgot.

Arnold asked Harris, "You're on your cellphone now, right?"

"I am."

"Is this the same phone Hacker called you on?"

"It is. Why?"

"Any idea how Hacker got that number?" Arnold asked, hoping to jog loose a potentially fruitful thread to pursue.

Harris replied without hesitating.

"That's one of the first questions that crossed my mind. That information is in the public domain because it's listed at the back of the main consent form in a section that contains contact information for both me and our medical director. It lists our names, cellphone numbers, and office address. In other words, that information's readily available to anyone with a copy of the consent."

Arnold jotted this point down as definitely noteworthy. Even scribbled two quick asterisks and an underline next to the note.

"Hold on a moment," he told Harris, while jotting an additional note that Bosko's family undoubtedly had that consent form and therefore had Harris's cell phone number. It was, admittedly, an anemic association, but an association definitely worth some follow-up consideration.

"That's it for me for now, but I'm sure other questions will probably pop up. Prisha?"

"I can't think of anything else. But, as Arnold said, I'm sure there'll be additional questions as we dig deeper. Thanks for the information. It's very helpful."

Call finished, Arnold remained staring at the phone, ruminating over the latest information.

After a few seconds, Prisha asked, "Ready to get back to it?"

As important as inspecting Elijah Brown's device firmware was, this new lead demanded further investigation. He asked, "You mind continuing on with that while I do some background checking on this Bosko thing?"

"Why? What're you thinking?"

Arnold burnt a few seconds putting vague associations into a coherent thought.

"Okay, try this on for size. The most atypical aspect to this disaster is that the extortionist isn't after money or anything of tangible value."

After weighing that statement a moment, he amended it with, "Let me phrase that slightly differently. He's not after anything of *apparent* value. Which I take to mean it's only of value to *him*. Don't know about you, but to me this whole thing's beginning to reek of revenge. What do you think? Make any sense?"

After taking time to answer, Prisha nodded. "Since you put it that way, yeah, you may be on to something." She shrugged. "What the hell, go for it."

Ideas began zipping through his mind.

"Stay right here while I do this, okay?"

"Wasn't planning to go anywhere. I'm the one still working through the code."

"It'll only take a few minutes."

Satisfied that they were still working together, Arnold turned his attention to reorganizing his notes into a more coherent and logical stream of information. He underlined the part of his notes that mentioned that the patient's death was the result of a preventable error. Once he'd rewritten the notes for clarity, he filed them point by point in the database.

Finished, he sat back and asked himself, *so what?*

Although he was certain the preventable-error part was relevant, he wasn't sure how or where it applied to the case.

Dead end? Was he fixating on nothing?

Maybe.

He'd focused so intently on documenting the data accurately that he'd lost track of the logic that had flashed through his mind while transcribing it. He now worked on reconstructing it. Arnold loved flow charts. Probably as a holdover from writing code. So, he broke the issue down to a yes-or-no, either/or logic pattern and it went like this: Alfred Bosko died in a clinical trial of a device that, if it'd worked as intended, should've kept him alive. But it didn't. Why? Because the leads weren't attached. End result: he died because the device that should've kept him alive couldn't save his life. Whose fault was that?

Ah. Now this is where perception was key.

One answer was Harris's point of view: Bosko's genetics gave him a bad heart and in the end, this was what killed him.

Another perception was that the Cor-Pace device should've prevented his death but didn't. Whose fault was that?

Voilà.

But was that enough for a sellable motive? That remained to be seen. But this was the best they had at the moment. Making the next question: was that motive strong enough to want to shut down the entire clinical trial?

That'd be a huge stretch for some people, but probably not for some others.

Arnold logged into the King County Death record website to search for Bosko's death certificate, found it, and stored a copy in the database.

After signing out of that website, he searched *The Seattle Times* for an obituary in the days immediately following Bosko's death. *Bingo.* He uploaded a copy into the database too. With the information securely stored, he poured a fresh cup of coffee, rotated through a few stretches, then returned to the table to read the obit.

Then reread it.

Alfred Bosko was survived by a loving wife of thirty-five years, Margo, and an equally loving son, Alfred Bosko Jr.

"Hey Prisha, I may have found something."

She glanced up from her work.

"Yeah? What?"

After filling her in on Bosko's obituary, he said, "I think I should devote some time digging into the son. You agree?"

He wanted her buy-in since she'd be the one left with the tedious task of plowing through the firmware line by freaking line. Getting it was especially critical after listening to Vihaan's whining accusation of being assigned only the team's shit jobs. Didn't want her thinking that he was dumping on her too.

"Because...?"

"Well, because this is our only tangible thread for a possible motive."

"A possible motive..." she echoed, as if suspicious of this as justification to slough off the drudgery.

"Yeah, think about it. Pops dies because a lead in this life-saving device isn't connected. That could be a righteous enough reason to really piss you off, right?"

She scoffed. "I figured out that part all on my own, dude. Just think it's a stretch to get from there to first-degree murder. And besides, it sounds like the lead became disconnected rather than not connected. There's a difference."

"Not if it happens to your father. And besides, it's the only thread we have at the moment."

Silence.

"Tell you what, I'll just knock off a quick plunge into the kid and if nothing of interest jumps out at me, I'll be back to help with the code. Deal?"

"You da boss, massa," she replied.

Ah, Christ.

Arnold massaged the fatigue-ache blossoming in his right temple.

"Thirty minutes. That's all, okay? You can set a timer if it makes you feel better."

More silence.

Arnold was about to defend his position once again but decided, screw it, just get to work.

"Promise I won't take more than that."

Prisha went back to the firmware code and Arnold ran Alfred Bosko Jr.'s name through all the major search engines, compiling a list of links. With that complete, he began quickly sorting through them one by one.

Then, *voilà.* Got an interesting hit. Sending him down an entirely different rabbit hole.

He quickly accumulated several items of interest.

Eyes closed, he sat back to tie together the various scraps of information just uncovered.

"Yo, Prisha, think I have something for us."

"Hold on. Let me mark my place. Last time you distracted me I had to backtrack. I hate that."

Arnold waited.

A moment later, "Okay, shoot."

"Turns out Alfred Junior's a pretty interesting dude, but I'll just recap the high points. For starters, the guy's, like, crazy smart. He graduated Lakeside. Know about that school?" he asked, since Prisha grew up in New York he didn't know how much she and Vihaan knew about the local area.

"No. What about it?"

"It's a private school for grades five through twelve. And like a lot of private schools with such high luster, it costs a shitload to attend. I have no idea if our friend received financial aid, but regardless, it must've cost *beaucoup* bucks. From there he went to the U-Dub," meaning the University of Washington, "and got a BS in, get this, *computer sciences*." He paused to let this sink in. "Then he turned around and scored admission to the Paul G. Allen Ph.D. program."

"Never heard of it, but from your tone, I guess I'm supposed to be impressed."

"Paul Allen? As in the Microsoft Paul Allen?"

"Don't be a dipshit. Of course, I know who *he* is. I've just never heard of that particular program is all. Don't be getting all uppity on me about it, okay?"

"Got it." Pause. "Well, it's a post-grad program at U-Dub, and admission is ultra-competitive. I mean, like, they get upward of 2,500 applications internationally for fifty to sixty openings." Another dramatic pause. "Given his history in software design, I'd say it's totally appropriate we tag him as a person of interest."

Several seconds of silence passed before Prisha nodded.

"Yeah, you're right. When you put it in that context, no way can I disagree."

Arnold couldn't suppress a smile. Progress. Or so he hoped.

"In that case, I think it's time to check-in with the rest of the team for a three-sixty update."

Prisha nodded again. "I'll switch over." Then was gone.

When Arnold changed to the main chat room, Mays, Ito, Lopez, Prisha and Vihaan were laughing at a joke. Prisha asked Arnold, "What took you so long?"

"Wanted to freshen up my coffee and start a new pot. So, what up?"

"Michelle?" Prisha said.

After clearing her throat, Mays said, "You were right. We found and removed a key stroke logger from Dawn's workstation. Meaning we now know for sure how that butt-wipe copped the database password."

Arnold: "Well, that answers that question. What we still don't know is how he broke into the network, right?"

Vihaan stated the obvious: "Odds are he tricked someone— probably Dawn—into biting on a phishing scam. But whatever he used, it must be pretty sophisticated because we haven't been able to find it yet."

Arnold was impressed. This was one of the exceedingly rare times when Vihaan had actually made a quasi-constructive comment instead of bitching about their workload.

He asked, "Anything else before Prisha and I report?"

"What? Finding the key stroke logger isn't enough?" Lopez asked, jokingly.

"Not even close," Arnold replied, all grins, as if holding a Royal Flush. "Okay, here goes; so far we haven't found anything of value in Brown's firmware, but we do have one item we think is worth pursuing further."

Prisha added, "Drum roll, please."

"But first," Arnold went on, dragging out the suspense like a TV announcer. "I want to give Vihaan credit for posing a pivotal question. Why would someone want to sabotage Cor-Pace? I mean, think about it. What's in it for them?"

Clearly rhetorical.

Not surprising, no one took the bait.

Arnold walked them through his phone conversation with Harris and how that led to researching Alfred Bosko Senior's background, which in turn led him to discover his highly computer-literate son, Alfred Jr.

At which point, Mays exclaimed, "Holy steaming dog shit!" Then, after a brief pause: "Hang on a minute. I just remembered something."

Arnold experienced a jolt of excitement of something about to break loose. He could feel it.

The sysadmin appeared too busy on her keyboard to elaborate. A moment later she glanced back into the webcam with an apologetic expression.

"There was this big blow-up a few weeks after Bosko's death. Reason I remember it so vividly is that we discussed the complication in a team meeting. Hold on while I pull up the minutes from that meeting."

No one spoke as she resumed searching, complete with more background key clicking.

A half-minute later, she told the group, "Yeah, here we go...it was a royal fuckup of gargantuan proportions—if you'll excuse my choice of words—but that pretty much describes it." She gave a sigh of regret, followed by, "I need to preface this by saying that once a patient enrolls in the study, they're plugged into the research protocol that's *strictly* adhered to. There's absolutely zero flexibility. None at all. So..." she inhaled deeply, "what happened was about ten days after Bosko died, the protocol automatically sent him a Quality-of-Life questionnaire to complete. I mean, that questionnaire is hard-wired into the protocol, and is supposed to be filled out within a rigidly specified number of days after enrollment. No one thought to stop the protocol after he died. Don't ask me why. I'm just telling you what happened. Anyway, his son—the guy you just mentioned—sent it back with a scorching email. I mean this thing was burn-your-hair-off-scathing. Hang tight and I'll pull up a copy. Should only take a minute or two."

More background key clicking.

Arnold texted Prisha: GOTTA BE HIM, RIGHT?

Prisha: RIGHT

"Okay," Mays said a moment later, "here it is. And aw shit, wouldn't you know it, it has an attachment. Anyone willing to bet it's *not* malware?"

No one took her up on the offer.

"Well? You going to scan it or what?" Arnold asked, wanting to keep things moving, thinking that without doubt, a malware scan would tell them exactly what to search for in the Cor-Pace network. By now, each passing second was making him see the Friday deadline approaching at Warp speed.

"Already doing that," Mays replied. A moment later, she exclaimed, "Got it. Yep, a RAT."

A remote access trojan.

Arnold: "Okay, so we now know how he hacked your network and encrypted database." Then, shaking his head, added, "Nothing fancier than the basic tools of the trade."

"As of now," piped in Prisha, "we have several pieces of evidence—albeit some indirect—to implicate Alfred Bosko Jr. as the hacker. To top it off, we have a plausible motive for him to want to shut down the trial. I don't know about you guys, but I think it's time for another serious talk with Harris and Cain about asking the FBI for help on this."

"Amen," Arnold said with mixed enthusiasm. "But the last time I tried to sell Harris the idea, he made it painfully clear he wants this investigation kept away from law enforcement."

"We get that, Boss. But that was before we had any of this new intel," Lopez countered. "This shit changes everything."

"I know, I know," Arnold shot back. "But I suspect he'll simply twist it around by pointing out that our progress just validates his initial position that we can work this case faster than the Feds. In other words, he'll want us to keep at it instead of handing it off. He'll claim that handing it off risks getting press coverage. He'd be dead set against that."

Prisha said, "I gotta say, having experienced the same song and dance as Arnold did, I agree with what he just said. On the other hand, I think it'd be smart to at least go on record as having advised them to involve the Feds. In other words, I think we need to take it up a step and record the call. I want to cover our asses if this mess blows up into the disaster it looks like it's gonna be. Also, I suggest we'll improve our odds of success if we go through Mr. Cain first. After all, as their corporate lawyer, I have to believe he is looking for a way to cover his ass too."

Nodding approval, Arnold said, "Great suggestion. Why don't you guys take a breather while I call Mr. Cain. I'll text you his answer."

"Deal!" chimed in Lopez.

CHAPTER 13

CAIN ANSWERED ON the third ring with, "Arnold?" in a haggard sleep-deprived voice.

"Yes sir, it's me. And I'm calling about the case. We've made some real progress but are at a point where we need solid legal advice."

The lawyer hesitated as if worried about what he might be getting into.

"If I can provide it, I certainly will."

"Oh, and before I continue, I want you to know I'm recording this call. Okay?"

Cain remained silent for several seconds before saying, "I see," in a tone filled with suspicious caution. "Proceed."

Arnold went on to describe the circumstantial evidence they'd accumulated to suggest that Alfred Bosko Jr. could well be the hacker.

When Arnold finished, Cain asked, "You just presented some excellent work, son, but why are you telling me this?"

"Because now, more than ever, I feel that the FBI should be running this investigation, not us."

Several additional seconds of silence followed.

The lawyer finally responded with, "At this point, what could the FBI do that you haven't been able to?"

Having anticipated this question, Arnold had his answer cued up, ready to go. "For starters, they could obtain a warrant to search his computer."

Again, Cain didn't answer immediately. Arnold suspected he was choosing his next words very prudently. And again, he flashed on the disturbing suspicion that Mr. Cain might continue to support Harris's stance. On the other hand, being aware that their conversation was being recorded...

Finally, Cain spoke: "At first glance, your point makes perfect sense. But the problem is that for the Feds to secure a search warrant for Mr. Bosko's electronic devices, they must present a convincing case to the Federal Magistrate. From what you've described, you fail to meet the bar for sufficient probable cause to win a search warrant."

Arnold wanted to scream. His head felt like it was about to explode.

"But we're trying to prevent this guy from killing someone."

"So *you* say. Personally? I believe you. Most likely because I have some skin in this game." Another pause. "Son, what I'm telling you is that from the standpoint of a judge hearing this information *de novo*, you have yet to accumulate enough *hard* evidence to win that argument. I'm not sure how I can express this opinion more clearly and concisely."

The only way they were going to be able to obtain more evidence would be to figure out a way to break into Bosko's computer. That would not only be extremely time-consuming under any circumstance, but considering this dude's apparent skill level, it seemed close to impossible. Especially given the looming deadline.

Was hacking Bosko's network what Mr. Cain was suggesting they do? If so, he wanted that on the recording.

"So, for the record, what're you telling me to do?"

"Son, I'm not telling you to do anything. You asked for my opinion, and that's exactly what I gave you. It's my professional opinion that before the FBI stands a good chance of securing a search warrant for Mr. Bosko's digital devices, they need more compelling evidence to implicate him as the person behind this fiasco. To date, you don't have that evidence."

And there it was. The implied marching order.

"In other words, you want us to find more evidence?" Arnold said in a tone dripping with his frustration. "The only way we can possibly do that is to break into his network. Which, I shouldn't have to remind you, is illegal."

Dead silence.

A moment later, Arnold asked, "Is that what you're suggesting we do?"

More silence.

Yeah, what did he expect after telling the lawyer he was recording them?

CHAPTER 14

AFTER A QUICK break to throw together a PB&J on whole wheat, which he washed down with a Diet Pepsi, Arnold reconvened the team to break the bad news.

Vihaan was the first person to fracture the stunned silence.

"Know what I think? I think we've done our part and it's now up to Cor-Pace to take this mess to the next level. After all, they need to shoulder some responsibility for their own fate instead of sloughing it all on us."

"While I agree with the last part," Arnold shot back. "We haven't finished what we agreed to do."

"Which is?" Vihaan challenged.

Arnold realized he was getting into a pissing match with him.

Why? Fatigue? Frustration? Because of his allegations? All of the above?

He sucked in a deep breath, said, "Sorry, dude. Nerves." Then in a more even tone: "We made a commitment to Mr. Cain and Mr. Harris to put forth our best effort, right? I, for one, don't want to back out now. Prisha and I haven't finished reviewing the firmware and you guys haven't locked down the network enough to ensure that this asshole can't come back to play games again. I'll bet you he still has a backdoor hidden somewhere in there."

"Well, shit," Lopez said, "isn't that sort of like closing the barn door after the fact? I mean, dude's got all the serial numbers. At this point *he don't need no stinkin' backdoor!*" in an exaggerated *Blazing Saddles* Mexican accent. "Maybe Cain doesn't buy Bosko as our guy just yet, but we're all convinced he's good for it. And besides, at the moment he's our one and only person of interest. I suggest we take a huge gamble and put a hundred percent of our effort into a deep dive on him instead of trying to lock the barn door."

"I totally agree," Arnold answered. "But we committed to helping secure their network. I don't want to get a reputation for backing out on our commitments. Meanwhile Prisha and I'll finish checking Brown's firmware for a possible hint. Once we've crossed those two items off our list, then yeah, I'm all for putting all of our effort on him." He paused. "Anyone disagree?"

No one took issue with the plan.

"Okay then," Prisha said. "Let's get back to it."

Once back in their separate chat room, Arnold and Prisha picked up doping out the firmware code, taking turns reading off the instructions and then drawing a line through the printout.

Arnold's phone rang. It was resting on its charge pad to the left of his laptop. A quick glance at the caller ID. Not a name he recognized. Spam? Answer it?

Shit! Might as well. His concentration and train of thought were totally trashed now anyway.

He told Prisha, "Hang on while I take this."

"You don't want me to keep going?"

"Naw. This'll only take a second. Looks like a wrong number." He swiped ACCEPT and barked, "Hello?"

She asked, "Why are you ignoring my texts?" in a demanding but instantly recognizable voice.

"Aw Jesus."

He raised his glasses to palm-wipe his face, anger and frustration bubbling up in his chest.

"I thought I was crystalline. I'm *working*. I can't afford to be interrupted when I'm focusing. Why are you having such a hard time understanding this?"

"Working too hard to answer a text?" she said, her tone growing petulant.

A tsunami of emotions crashed on him. Most of all, being supremely pissed at the interruptions despite having explained multiple times just how intense this job was. But he was even more annoyed at himself for feeling so let down that this relationship wasn't turning out to be as healthy as he'd initially envisioned it.

Man, you really know how to pick them.

"Look, Noriko, I don't know how to be any clearer about this but listen to me very carefully. I'm working an extremely difficult time-sensitive job, meaning I don't have time for chit chat. With you or anyone. Please do *not* call back. I'll call you when I have a moment to chat. I'm hanging up now."

"Don't you dare hang up on—"

After disconnecting, Arnold blocked the number she'd just called from.

"Girlfriend issues?" Prisha asked.

Shit, didn't mute the laptop microphone.

With his face starting into the space-heater thing, he nodded.

"Yeah, something like that."

"Oh goodie, one more topic to discuss when the dust settles, because while you were dealing with that, I came across something I think you just might be interested in. Go down two lines from where you were when you took the call."

"Give me a moment to work my way down there."

Muttering, he found the line he'd last been on before the interruption, then carefully moved down to line 283 of Elijah Brown's firmware. Comparing it word for word to the standard Cor-Pace firmware showed that several instructions had been added.

Arnold whistled softly.

"Bingo. You found a definite patch." Meaning a place where instructions had been altered or inserted. "What's your take on it?"

"I haven't had all that long to completely dope it out, but it looks to me that it allows another device to interfere with its normal function. Whadaya think?"

Pinching his lips, Arnold studied the extra instructions for several seconds.

"Yep, think you're right. Or at least, it looks that way to me."

"As outrageous as this might sound, that couldn't be a phone number, could it?"

Sitting back, eyeing the added instructions, Arnold slowly worked through the code immediately before and after the lines in an attempt to reconstruct the purpose of the modification.

"It's totally unbelievable, but it looks like that to me too." He blinked, looked at it again. "Just for the hell of it, I'm going to dial that number and see what happens?"

She pushed a loose strand of black hair from her forehead. "The thought did cross my mind...but I wanted to run it past you first. See any downside to doing that?"

"Good question," Arnold mused. "Hard to believe someone smart enough to worm their way into an encrypted database would be dumb enough to leave their phone number behind, but I guess this is precisely the reason we're looking at it so closely, right?"

After finger-combing his hair and pushing his glasses back up his nose, he said, "What're you thinking? It could be a trip wire?"

"Like if someone calls that number, he'll know someone's on to him?" Prisha asked with a note of doubt.

"Exactly. But listening to you say it just now...that doesn't really make much sense. I'm just thinking out loud. I mean how often do you get a wrong number? Not often, but it does happen, right?"

"Right, but that's exactly why I wanted to run it past you before trying it. Wanted to share the responsibility of making that decision."

"The scary thing is, I really don't see much risk in it. Which, in itself, is a tad bit creepy. Because there's always a downside, right?"

"Right."

"Well hell, let me give it a try," he said, putting the phone on speaker. He dialed the number, then held the phone so Prisha could see the screen while listening. They heard the pause of a call working its way through various switches, then an aborted ring that abruptly transferred to a recorded message: *The Verizon number you are trying to reach is not in service.*

Bingo.

Disconnecting the call, Arnold set the phone next to the laptop, said, "Let me put this in the database before I forget."

After a moment, Prisha asked, "Get both points? The phone number and that it's on the Verizon network?"

"I did. I also added that the number looks like it might be a TracFone."

"While you were doing that, I Googled it, but it didn't hit on anything. You might want to add that too."

"Good point." Arnold paused to add that.

"Okay, done. Now that we have a tangible lead, I'm going to ask Mr. Fisher if he can run it."

Prisha said, "Should we share this with the rest of the team first?"

After considering the suggestion, Arnold replied, "Yeah, probably a good time for another three-sixty. This thing's moving faster than a speeding bullet."

"Now all we need is for Superman to bail us out."

Back in the main chat room, Arnold updated the rest of the team about the phone number embedded in Mr. Brown's device's firmware.

When finished, he asked, "Anything new on your end?"

"Unfortunately, no," Lopez reported for the group. "Mays and I are still working on sanitizing their network. Vihaan, got anything new for us?"

Vihaan cleared his throat. "We decided that I should put my effort into researching our new BFF."

The group decided, or did you demand it? Did it make any difference? No, not really.

"And?" Arnold asked.

"Apparently our friend lives at home with his mom and presently isn't employed or going to school."

"Good to know," Arnold told him. "You put it in the database?"

"Uh...not yet."

"Please do it now before you forget."

"Doing it now," Vihaan said.

After what Arnold felt was an awkward pause, Ito—who seldom voiced an opinion during team meetings—said, "That phone number is a pretty compelling reason to involve the FBI."

Lopez said, "I second that."

Arnold scratched the back of his head, thinking.

Yeah, probably time.

Besides, he'd heard that confession was good for the soul.

"Okay guys, it's time to fess up." Arnold paused, glanced away from the webcam a beat, then back at the lens. "I've contacted him already. Did it several hours ago, in fact. I wanted our asses covered in case this thing blows up in our faces. Which I think it's got an extremely good chance of doing. Yeah, I'm super-aware that Mr. Harris has been more than emphatic about not wanting them involved, but I saw no other option. Anyone have a problem with that?"

When no one said a word, Arnold said, "Good. I'll ask him to run the number for us. I suspect he'll do it."

"I have a suggestion," Prisha offered. Then, without waiting for an answer, went on to say, "Before doing that, let's get Cain and Harris on a conference call and, like, really emphasize that we see no other way to move this thing forward without involving Fisher. See if that changes their position."

Arnold considered her suggestion a moment, shrugged, said, "Hey, might as well. I mean, what do we have to lose, right? All they can do is to tell us no again. Which won't change what we plan to do anyway. Want to be on the call with me?"

"Why not?" she said, then yawned. "Sorry."

After corralling Cain, Harris, and Prisha on a conference call, Arnold brought the two non-team members up to date on their progress, summarizing it by saying, "Essentially, we have an excellent case— although admittedly circumstantial—pointing to one person as our hacker. Additionally, we have a cellphone number the hacker added to Mr. Brown's device. Our problem is we don't know if the two are connected. If we can show a definite link between them, it'd go a long way in confirming your hacker's identity and getting that search warrant."

"Have you tried Googling the number?" Harris asked.

"Oh, give me a freaking break." Arnold snapped, mildly offended. "Of course we did."

He quickly reminded himself that everyone involved in this case was on edge due to sleep-deprivation-fueled stress. But he didn't apologize for sounding harsh. Instead, he simply added, "It's not readily available."

"We have the utmost confidence in you, son," Cain responded gently in an apparent attempt to smooth over raw edges. "However, these are questions we need to ask, so please don't take offense when we do our job. Nothing more, nothing less. Why don't all of us just take a deep breath and then, Arnold can finish his report."

Arnold said, "Given what we know, I believe the time's perfect time to ask the FBI for help. In particular, to ask them to run the number and if it turns out to be associated with our person of interest we could obtain a search warrant for his digital devices."

Mr. Cain said, "You've done some excellent work, son. And your conclusion makes sense. But this, of course, is John's decision. What do you think, John? Can you appreciate Arnold's reasoning?"

"I can see *why* he voiced that opinion," Harris replied, as if this were a discussion just between the two of them. "I just don't come to the same conclusion. The amount of information his team's been able to amass in a relatively short period of time is extremely impressive..."

"But?" Arnold asked, since Harris's unfinished sentence implied a reservation. And he was pretty sure what he was about to say.

"But," Harris continued, "the progress you've made simply validates my original thesis that as a group of hackers, you can move more efficiently and expeditiously in this arena than can the FBI. They, after all, have various legal hoops to jump through that you don't need to bother with. Obtaining a search warrant is a perfect example. Obtaining one would probably take days. Time we simply don't have."

"You know that for a fact?" Arnold asked.

When Harris didn't reply, Arnold pushed it.

"It's critical to look at the contents of his digital devices."

"I agree."

Confused, Arnold asked, "Sounds like you just agreed with me, yet you don't want the FBI involved? I don't get it. What am I missing?"

"Your team is a group of accomplished hackers, isn't it?" Harris replied.

Not liking the tone of where this was heading, Arnold shot back. "Yes, but we operate legally."

He cringed at how pompously self-righteous his words sounded. As if his team was on the side of the angels. Hardly.

"That may well be," Harris shot back, "but breaking into computers is what you do, isn't it?" He made it a statement instead of a question.

Why even bother trying to answer the when-did-you-stop-beating-your-wife question? What would it achieve? Absolutely nothing.

Arnold asked, "Where precisely are you going with this, Mr. Harris?" Despite knowing the answer.

"'Where is this going?' you ask in feigned innocence. As if you have no idea. Which makes me wonder if you're recording this conversation as some sort of future bargaining chip. Well, Mr. Gold, at this point I could care less. My main concern is saving our company and the clinical trial. Take a moment to look at the big picture from my perspective." Harris paused for effect before continuing with, "In a very short period of time you've gathered excellent—albeit circumstantial—evidence to suggest that Alfred Bosko Jr. *could* be our hacker. At this point you have two choices. The first is to solve our problem directly by breaking into his computer and destroying his ability to continue his reign of terror and possibly commit a murder. Or you can ask the FBI to do the job for you—which they may or may not elect to do—at which point the whole investigation becomes bogged down in legal machinations. Which option would you choose?"

Arnold blew an audible sigh. This guy simply wouldn't budge as the sand continued slipping through the hourglass. Harris had no idea of the full potential of the FBI's capabilities in this arena.

"Well?" Harris asked.

When Arnold didn't answer immediately, the CEO asked, "Noah?"

"I don't believe I have the expertise to answer you, John, so I'll defer judgement to Arnold."

Jesus, talk about a non-answer.

All eyes were on him now.

"Oh, man!" Massaging his forehead, Arnold started in with, "Look, Mr. Harris, this isn't a Hollywood hacker movie where cyberpunks gain access to computers by typing a few commands on a scrolling screen of multicolor computer code. This is real life, and real life just doesn't work that way. In this particular case, we're up against someone who's totally computer-literate and very canny. Yeah, sure, given enough time—which we don't have—we might be able to devise a way to fake him out and sneak into one computer. Okay, say we could do that. Then what? Odds are we'll find nothing of value. You want to know why? Because no doubt a guy like Bosko has several computers laying around, making it extremely likely that the computer he used to diddle your devices is *not* his everyday machine. Meaning the target computer probably isn't even taken out of a closet and turned on except for the very specific times he needs it. You following any of this?"

"Don't be condescending," Harris shot back.

Asshole.

"In that case, I'll continue," Arnold said, no longer caring if he offended the CEO. The man needed to understand what they were up against. "Most importantly—and this is critical, so listen up—because he's very skilled at computing practices, it's a safe bet he backs up everything on at least two external hard drives as well as a couple of cloud storage sites. Which means that if we happened to luck out and find a machine with your serial numbers on it and then trash that machine, he still has them. In other words, this won't solve the threat to you and your company. Finally—and this too is very critical—if he really *is* your hacker, when and if law enforcement finally does seize the evidence, we don't want any shred of evidence of us ever being in his network. Know why? Because a good defense attorney will claim we set him up. What I'm telling you, Mr. Harris, is I guarantee that the FBI eventually *will* need to be involved in this. Especially if, God forbid, your hacker actually murders one of your patients. At which point you'll have no choice but to involve them." Arnold paused to catch his breath. "Basically, we'll just be wasting precious time."

Harris immediately resumed his offense.

"I understand what you just said, Arnold, but at this point I have more faith in you and your team than I do in a large bureaucracy. We need to do *something* to prevent Bosko from inflicting any more damage."

"News flash, Mr. Harris," Arnold replied while grappling to rein in his frustration at someone so pigheaded, "we have *no* tangible proof that he is or isn't our hacker. Yes, we have *some* very intriguing circumstantial evidence, but nothing conclusive. That's precisely why I urge you to ask the FBI for help on this. We've taken this about as far as we can. They can take it the rest of the way."

"Gentlemen," Cain said. "It's clear we're all enmeshed in a very stressful situation and are deadlocked. Presently this debate isn't serving a productive purpose. I suggest we take a one-hour break to consider what's just been said and then reconvene to see if we can arrive at a productive path forward. What do you say, John?"

"Noah, we simply can't afford the time."

Cain replied forcefully, "Nor can we afford to make a mistake, John. Having been in extremely taxing situations before, I can tell you that everyone needs to dial back their emotions so we can all see things more objectively. What do you say, Arnold?"

"We'll get back to you," Arnold said before cutting the connection in complete frustration over Harris's short-sightedness. And immediately regretted his childish action. Now, more than ever, he felt vindicated for having already notified Agent Fisher of this rapidly evolving clusterfuck.

CHAPTER 15

WITH THE ENTIRE team in the chat room, Arnold narrated a concise recap of the frustrating conversation with Mr. Cain and Mr. Harris.

He finished by asking Prisha, "Anything you'd like to add to what I just said?"

"Nope. That's exactly how I heard it go down."

After momentary silence, Arnold said, "I guess we're left with three options. One: we simply walk away from the case. Two: we brainstorm a way to break into Bosko's computer to see what's there. Three: we come clean and admit to Mr. Harris that we've already notified the FBI."

Prisha shot back.

"I dunno, man, I personally don't like walking out in the middle of a job just because it's tough. I sure as hell don't want the word leaking out that we did that. And you know for sure that's what's going to happen if we do. You want our reputation to take a hit like that? I don't."

"Valid point," Arnold agreed. "I hadn't considered that."

"Same thing applies to option number three. I'm not really sure how it's going to play if word leaks that we ratted out our employer. On the other hand, if we're hired to do an impossible task with an impossible deadline and don't come through, well, that *is* understandable. Any tarnish to our reputation would be minimal. If any. Like you've told us before, we can't possibly win one hundred percent of the time."

Dead silence.

When no one else spoke up, Arnold muttered, "Oh man, trying to come up with a way to hack a skilled hacker is going to be like crazy-dicey."

Prisha said, "No shit. That's why I suggest that before we waste time working on it, you need to have a serious discussion with Agent Fisher about what we'd be doing. Not only that, but I also think you need to record it to help indemnify our collective asses if things go off the rails."

"Wow. I like that idea," Lopez said enthusiastically. "Like it a lot."

"I don't," Vihaan immediately said. "In fact, I totally disagree with trying to take on this guy. If he *is* our hacker, he's already shown us what a crazy-ass whack job he is. I just don't see one bit of upside to going up against a man like that. Especially in the limited amount of time we have. We'd be scrambling."

Arnold decided, given Vihaan's raw personal feelings toward him, to wait to see if another team member voiced a rebuttal.

"News flash, Vihaan," Ito said. "Our jobs are a risky business. What's wrong with upping the ante? Besides, what's the worst that can happen? We're unable to break into his network by Friday? So what? That's not our fault, man."

"So what? Are you serious? Someone might die if Bosko isn't neutralized by the weekend," Vihaan shot back. "Why not offload that responsibility to the Feds?"

"Okay," Ito continued. "For the sake of argument let's say that does happen. Whose fault is that? I can tell you whose fault it ain't. Ain't ours, bro. The fact remains that any blame lands squarely on Harris for not siccing the FBI cybercrime unit on this asshole the moment the first call was made. Don't even try to deny it. You know that's the truth."

"I still think we'd be taking an unnecessary risk by going up against this dude," Vihaan muttered.

Arnold was pleased that Ito was pushing back instead of him. It was also comforting to know that he wasn't the only one annoyed over Vihaan's Nervous Nelly conservatism.

Prisha: "Sounds like we've made a decision. So, bossman, why don't you ask Fisher to run that number while the rest of us try to get super-creative and work on a plan for stealing Bosko's network."

When the recording finished advising him to leave a message, Arnold said, "Mr. Fisher, Arnold Gold again. I need to update you about the case and get your advice. It's ultra-important, so call me soon as you can. Thanks."

Call finished, Arnold poured another cup of black coffee, then stood with the small of his back against the stainless-steel kitchen counter, wracking his brain for a clever way to get past Bosko's firewall.

James Brown broke his concentration.

"Gold. Fisher. What do you have for me?"

After thanking him for returning his call, Arold updated him on the status of the case and asked if he could find the name of the person registered to the Verizon phone number.

"That's easy enough to request, but you realize to get an answer will take more time than you have."

Arnold knew that Mr. Fisher would need a warrant before Verizon would release that information. Even after submitting it, several days would probably pass before the results were available.

"I know, but isn't there a way you can possibly expedite the process? I mean, people's lives are at risk here."

"I'll submit a request, but suggest you work on finding the answer on your own."

"And how do I do that?" Arnold asked with growing frustration.

"Come on, Gold, think. He uses a computer and probably has his Verizon bills on it. And, while you're at it, try to stumble onto some evidence relevant to the Cor-Pace hack."

Arnold stared in disbelief at the phone in his hand, then brought it up to his ear again. "Just to be crystalline, did you just give me permission to hack his computer?"

"Permission? I assume you're joking. I can't give you permission to commit an illegal act, but as my CI, I can and will use whatever information you pass on to me to build a case for a formal search of his digital devices."

After a few seconds of silence, Fisher added, "If you're waiting for additional clarification, Gold, I can assure you that no legal action will be brought against you. Just in case that's what you're asking."

"Yeah, got it," he answered, unable to mask the disappointment from his voice.

After his less-than-satisfying exchange with Fisher, Arnold desperately wanted to hear something good, like an amazing plan for worming their way into Bosko's network. He switched over to the group in the chat room and asked, "Any progress?"

"You first," Prisha said. "How'd your chat with Fisher go?"

Arnold gave a disappointed headshake.

"First the good. Fisher agrees that we have sufficient evidence to make Bosko a serious person of interest. Which means he'll go to work on Verizon. But there's a catch: it could take a week or more for the warrant to work through the process."

After a pause for that to sink in, he added, "Now the bad news. Before he'll even ask a magistrate for a search warrant, he wants us to get him more evidence to shore up his case."

"Such as?" Lopez asked.

"I don't know…a copy of the encrypted database files, maybe. Just about anything that might implicate him directly. Let's face it, guys: the odds are pretty slim we're getting anything for him before Friday."

He waited for the bad news to really sink in.

"So, on that unhappy news," Arnold continued, finished with his summary, "what ingenious plan have you guys come up with?"

Prisha spoke for the group: "We're working on a concept that feels like it has promise, but we're not even close to an executable plan yet."

"Yeah?" Arnold asked, feeling a faint spark of hope. "Tell me about it."

"Okay. It goes something like this: given our time restriction, we're kicking around the idea of taking a gamble and contacting him directly with a cover story."

After a few seconds of silence, Arnold asked impatiently, "Yeah, then what?"

Immediately, he regretted sounding so harsh. They were all maximally stressed at having such a loser job crammed down their throats. He didn't need to fan that flame.

He amended his last words with, "Sorry. I didn't mean to sound like that."

"We did some searching," Prisha went on as if nothing had happened, "and found that he's on two dating sites: eHarmony and Christian Mingle. We were just tossing around the idea of opening an eHarmony account to set up a date with him."

Having never used a dating app before, Arnold had no idea how much work signing up for one might entail. But Howie—his deceased best friend—had. And he remembered, quite vividly, Howie bitching about how time-consuming signing up could be, what with answering all the questions.

Arnold said, "I love the concept of going straight for a personal meet. But we need to figure out a scam to communicate directly with him instead of going through a dating app."

"Yeah? Well, I love the idea of going through the dating app," Vihaan said. "I don't want to give up on it."

Which convinced Arnold that it'd been his idea.

"Naw, Arnold's right," Prisha answered. "We need to go for something more direct."

Vihaan: "Why?" The one word, weighted to be challenging.

"Because," Prisha answered, "we'd be doing it for a shot at infecting his computer. At least, that's what I think this is all about. Right, Arnold?"

Arnold instantly knew where she was going with this. Another example of being completely in sync. "She's right."

"Why can't we do that through a dating site?" Vihaan persisted.

Prisha answered, "There's no way we'd be able to sneak malware through those sites. Their filters would nail us for sure."

Arnold jumped in with, "She's right. The only way we stand a chance of getting hooks in him is to find a way to communicate *outside* a dating app. Have you guys checked out any of the less problematic social-media sites, like Facebook?"

"I did," Lopez said. "Dude's on all the usual suspects. Facebook, WhatsApp, Instagram, and X, but interestingly he's not on any of the Chinese-based ones like TikTok."

"Which is just one more reason to suspect the guy's on the paranoid side," Vihaan tossed into the conversation.

Ito said, "Well if he *is* our guy, being paranoid improves his chances of not getting caught."

Arnold realized he'd just checked his watch. And he'd been doing this habitually since the start of this case. A definitely counterproductive thing to do because it only amped up his anxiety.

"Whatdaya think about reaching out to him on Facebook?" Prisha asked the group.

When no one responded, she expanded her train of thought with, "Yeah, yeah, yeah, I know, it's not as popular as a couple years back, but he does have an account, so chances are we can catch his attention, especially if we work with Messenger."

Vihaan asked, "And do what?" There was a slight confrontational edge to his voice.

"I dunno," she said, throwing up her hands, "get him to meet for coffee maybe. But we gotta come up with *something* that gives us a chance to check his phone. Maybe let him think he has a shot at hooking up."

"And who're we going to get to do that? Not you," Vihaan said adamantly.

"I don't see why not," she replied just as adamantly.

Oh man, here we go.

"Hey guys," Arnold interjected, "we can fine tune the details on the fly, but we need to establish some sort of rapport with him, and this is the best suggestion I've heard so far."

"Totally agree," Lopez echoed.

Silence.

"Okay then," Arnold said. "Let's take a vote. Does everyone agree with setting up a Facebook account for this purpose?"

When no one disagreed, Prisha offered, "I'll get started on it."

"Hold on," Vihaan quickly interjected. "You don't intend to use your real name, do you?"

"Oh for christsake, husband, of course not, but I will need to post a real picture."

"Why?" Vihaan challenged.

"We just went over this," she answered, clearly unable to hide her annoyance. "Because I want to meet him for coffee and perhaps get a chance to see his phone. That's why."

Vihaan shook his head. "Oh no you won't. I forbid you to come on to him like that."

Prisha: "Don't be silly."

"Wait," Lopez interjected before tensions could get out of hand, "there may be a more pragmatic reason to use someone else. Don't take this the wrong way, girl, but I'm wondering if there's a remote chance that he's got a thing against Asians. Don't forget he's not signed up for any of the Chinese social media sites. Especially TikTok."

Arnold gave a silent sigh of relief. Lopez just defused a potential fight. He quickly chimed in with, "Wow, good point. I mean, with time running out, why risk it, right?"

"Oh man," Ito interjected. "Who does that leave us?"

Expecting pushback from Prisha, Arnold suggested, "How about using Kara? It's a perfect job for her. After all, she really came through for us on the pen-test."

He was referring to Kara Winston, a paralegal at the law firm of Cain, Tidwell, Stowell. Arnold had run into her—literally—while working a ransomware case for the firm.

After noticing that Arnold had a "thing" for the little red-haired cutie, Prisha warned him to not do anything stupid that could jeopardize Mr. Cain's enthusiastic support for their company. But Arnold had already tumbled to that potential landmine and was going out of his way to avoid creating an issue. But this only seemed to increase her lure.

Prisha said, "Know what? That's a great suggestion. She'd be perfect. Assuming, of course, she'll do it for us. Especially on such short notice. How about calling her to ask if she can meet us tonight after work?"

After recovering from the shock of Prisha's enthusiastic buy-in, he checked his watch. It was getting late in the workday.

Too late to still reach her at the office?

"I'll put it on speakerphone," he offered so Prisha could hear that the conversation was legitimate.

He dialed her direct line. After only two rings she picked up with, "Well, well, well...Arnold Gold, how they hanging, dude?"

He swallowed a sarcastic comeback, said, "Watch it, girl. You're on speakerphone with the team."

"Why didn't you warn me?"

"Like you gave me a chance? Anyhoo...the reason for this call is to ask if you can drop by my place after work to help us with something hugely important. Apologies for the short notice, but we're under a gonzo time crunch and, like I said, it's super-important."

"We? As in the team?"

"Yep. We're working an extremely problematic case and could really use your help."

"Yeah? Unfortunately, I already have plans." Pause. "Just out of curiosity, what'd you have in mind?"

Aww man.

Raking fingers through his hair, he debated how much to disclose. Or, because of working for Mr. Cain, did she already know about the Cor-Pace disaster? Or was the lawyer playing it close to the vest? And if she knew about this mess, did he risk blowback by disclosing confidential information?

Jesus.

"Look, I really can't discuss this on the phone. All I can tell you is that it's ultra-highly sensitive and we're working under a super-time crunch and could really use your help."

There! Enough said.

He'd leave it at that and hope he'd piqued her interest enough to reel her in.

"I have to admit, you do make it sound intriguing, but I need to know more than that if you expect me to cancel my plans."

Aw man.

After spending a moment organizing his thoughts, he walked her through a bare-bones sketch of the situation without naming the company, Mr. Harris, or her boss.

After he finished, she remained silent for several seconds. Then, "Okay, I'm in. I'll cancel my plans, which, by the way, included dinner. So, bro, what're you serving as compensation?" Then quickly added, "As if I can't guess."

Massively relieved that she was on board, he gave a silent fist-pump.

"I'll have your favorite Flavio's waiting."

"Why'd I even bother to ask?"

"In the meantime, could you please send me a couple pictures of yourself that we can use?"

"Of course. But for God's sake, do *not* use my real name. We clear on this?"

"Well, duh! I'm hurt you even mentioned it."

"Too bad. You're a big boy. You can take it. At the risk of further deepening your wound, please verify that we're absolutely clear on this."

"Alright already. I won't use your real name," Arnold said, rolling his eyes. "So, we good?"

"Totally."

"What time can I expect you?"

"Mmmm, sixish, give or take."

CHAPTER 16

ONCE ARNOLD DISCONNECTED the call, the group began setting up Kara's bogus Facebook account and background. Their first obstacle was choosing her pseudonym.

"Anyone have a suggestion of where to start?" Lopez asked the group.

No one came up with a suggestion.

A moment later, two photos of Kara popped up in Arnold's email account. Probably sent directly from her phone.

"Hold on. I just got a couple of snapshots. I'll put them on up the screen to hopefully inspire us."

Both shots were selfies. One with what appeared to be the Grand Canyon in the background. The other with friends in a restaurant that Arnold recognized as the Pink Door, an extremely popular Italian restaurant on the periphery of the Pike Place Market.

"This is helpful," Prisha said. "Given her red hair and green eyes, I gotta say we go for an Irish-sounding name."

"That feels right," Ito seconded.

"The floor is now officially open for suggestions. Anyone?" Prisha asked.

Arnold flashed on a red-haired girl in his grade-school class, so offered, "How about Sharon?"

"Or Erin," Vihaan immediately countered.

"I like Sharon better," Lopez said. "It doesn't sound so common, like a setup. Don't forget we're dealing with a guy who's got every right to be super suspicious. At least I'd be if I were in his loafers."

Having already moved on, Arnold pulled up a Google search of common Irish surnames on his laptop. Scrolling the list, he stopped at one in particular.

"How does Sweeny grab you for a last name, guys?"

"Sharon Sweeny, huh…works for me," Prisha said.

Before they wasted any more time debating the issue, Arnold said, "Sold! Okay, so now we need to generate a bio and a few photos based on what we have on her. Anyone want to volunteer to throw together a first draft?"

Lopez: "I'll do it. Well, actually I won't do it myself. I'll feed the pictures and a few other likely scenarios into ChatGPT and see what it comes up with."

Prisha guffawed. "Perfect. We've got so much else to do so might as well. One suggestion though; since the ultimate goal is to lure him into a face-to-face meeting, I'd stick close enough to the truth to keep her from being tripped up if they do meet and he starts to grill her." She paused. "Okay, try this one on for size: she's first-year law at UW. With this as a cover, she can bullshit her way through just about any test question he throws at her. Go ahead and run with that as the backbone to your story. Then use these snapshots to generate five or six additional ones of her with friends. You know, stereotypical shit like a backyard barbecue, playing with a cute little doggie, blowing out candles at a party, etcetera etcetera. In the meantime, we'll work on generating a background on her friends along with some fake exchanges. Once we have her look credible, I'll whip off an enthusiastic friend request to him."

A half hour later, a very attractive Sharon Sweeny sent Alfred Bosko Jr. a Facebook friend request. Although the entire team had the password and account name, they agreed that to preserve consistency, only Kara should write any subsequent communication.

With the hook baited and dangling, there was nothing more to do to move this part of the case along. In fact, there was nothing more they could think of doing to move anything along. They would either get a lead into Bosko's computer with this Hail Mary play or they wouldn't. The only thing to do now was sit on their hands and wait.

Arnold told the group, "Seems to me this is the perfect time to catch a few Zs. Or am I missing something?"

"Nope, you're absolutely right," Prisha answered for the group. "I know I could sure use a nap. Let's reconvene at six, about the time Kara's set to arrive. In the meantime, I figure if Bosko takes the bait, he might have a few questions for her, so I'll keep working on prepping for them."

"I'll help you," Arnold offered.

Vihaan jumped in with, "I will too."

"Hey, you guys are welcome to continue your After-You-Alphonse routine, but I'm taking the opportunity to crash," Lopez said.

"Me too," Ito echoed.

"Fine. The three of us will work on it," Arnold said, sensing continued tension between the two Patels. Mostly from Vihaan. Prisha just seemed to be mildly pissed.

Lopez and Ito signed out of the chat room. Mays had left the chat room a couple of hours ago when the group changed their priority to entrapping Bosko.

"What's your greatest concern?" Prisha asked Arnold.

"Well, if I were him and on the paranoid side, the first thing that'd pop to mind would be, 'How did you get my name?' Seems to me, selling an answer would be easier if we could find a common point of intersection."

Prisha: "Ahh, good one."

Arnold: "Hold on, I want to check something."

Vihaan: "What?"

Arnold: "Hasn't he bounced around from job to job quite a bit?"

"Yes, he has." Vihaan again.

Arnold: "Give me a minute or two to sign into LinkedIn and check out what's going on there."

A little over two years ago, Arnold had established a LinkedIn account under the name of Justin Case to be used for exactly this type of snooping. A moment later he was sharing his screen with Prisha and Vihaan.

"What I'm thinking," he said, "is we scout out someone he worked with in the distant past to use as a link. Someone we feel is peripheral enough that odds are they're not BFFs now. Just in case he tries to verify our story."

"Preferably, a woman," Prisha added.

"Why's that?" Arnold asked, feeling vaguely discriminated against by the Sisterhood.

"Well, because the biggest risk to this is that he's still in contact with whoever we end up using as the link. And I get the distinct feeling that Bosko's the type of guy who's less likely to have long-term friendships with females."

"Guess that makes sense," Arnold mumbled as he started to work through the website.

While Arnold was digging into LinkedIn, Vihaan offered, "Another risk is that if he answers Sharon's friend request, he'll be wary of being trolled by a chatbot."

Neither Arnold nor Prisha responded.

"My point," Vihaan said defensively, "is she should be prepared to validate that she's a human."

"I don't follow that one," Arnold said. "That's why they're going to set up a meeting, right?"

"Yes, but that's the thing," Vihaan responded. "Kara's way too attractive for a guy like him."

"That's a pretty nasty thing to say," Prisha replied.

"Hey, I'm just saying, that's the way things are. Or at least, that's the way I see it."

Arnold was just about to intervene in what was beginning to feel like a family feud, when Prisha said, "Bingo. Bosko just responded to the friend request. He wants to know how she got his name, so what do we say?"

Arnold's phone started in on his custom ringtone.

He said, "Go ahead and start brainstorming while I take this call," and picked up the phone for a closer look. Didn't recognize the name on the screen.

Dump the call or answer it? Might as well take it since he was already distracted.

He answered with, "Yes?"

"Why haven't you called or texted?"

Took a moment to for her voice to register. "Noriko?"

"Yes. I'm using a friend's phone since apparently you won't answer calls from my number."

Aw Jesus.

"Look, haven't we been through this already? Too many times, in fact," he replied making no attempt to mask his irritation. "I'm working an extremely tough job, and I just don't have time for this. What does it take for you to understand this?"

Just then his doorbell rang.

Phone in hand, he blew through the living room to answer the door as she was saying, "I don't believe you can't find a few minutes now and then to call me. You haven't even texted. Why is that?"

Fuck.

"I just told you why. Was what I said muddled or confusing? Why are you having such a problem understanding this?"

Soon as Arnold opened the door, Kara breezed past saying, "Hey, studly, did you remember to pick up dinner?"

"Whoa, who's that?" Noriko demanded in a voice dripping with accusation.

Putting fingertips to lips, Kara said, "Oops," then mouthed, "Sorry."

Fuck!

He realized his iPhone was still on speaker.

Arnold just shook his head at her while telling Noriko, "Like I told you, I'm working. She's part of the team."

"Oh, I bet she is, *studly*." Noriko cut the call.

For several seconds, Arnold stood perfectly still looking at his phone.

Call her back? If so, say what?

Part of him wanted to smooth over the situation despite knowing that any attempt to do so would mire him in a lengthy conversation. And besides, he seriously doubted that her ears would be open at this point. No, he flat-out couldn't afford the time, especially with Kara here and ready to work.

Okay, so what did that say about his feelings toward Noriko?

Interesting question.

Finally shutting the front door, he called out to Kara, "Domestic issues." As if that wasn't flagrantly apparent.

Back in the kitchen, he asked, "Would you like a beer with dinner? I'm sort of attached to a new IPA. Bodhizafa. Ever tried it? From Georgetown Brewery." Referring to a Seattle neighborhood bordering the south of downtown.

"Nope, never heard of it. Are you having one?" she asked, shrugging off her coat to hang over the back of her usual chair.

He briefly considered saying yes but decided the alcohol stood a good chance of making him drowsy, which he couldn't risk right now.

"Naw. Not with this job in play."

Smiling at him, she slipped into her chair saying, "In that case, I won't either."

Arnold pulled two wine tumblers from the above-counter cupboard.

"Water then?"

"Please. No ice."

"Roger that."

After setting the pizza on the kitchen table along with a couple of paper plates and a roll of paper napkins, he filled the tumblers with tap water and set them in place before sitting down.

"What's the latest breaking news on the case?" she asked, her sparkling green eyes radiating enthusiasm.

"Good news. Our target accepted your friend request, like, almost instantly. Here."

He rotated the laptop so she could read the screen, then pushed it closer to her. He kept the free-standing monitor set to the chat room.

She scanned Bosko's reply to the friend request and then took a moment to study her profile.

"Sharon Sweeny, huh. Nice riff on the Irish twist. What's your take on how to answer it? I don't want to come across as *too* eager."

Before he could open his mouth to respond, she held up a just-a-moment finger.

"Before I type a word, I need to know a hell of a lot more about what's going on and why. When you briefed me, it was just that: brief. I suspect you didn't let me in on what sounds like a monster case. Why the mystery?"

Shaking his head, Arnold exhaled.

Girl had a point.

Sliding a tranche of pizza from the box onto a paper plate, he began with, "What I'm about to disclose is, like, totally hyper-sensitive classified material. It stays with the team. You totally cool with that?"

"Yeah, I pinky-swear and all that shit. Now out with it, Mr. Tight Lips."

She turned her attention to following his lead with the pizza.

He walked her through a detailed synopsis of the story that prompted John Harris to arm-twist her boss into pressuring Gold and Associates to conduct a forensic investigation rather than turn a clear-cut extortion case over to the FBI. Which clearly would've been the sane course of action. But no, they didn't buy it, so here they were, like it or not.

"That's total craziness," she said when he finished that part. "I can't believe Noah would stand for that."

"Well, believe it, he did. Plus, you have no idea how hard those two put the thumbscrews on Prisha and me to work this Hindenburg of a case even after I made it crystalline that I thought it was a monster mistake to not involve the Feds. But Harris is convinced they can't possibly work it fast enough to shut down our hacker before Friday."

With wide-eyed shock, she asked, "And he thinks you can?"

Arnold just spread his hands and shrugged.

Holding her slice of pizza up to her mouth, ready for her first bite, she seemed to mull over what he'd told her. Then, "Okay, so what's up with this Bosko dude?" She took a bite.

Arnold walked her through their circumstantial evidence tying Bosko to the hack.

She appeared to mull this over too while chewing pizza.

A moment later, after washing it down with a drink of water, she said, "So here we sit with your prime suspect wanting to hook up via Facebook. Any suggestions on what tone I should take?"

Arnold gave a sarcastic laugh.

"You're asking me, the social media retard? That's one of the reasons I wanted your help on this."

"Yeah, I got that, but guess what I'm really asking is—since we're racing the clock here—you want me to come across as guarded or hot-to-trot?"

"Okay, I see what you're asking. Hmmm. Good question."

Fingers laced behind his head, he sat back to think. A moment later, said, "I'll leave that part up to you since you're more experienced at these things. Just keep in mind, from everything we've been able to dig up about this guy, he's definitely on the paranoid end of the spectrum. We don't want to do anything to freak him."

She continued to stare at the screen, apparently deep in thought. She finally said, "Know what? I'll take you up on that beer now."

He was up, out of the chair, heading for the fridge.

"I'm on it. Stay focused."

A moment later, he handed her an opened can of IPA.

She took a swig, then smacked her lips and said, "This goes so much better with pizza than water." Holding out the can for another appraisal: "Bodhizafa? Never heard of it. Nice find. Where do you buy it?"

She shoved aside her glass of water to make room for the can.

"Last time we were at the 5-Point it was on tap. I liked it, so picked up a six-pack at Met Market," he answered, sliding back into his seat.

Silence.

"How about something along the lines of you don't like to go through the hassle of using dating sites like eHarmony—since we know he has an account there—and you're looking for men to meet in the city. Then throw in something to the effect that he looks interesting."

Kara nodded, took another bite of pizza, sat back, seemingly to give his suggestion serious consideration.

Arnold waited. Took another bite of pizza. Waited some more.

Then, after degreasing her fingers with a paper napkin, Kara began to type. Finished, she turned the laptop so that he could read and approve the text before hitting send.

Her post turned out to be an almost word-for-word transcription of his suggestion. After making a few modifications, Arnold returned the laptop to her with, "Here you go. What do you think?"

"Perfect. Let's see if he bites." She quickly amended that with, "Or rather, how aggressively he bites."

After posting her reply, she sat back, looked him in the eye, asked, "Explain to me again why Harris is so dead set against handing this mess over to the FBI? I mean, that seems like such a no-brainer."

To him, her tone reaffirmed two important points: he'd been right to recommend that Harris do that from the get-go. Same for going against the CEO's wishes and informing Agent Fisher of the quagmire.

Tell her that part? Naw, probably best not to.

Probably best to keep that part under wraps. Especially seeing how she worked for Mr. Cain. A point that also kept him from wisecracking: *Because they're just being stupid.* It'd be just his luck for a derogatory remark like that to inadvertently wend its way back to the lawyer. Because low as the odds were, that'd be quintessential Arnold Gold luck.

Instead, he parroted Mr. Harris's stated belief that a group of skilled hackers unconstrained by the shackles of law could work this issue more expeditiously than any law enforcement agency, blah blah, and blah. He judiciously resisted adding that neither Mr. Cain nor Mr. Harris apparently appreciated the caliber of the FBI's cyber squad.

Kara, who was listening intently, casually glanced at the laptop screen, sat bolt upright exclaiming, "Whoa. Our friend just answered.

And looks to be one very enthusiastic dude, too."

When she didn't embellish, he asked, "Out with it. What's he say?"

With a wry smile, she answered, "Quote, *'What do you have in mind?'*"

Arnold shrugged. *So?*

"Help me out here. How do you want me to respond? Give me some inspiration."

"I hate to admit it, Kara, but I have absolutely no experience with online hookups. You're better off relying on your own judgment. My only advice is to give him the impression that you're definitely looking to hook up but are unwilling to commit until you've seen him in the flesh. Move too quickly and odds are he'll freak, and we don't want to risk losing him now."

She glanced away from the screen, appearing to mentally edit her response before returning to the keyboard.

Finished, she sat back, asked, "How's this sound? 'Don't know yet. Depends.'" Pause. "Does that sound enticing but totally ambiguous?"

Arnold laughed, "Pretty damn good. Both realistic and tempting. And most importantly, it shouldn't punch any paranoid buttons."

"You saying it's good to post?"

Arnold ran through it one more time but again couldn't see any nuance that might push Bosko's suspicion buttons.

"Think so."

"That doesn't sound particularly enthusiastic."

"Then let me put it this way. I can't come up with anything better than that, so go ahead, send it and let's see what shakes out."

As the words left his mouth, Arnold realized that his fatigue-fueled stress was gutting his creativity. Not only that, but this was the first job in which he was mentally prepared for the team to take a hit. This could well be their Waterloo.

She posted her reply, then sat back with a pensive expression.

Watching her, Arnold asked, "What?"

She hesitated a beat.

"Now comes the tricky part. Say he snaps up the bait and wants to meet. Then what? I really need some guidance on this."

Arnold went back over the plan he'd been sculpting for the past two hours. It appeared to be solid. Which, in itself, was a bit scary. Had to be missing something. What?

Stop it. You're freaking yourself out.

She was staring at him, waiting.

Finger-combing his hair, he finally said, "I suggest you set up a brief face-to-face in a very public place with lots of people around so we can keep watch on you when you're physically close to him. Use the excuse that before you take anything to the next level, you want to be sure he's the same person as the Facebook picture and not someone messing with you. This should play to his paranoid nature. And it wouldn't surprise me if in the end, it actually ups your stock with him. Push him to meet in-person tomorrow evening if possible."

"Why not for tonight?"

"Because you need to not come across as too eager. For sure, that'd be a huge red flag for him."

After a beat, she nodded.

"Yeah, sounds about right," then, after another beat: "Since you've been putting a ton of thought into this, where should I suggest this meeting take place?"

No. Actually, he hadn't given it as much thought as he should've.

A knee-jerk response had been to suggest a Starbucks but then realized that the shops he knew of were shuttered by six PM and daytime wouldn't work for Kara because of her job. A bar? Naw, too noisy. A restaurant? Not for a brief encounter. Hold on…what about an outdoor restaurant? One where people would be milling about so he could easily mix in without being noticed.

Then, it hit: "What about Dick's Drive-In on Broadway? That's just about the perfect spot."

Kara sat up, eyeing the laptop screen.

"Wow, talk about eager."

Arnold craned his neck for a glance.

"From Bosko?"

"Uh-huh."

"That was quick. What's he say?"

"One word: '*Meaning?*'"

It took a moment for Arnold to insert the response into the context of their prior exchange, but then he got it.

Grinning widely, he said, "Perfect. Hook, line, and sinker."

"Hmmm...." Kara was sitting still except for tapping her lips with her right index finger, apparently thinking.

Arnold waited.

Moments later, a devious smile began to curl the corners of her lips. Leaning forward, she started typing, reading aloud as the keys clicked, *I think you know exactly what I mean, so I don't think I need to spell it out to you.*

"Aw man!" Arnold said with a woeful headshake. "Dude's bound to be a stone-cold goner when he reads that."

"We'll see," she replied warily. "Need I remind you of your warning that he's on the super-paranoid side, in which case all bets are off."

He stopped laughing. "I don't remember betting on this."

Glancing up from the screen, she said, "Figure of speech, fool."

"Seriously, I'm giving odds of ten-to-one he believes he's got a good shot at hooking up. Nice job."

"We'll see. I reserve judgment until we read his response to this. Or if he simply walks away."

She paused for another bite of pizza, then chewed while again degreasing her fingers on a paper napkin. After washing it down with a swig of beer, she asked, "If you want to bet, why not bet on what his next move will be?"

Arnold shook his head.

"You're asking Mister Social Retard?" After a sarcastic laugh, he added, "I don't have a clue. Why? What're you thinking?"

"If my off-the-cuff impression of this turkey's anywhere close to accurate, he'll want to go straight for a picture exchange."

Even after an instant replay, her comment didn't make sense.

"A what?"

She studied him with a furrowed brow for a beat before asking, "Seriously? You're not messing with me, are you?"

Arnold shook his head. "No, I'm serious. I'm asking on account of I have no idea what you're talking about. This way of hooking up isn't in my wheelhouse. Then again, I guess when it comes to social interactions like this, I don't have a wheelhouse."

Which was a gross understatement. Given his lack of dating history, his wheelhouse was perhaps the size of a thimble.

"Ah, here we go," she announced with a satisfied smile. "Reading from the Book of Bosko: *You up for sending a few more pictures?*"

Arnold responded with another shrug.

"I still don't get it. What's wrong with that?"

She flashed him a look of stunned disbelief.

"Dude! He's asking for pictures of my boobs."

After a moment of surprised silence, Arnold managed to mutter, "Oh..." as the shock began to dissipate.

Shock over Bosko's unabashed intimate request to a person he'd only met online mere minutes ago. Shock at himself for being so out of touch that he had no freaking clue about his peers' contemporary mores.

Was social-media life now so impersonal that cutting straight to the chase risked little consequence?

If a new virtual friend says no, simply keep panning the stream until that gold nugget shows up. Or was this an uber-pragmatic approach to simplify snagging like-minded friends? It was certainly less problematic than his one dreadful experience at speed dating: sitting face-to-face with someone and having to make conversation for however many minutes the rules required. Looking for a fuck buddy? Troll online. Takes much less effort. But lastly, he was shocked at what Kara appeared to accept as normal social-media protocol.

Which begged the question: had he expected her to be above...above what? Above the social norms of her peers? Put in that light, he became even more disappointed in himself for realizing that his comfort zone was more than two standard deviations from the norm. *He* was the misfit, not her, and not Bosko.

Massaging the back of his neck, he tried to come across as casual by asking, "How do you plan to respond to that?"

It was asked partly out of curiosity and partly out of prurient interest, since he'd be more than happy to accept the job as photographer.

She studied him a beat as if suddenly clairvoyant.

He could feel his face reddening.

"Correct me if I'm way off in the weeds on this," she said with a devilish sly grin. "But isn't this the point where you sagely tell me this is the perfect opportunity to send a chunk of malware to his machine?"

Holy shit. Score one for Kara!

He was so bogged down in his own Victorian hangups that he'd been blinded to a perfect opportunity. Couldn't ask for a more perfect setup—especially when dealing with a paranoid asshole like Bosko—to slip some malware into his computer. Wasn't guaranteed to get past him, especially considering the target's expertise, but hey, worth a shot.

He was aware that Kara hung around the fringes of hackerdom as a hobby of sorts, but had no idea of how sophisticated her chops might be. Well, this was a perfect opportunity to get a better read on the issue.

With a palm-thump to his forehead, he said, "Wow, you're absolutely right. And I assume by pointing it out to me, you already have a plan. Go ahead, tell me what you're thinking."

"Exactly what I mentioned. Attach a RAT to a picture. Soon as he clicks on the picture the malware embeds into his computer. That should stand a reasonable shot at working, shouldn't it?" she asked tentatively, perhaps self-conscious over being put on the spot.

Nodding thoughtfully, mind rocketing along in hyper-speed, Arnold started working through it.

"I like the concept. I especially like how you latched onto the opportunity. But the way things presently stand, I don't see how it has any shot at working."

"Because?"

"We're facing two problems. First, I don't see any way in hell we

143

can get malware past Facebook. Second, I think the odds of getting a Remote Access Trojan past his security are close to nil. Remember, dude's super-cybersecurity conscious."

She appeared to consider his points before nodding.

With an air of defeat, she said, "I see your point."

"On the other hand, we probably aren't going to get an opportunity like this again. I'd hate to not try to take advantage of it."

Eyes closed, Arnold sat back to focus on how to make this work.

A moment later, he offered, "We'd eliminate half of the problem if we can con him into moving over to email. Agreed?"

"Right. But I don't have any bogus email accounts and I sure as hell don't plan on giving him my real one."

Arnold laughed.

"Hell, girl, I can have a fistful of disposable bogus accounts for you in a few minutes."

She laughed.

"Right again. Let's do it. But why don't you work on that while I work on devising a strategy to get *him* to make the suggestion to move to email."

"Nice." With a sly smile, he said, "Go ahead, work on that while I set up an account."

She started drumming her fingers on the table with a distant look on her face.

Watching her, he decided that setting up the email was such a trivial task that he would be better off investing his energy to helping her.

"Any general strategy on how to sell this?" he asked.

She picked up the beer and started inspecting the can, as if it held the answer.

After a moment she said, "As a general rule, paranoids feel more comfortable dealing with those who hold similar concerns, so I'll pivot around that premise." Then, as she set the can back down: "I'll simply tell him I'm uncomfortable exchanging anything personal on Messenger. Period. I'll let him come up with what my reasons are. If he's as paranoid as you believe, he should have no problem coming up with several." Pause. "If he's really serious about swapping pics, then he'll suggest something as simple as email."

"Got it. Smart plan. Go ahead and send it while I sign you up for a new email account."

He pulled the notepad over to jot down a name and devise a password.

A moment later she asked, "What do you think?" and turned the laptop for him to read the screen.

While reading her message, a smile came over his face.

"Great job, girl."

"Good to go?"

"Yep."

She tapped enter then slid the laptop back to him. Took only a couple of minutes for Arnold to have a Gmail account set up under the name of Sharonsweeny312.

"What's a good password for you?" he asked.

Lips pressed into a straight line, she seemed to be giving this more thought than he anticipated. A moment later, she glanced back up at him.

"What're the odds he'll try hacking it?"

"Yeah, that crossed my mind too. Probably sooner or later. That's why I asked. It all depends on how long this non-relationship ruse persists. Hopefully it'll be over by the weekend."

"Hopefully. But if it isn't…" She shook her head. "I'm getting a seriously bad vibe about this guy. I don't want to leave the slightest thread he could use to find out who I really am."

"Just make damn sure you don't put the account on any of your own devices. I'll make sure this one's long gone by Saturday morning. Okay?"

And with SAM providing his own digital security, Arnold was damn sure that Bosko wouldn't be sneaking into his network.

"Yeah, that'll work." She paused to brush the corner of her right eye. "Ahh, where were we? Oh, right, a password." Another devilish grin morphed across her face. "How about BarelyLegal21!. That should get him all hot and bothered if he does snoop it out."

Again, Arnold laughed. "You're dangerous. You know that, don't you." Not a question.

After he put the final touches on the email account, she asked, "Okay, since you don't think we can sneak a RAT past his firewall, how do you propose we get our hooks into his computer?"

He raised an index finger to buy more time before explaining. Although his plan seemed solid, he worried that the relentless pressure from Friday's rapidly approaching deadline was distracting enough to overlook an obvious glitch. He went back over the idea, looking for mistakes. He was *pretty* sure that his choice was solid. But being only pretty sure wasn't sufficient to tamp down the anxious butterflies in his gut. The flip side, of course, was that it was the best he could come up with in a time-sensitive situation. He needed to get on with it. The fatalist side of him decided that it would work, or it wouldn't. It was the best he could do for now.

"Optimally, I think it's best to stage this. Much as I want it over as quickly as possible, we can't afford to mess up. I think we—or rather you—need to start by gaining his confidence. And the best way to do this is to convince him you're not a threat. That's a delicate balancing act. He's got to believe that you will actually hook up if he's really who he claims to be. Yet you can't seem too eager on account of that's a sure way to ping his paranoid sensors. Yeah, I know it's a fine line to walk, but I think that's how we need to play it."

"I get all that," Kara said a bit impatiently. "That's not what I'm asking."

Arnold raised his palm.

"Hang on, I'm getting there. For the moment, we send him an innocuous picture along with the caveat that you're not about to send anything more *personal* until you know for sure he is who he claims to be instead of some kind of perv trolling the net."

"That's it?" she said, eyeing him askance.

He raised his eyebrows.

"What, you want more?"

She seemed to reconsider her question, then shook her head.

"Nope, guess not." Pause. "That shouldn't be too hard to

compose."

She frowned at the laptop for a moment before starting to type her reply. Finished, she angled the screen for him to read.

Arnold carefully read through the email twice before finally agreeing, "Yeah, that should do it."

As her index finger tapped ENTER, she exclaimed, "There!" as if bestowing the message with some sort of super-galactic power. With a sigh, she sat back, eyeing her half-eaten slice of pizza, perhaps contemplating exactly how much more she could—or should—consume.

Resignedly pushing away her plate, she proclaimed, "You still haven't explained how we plan to get into his computer."

"Hang on, I'm putting the final touches on that…" he said, trailing off.

They sat like that. Silent. Kara sipping her IPA with one eye on the laptop screen, yet a distant look about her.

Suddenly, she sat upright, with both eyes locked into the screen.

"Oh man, what we have here is one eager dude. He's demanding I send a selfie within the next five minutes to make sure I'm not a chatbot. What do I do?"

"Send one to him," Arnold replied as if the answer was screamingly self-explanatory. He started to look around the immediate area for an appropriate background, one that didn't include any interior of his home. Something plain vanilla that could be from any neighborhood in the city.

He stood and zeroed in on the back deck.

"Tell him you need to put some clothes on, so it might take a little longer than five minutes. That should keep his interest up. Then add that he needs to send a selfie too. Oh, and add that he needs to send it at the same time you send yours."

He hoped to get lucky and have Bosko's shot include some useful background details. Although he had no idea what those might be.

Another sneaky smile flickered across her lips. "I like it," she said, clearly getting into the game.

So much so, that Arnold decided she might just be a natural when it came to social engineering.

After sending Bosko her response, she picked up her phone and glanced around.

"Where do you want to take it?"

"Not in here." Then, pointing at the French doors: "Out there on the back porch. Here, give me your phone," he said, holding out his hand.

After handing over her phone, she walked out to the back deck and turned to him. "Tell me where to stand."

Arnold motioned her to the edge of the porch with her back to the alley, then went down on one knee to angle the shot toward mostly darkening sky to exclude any identifiable background, then moved close enough to give the impression of a selfie. He snapped off three consecutive shots.

"There. That should do it," he said, handing her the phone.

At the kitchen table again, while Kara was editing the snapshot, Arnold brought the other team members up to speed on their plan.

"What do you think?" she asked, holding up the phone for him to see.

He took the phone from her and studied the background. Nope, nothing that might disclose his location. Satisfied, he returned it.

"That's perfect. What we need to do now is copy that shot from your iCloud Photos folder to my desktop. You want to do it, or you want me to?"

"I got it...unless, of course, I can't remember my Apple password."

With a disconcerting frown, she seemed to ponder that a moment before typing a series of commands into his laptop. A moment later, she beamed.

"Whew! Pulled that one out of the depths. Wasn't sure I could do it."

After a moment of furious typing, she flashed a broad smile.

"It's on your desktop."

Arnold retrieved his laptop, double-checked the picture, and nodded approval. The lighting caught her perfectly, making her look as cute as ever. Bosko should love it. Stage 1 of their plan was now good to go.

Grinning at her. "Ever heard of the Zero-Font trick?"

A shake of her head. "Nope. Never."

Surprising him. He turned to the extra monitor, asked, "Hey Prisha, you been following this?"

Prisha glanced at her webcam.

"Not super-closely but have a general idea what's going on. You just mentioned the Zero-Font trick, right?"

"Yep. You want to explain it to her while I get to work?"

"Sure, no problem." Pause. "So, Kara, it's an ultra-cool trick. It so happens that the HTML font—those underlined hyperlink commands that web browsers use to take you to websites—can be set to a zero-size font. In other words, the underlined type is too small to be seen. They're, like, invisible, but still operable. He plans to embed your picture with a series of commands so that, when Bosko clicks on your picture, the commands embed a trap door in his computer. Cool, huh?"

Kara laughed. "Wow, how insanely cool! How come I've never heard of this before?"

Ignoring the obvious answer, Prisha asked Arnold, "I assume you'll want us to use the spread offense on this one?"

Which was their code name for deploying the team in a coordinated attack. One in which each person had pre-defined collaborative responsibilities. By synchronizing a series of sequential steps, they maximized their odds of sneaking in an alternate route into Bosko's machine before his anti-malware software could detect and neutralize their initial one.

Arnold: "Yeah, it's the perfect situation for deploying it. I'll get things set up on this end if you get the team set up and ready to go."

As Arnold began typing, he told Kara, "Luckily I have a few pre-coded Zero-Font scripts that'll work." He typed a series of commands and scrolled through several options. After reviewing five, he muttered, "Oh man, got the perfect one right here."

A moment later, he announced to the group, "Okay, sports fans,

I'm all set. Everyone ready?"

He then told them which script he would use so that they would be ready to pounce the moment that Bosko clicked open the picture.

After each team member confirmed that they were in place and ready, Arnold said to Kara, "First thing we need to do is have you migrate him from Messenger to email."

She thumped the heel of her palm against her temple, said, "Wow, totally blanked on that step."

Kara typed: DON'T WANT TO DO THIS ON MESSENGER, ESPECIALLY IF WE PLAN ON TAKING THIS TO THE NEXT LEVEL.

Bosko: WHY NOT?

She glanced at Arnold for help.

Arnold said, "Don't be too accommodating and eager. Stand your ground."

Kara: WHAT DIFFERENCE DOES IT MAKE TO YOU?

Bosko: THE HELL WITH IT THEN.

Arnold: "Call his bluff, girl."

Kara shrugged. "Okay…you're the gambler."

Kara: FINE. YOUR CALL, BRO.

They sat watching the screen. A minute ticked slowly past.

No response.

"Uh-oh," Kara muttered, reaching for her beer.

CHAPTER 17

ARNOLD FINGER-COMBED his hair and worried.

Had he misjudged Bosko enough to blow this opportunity?

Perhaps. But he didn't want to give up just yet.

"Keep the faith. Let him stew. He'll come around."

He assured himself that if he were in Bosko's shoes he'd certainly come around.

But he wasn't in Bosko's shoes, and wasn't paranoid, so what did he know?

Arnold pushed out of the chair and started to pace while Kara thoughtfully sipped her can of IPA.

"What if he doesn't answer?" she finally asked.

Good question. He had no response for her, but didn't want to admit it. He said, "Then we go to Plan B," with an edge of confidence that surprised him.

"Which is?"

Shit.

He threw up his arms.

"I don't know. But we'll figure out something."

"Oh great!" she said with more than a little twist of sarcasm.

"He'll come around," Arnold repeated, but with noticeably less conviction this time.

Pressing both palms to her temples, Kara glanced at the ceiling.

"Why do I let myself get sucked into these cases of yours? Not just physically, but emotionally. Like that last pen-test." She shook her head. "That one was a real doozie." Pause. "Now this. I probably won't even be able to sleep tonight."

Arnold stopped pacing to lock eyes with her.

"Admit it. You love it. You're basically a social engineering freak at heart."

Glancing back at the screen, she asked, "How much more time are we going to give this yo-yo before we pack it in?"

Arnold made a show of glancing at his watch. "Two minutes, thirty-five seconds." Then threw up his hands again. "Jesus, how do I know? Until we're convinced that he's bailed. Which I'm not."

Kara blew an audible breath. "Aw, man…"

Then her posture straightened as her eyes locked onto the laptop screen.

"Hold it. He's back!"

Arnold stepped behind her to look over her shoulder.

Bosko: STILL THERE?

Kara: YEP

Bosko: WHAT'S YOUR EMAIL?

Kara sent him the address along with, CHAT ON MESSENGER, BUT EXCHANGE PICS ON EMAIL

Bosko: WHATEVER

A moment later an email popped up in the Sharon Sweeny account.

Kara typed: GOT A PICTURE OF YOURSELF?

Bosko: YES

KARA: READY WHEN U R

Bosko: ME2

Kara: SEND!

She tapped ENTER and the infected picture zipped off into cyberspace. A moment later a message arrived in Arnold's laptop.

"Hold it," Arnold said before she could mouse it open. "We need to make sure he's not doing the same thing to us as we're doing to him."

"Oh crap! I totally spaced on that. Obviously. He is, after all, a hacker," Kara answered, sliding the computer to him.

Arnold told Prisha, "Go!" so that the team would start in establishing a beachhead on Bosko's computer. He then opened the security software on the laptop. A moment later, Arnold said, "Okay, it's clean."

After opening the attachment, he studied Bosko's picture for a long moment. Guy looked to be in his late twenties or early thirties, about the same age range as himself, but with scraggly straight blond hair in a semi-surfer-dude look. Piercing dark hazel or black eyes. Arnold couldn't tell exactly which because of the glint. Had a cunning look about him, but Arnold wasn't sure if that was real or if his preconceived bias was prejudicing him. Bosko looked awfully young to have all the educational credits and work experience to his name, but then again, maybe the dude was one of those uber-smart misfits who blew through university during mid-puberty. Which would give him a massive leg up on life if he weren't so victimized by such a malignant personality. And now that he thought about it, that could explain a lot.

Sliding the computer back to Kara, he said, "Here you go."

A moment later Bosko was back with: HOW ABOUT A REAL PICTURE?

Kara: PERHAPS, BUT ONLY AFTER I SEE YOU IN PERSON.

Bosko: HOW BOUT NOW?

Arnold was now standing behind her, reading the screen over her shoulder. He reminded her, "Remember, don't come across as too eager," despite the growing urge to maintain momentum on this potential lead.

The sooner they got a shot at neutralizing this asshole the better.

Kara: BUSY NOW. TOMORROW 7 DICK'S ON BROADWAY

Bosko: THEN WHAT?

Kara: WE'LL SEE

Bosko: DON'T LEAVE ME LIKE THIS

Pushing the laptop back over to Arnold's side of the table, she said, "Dude's way too eager. I'm already getting a creepy bad feeling about him."

"Yeah, I know what you're saying."

Sitting down again, he pulled the laptop to him and switched back to the chat room where the team was congregated, Ito and Lopez working on locking down an extra back door into Bosko's machine while Vihaan was already back to work with Mays on sanitizing the Cor-Pace computer network.

He said to Prisha, "I think it's time we take another go at Mr. Cain and Harris, and I'd like you on the call. This a good time to set things up?"

Arnold realized he had no idea what time it was other than some hour in the evening.

"Go ahead and get them on the line while I take a quick break."

Arnold got Mr. Cain on the line, then patched in Mr. Harris, and finally Prisha.

He began with, "I have a confession to make, but before I go any further, I want assurances you'll hear me out completely before you say a word."

John Harris said, "Oh, please don't tell me—"

Arnold cut him off with, "That's right. I went ahead and contacted FBI Special Agent Fisher. I've worked with him before and can tell you he's a real no-nonsense straight shooter. I gave him a complete rundown on the situation including your reasons for *not* wanting to involve them."

He imagined Mr. Harris's face growing red with supreme anger, so he plowed ahead with: "And before you say anything, let me finish my explanation. The case we worked together was also extremely sensitive and complicated, so I can assure you that he'll keep your best interests in mind because believe me when I say you're officially in some very deep shit."

He paused briefly for a deep breath.

"I can't emphasize strongly enough that since we have a strong person of interest in play, it's critical for them to help us as much as possible, like running the phone number I mentioned. More important is that he's in the process of initiating a case file, so that *when* the time comes for you to ask for their help on this, they'll be set up and ready to move."

There! He'd fessed up.

Doing so brought him a sense of relief. Undoubtedly Mr. Cain would appear upset with him, but he suspected that that was more for Harris's benefit and in reality he was probably relieved by Arnold's action since it also helped cover his ass.

After a pronounced silence, Mr. Harris said, "I'm very disappointed that you went against my explicit wishes, Mr. Gold. This type of behavior isn't remotely close to what Noah led me to expect from you. I just hope that your Mr. Fisher can exercise the discretion you claim he's capable of."

Mr. Cain said, "With all due respect, John, I have faith in Arnold's judgment as it pertains to these matters. If he genuinely believes that enlisting Mr. Fisher's collaboration at this time is the appropriate course of action, then I support his decision. Let's face the reality of what we're dealing with: we have a truly awful situation on our hands, one in which people's lives are at stake. We have no room for error. And I, for one, want no regrets when this disaster finally resolves itself, one way or the other. I suggest that we put any recrimination behind us and move forward the best we can."

Arnold said, "Thank you both for supporting us," although he wasn't so sure he had Harris's wholehearted commitment anymore. "We'll get back to you if and when we have additional progress to report. Have a good night, gentlemen."

He dropped the call before either one could respond, figuring that if they had anything substantial to say, they'd call back.

Turning to Kara, Arnold said, "You did great. Thanks."

Their eyes met and held, Arnold fighting the urge to reach over and touch her face, and draw her closer...

Watch it, pal. We've been down this path before.

How many times had he debated this? How many times must he remind himself that she was off-limits?

He cleared his constricted throat, stood, stretched, said, "Prisha and I plan to be with you tomorrow during the encounter. I just need to work out the details of exactly how we plan to accomplish everything we need."

Translation: the evening is now officially over.

Rats!

Now also standing, she asked, "Why? You don't think I can handle this yo-yo?"

He shook his head. "Naw, that's not it at all. We know you can handle the situation when you two meet. But we have other objectives we want to get from the encounter. We need to figure out how best to get those."

Head cocked, hand on her hip, she flashed a look of disbelief as if her bullshit meter just pinged.

"Such as?"

Arnold shrugged.

Fair enough.

"Well, for one, we want to call our mystery number when we're able to hear if his phone rings."

"Oh," she said, as if she'd missed something obvious. Which she had.

For an awkward moment they remained standing eye-fucking each other, lightning bolts of raw attraction zapping back and forth between them, driving Arnold crazy.

A moment later, he said, "I'll walk you to your car."

Mr. Perfect Gentleman.

Mr. Frustrated Perfect Gentleman.

She swallowed, turned and headed for the front door.

"How do you plan on getting to work tomorrow?" he asked as they ambled to her car, Chance tagging along hoping there was something in it for a pooch.

"Hadn't given it a thought. Why?"

"Because Prisha and I plan to pick you up outside your office and drive you up to Dick's. I was thinking we could have dinner there."

Flashing an expression of disgust, she said, "A Dick's Deluxe for dinner. Yuck! You're not making any points, Gold."

"What, you don't like their burgers? Hard to believe. Oh well, you can eat afterwards, but we definitely are planning to be there as backup."

Then Arnold went on to explain the plan they had roughed out.

CHAPTER 18

"SORRY TO CALL so late," Arnold said to Special Agent Fisher. He was back at the kitchen table, toying with whether to have another few bites of pizza before rearranging the contents of the fridge to accommodate the remaining pieces. "But I want to bring you up to speed on our progress with the case."

He went on to explain that they'd successfully burrowed into Bosko's computer, but exactly how long they might survive there before being discovered and locked out was up for grabs.

"Nice work, Gold. I figured you'd engineer a way in. Hope you can find what you're looking for."

Arnold marveled at how adroitly the FBI agent could converse without uttering an incriminating word. After all, Fisher had been the one to suggest they break into Bosko's computer.

Then Arnold explained how Kara was now set up as a lure to get close enough to Bosko to, among other things, determine if the annotated phone number in Elijah Brown's firmware was his personal cell. Doubtful as that was.

Fisher said, "Now that I have a file open on this, go ahead and give me that number again, and I'll run a reverse look-up in the morning."

After Arnold recited him the number, Fisher asked, "When and where did you say your friend is meeting Bosko?"

"At the Dick's Drive-In. The one on Broadway. Seven tomorrow evening."

"Okay, that sounds relatively safe." Fisher stopped for a moment. "You'll stay close enough to keep an eye on her at all times?"

"I plan to. I'll play the part of just another loitering customer. Prisha Patel will actually be the one to accompany her into the area."

Arnold stopped his explanation, now uneasy about explaining how Kara was being used as a honeypot.

Just then his phone beeped. Another call waiting to be answered.

"Can you hold for one second? I got another call coming in and I want to make sure it's not Kara?"

Fisher said, "Have anything else for now?"

"No, not really."

"Then good night." And Fisher was gone.

Arnold glimpsed at the caller ID. Noriko.

What the hell?

Given the three-hour time difference, it was late Monday night there and early Tuesday morning here. He wasn't sure how he felt about the call but accepted it anyway.

"Yes?" he said, harshly. Too harsh, he knew.

"I just wanted to call back to ask how things are going. Or is your girlfriend still there?"

Aw Jesus! How do you deal with a question like that?

"My girlfriend? What are you talking about?"

"The one who you were talking to last time I called, *Studly*."

"That *was* Kara, and like I told you, she's not a girlfriend, she's part of the team."

"Know what, Arnold? I'm not sure I believe you because if that's the case, why haven't you mentioned her before? And why didn't I meet her when all your teammates came over to the island for a mini-vacation? Remember?"

She was referring to last month when the team had blown their 25K bonus from their last pen-test to fly Prisha, Vihaan, and Lopez to Honolulu for a celebratory mini-vacation. Arnold had had them over for a party on his back deck. Noriko had helped him put the party together.

He felt himself being sucked into a vortex of drama-quicksand and knew that any reply would mire him more deeply.

How do you deal with a situation like this?

On the one hand, it felt nice to have her care for him. The flip side was that her baseless accusation of having a "girlfriend" here was annoying and worrisome, and pointed a finger at potential problems down the road. More than that, however, was how blithely she ignored his repeated pleas to not be disturbed during this job. These constant interruptions, he found, were massively irritating.

She continued to wait for an answer to her question.

Answer or ignore it and move on?

Moving on seemed to be the safest course.

"The thing is, Noriko, at the moment I really don't have time to chitchat. Like I've told you too many times now, this job is time intensive. We're up against the clock on this."

"You can't really be serious. I mean, like, you're too busy twenty-four hours a day? That's impossible. I just don't believe it."

After a heavy sigh of resignation, "In that case I really don't know what to tell you other than I have to get back to work."

"Maybe I'd find your story more believable if you explained what this super-classified job is all about. So far you haven't said one word about it."

Massaging his forehead with his free hand, Arnold flirted with the idea of just hanging up but decided not to be an asshole. And besides, his concentration was already trashed. Instead, he said as evenly as possible, "That's because this job is *classified*. Meaning I'm not a liberty to tell *anyone anything*."

"Oh, come on, Arnold. You're making it sound like you're working on some sort of clandestine CIA operation instead of an IT issue." After a moment of silence, she asked, "Or have you lied to me about the work your company does?"

Jesus.

"No. I didn't lie to you about that. Or anything else. And yes, this is basically an IT issue. But believe me, I cannot and will not discuss it.

Maybe once it's a wrap, but not now. Do you understand what I'm telling you?"

"No, not at all. I understand the words you've said, but I'm not sure I believe you."

For a moment, Arnold just stared at his phone.

Was this conversation for real or nothing more than a bizarre auditory hallucination due to sleep deprivation?

"Did you just accuse me of lying?" he asked incredulously.

"Are you?" she responded pointedly.

As the initial shock over her question began to ebb, he realized that his hesitation in answering probably confirmed her suspicion. In other words, he was now officially hosed no matter what he said. When facing a situation like this, the best strategy, he believed, is to drop back ten yards and punt.

"Look Noriko, I am sorry, but I need to get back to work."

"No, Arnold, don't—"

"Sorry, Noriko. Good night."

After cutting the connection, he sat very still, reflecting on the little drama that had just played out.

Was he an asshole to cut her off like that?

Probably.

No, not probably, definitely.

Then why do it?

Because...

Well, because she'd forced the issue by calling despite repeated requests to not interrupt him while he's working this case. But from her perspective, was it even remotely credible that he was so laser-focused that he couldn't spare a few minutes to chat?

Naw.

Okay, sure, if put in those terms, he undoubtedly deserved a Giant Asshole Award.

And as long as he was being Mr. Honesty, how could she possibly know when it was a good time to call? No way she could. Making the more relevant question: Why didn't he call her during one of his breaks?

Well, duh, because he didn't think of it.

Yeah? And why not?

Yo, you've just wasted more time fretting about this than it would've taken to waste a few moments to chat with her.

Good point, but he still hadn't addressed the question: why didn't he take a moment out of his day to call her?

Well, if he was *really* truthful with himself, this job was an excuse to avoid her.

Okay, but why?

Hmmm…the most straightforward wiggle-out-of-it answer was that the gravity of this case prevented him from loosening up. It made him feel as if every unproductive minute was hurling the team toward a deadline that if missed, jeopardized some innocent person's life. A heavy responsibility, that. One he didn't want to bear. Not to mention that it'd be the team's first failure. Yet that outcome was looking unavoidable. And as long as he was being gut-wrenchingly truthful about this quagmire, he strongly resented having been shoehorned into it by Mr. Cain.

Yeah, yeah, yeah, this was all true.

But he was now starting to stray from his question about Noriko again. He needed to resolve it. If not right now, before he returned to Honolulu.

Arnold sucked in a deep breath. He felt bad about the way he'd treated her on the call, but like everything, his reaction was exactly that: a reaction. It didn't arise from a vacuum. Meaning something had provoked it.

What?

He knew the answer was…

"Yo, Arnold, you there?"

He glanced at the laptop screen and realized that Lopez just asked him a question.

"Roger that."

"We just found a chunk of code in one of the routers that I swear is a RAT."

This had to be one of Bosko's ports of entry into the Cor-Pace network.

"Cool. Appreciate the update." Arnold didn't insult him by asking if they'd removed it. "Prisha, you on?"

"That I am."

Arnold finger-combed his curly black hair while weighing their situation.

"Look, we can assume that by now our hacker probably has one more backdoor still available, so we need to keep trying to sniff it out. But I also think we're at the point where our efficiency is beginning to take a huge hit from fatigue. What do you think about all of us knocking off for a four-hour nap?"

He realized that if it weren't for daylight on the other side of the windows, he had no idea if it was night or day, even though he was pretty sure this was Tuesday.

"Oh, man, I totally agree. We all sure could use it."

He checked the list of team members logged into the chat room. Everyone was present, but just to be certain they were at their computers and paying attention, he took a quick rollcall and checked the time.

"Okay then. Let's reconvene at four o'clock this afternoon," he said, giving them a few extra minutes.

Upstairs, Arnold instructed Alexa to wake him at quarter to four, then collapsed on the bed. His brain immediately zonked out.

CHAPTER 19

Prisha

PRISHA HEADED INTO the one bedroom in their small apartment, Vihaan on her heels, saying, "Why do I have to be the one who's sitting in front of the monitor while you're out with Arnold doing all the cool stuff?"

She spun around to face him, eyes blazing, hands on her hips.

"For christsake, Vihaan, give it a rest. We both need to sleep."

He reached out, took hold of her arm.

"No, I'm serious. I don't see why I'm always the one who gets stuck with the shit jobs while you're off playing around with Arnold."

A surge of adrenaline-fueled anger spiked through her arteries, tingling her fingertips and toes. She tore his hand from her arm and drilled him with hard eyes.

"Don't you ever lay a hand on me like that again!"

Vihaan took a step back, eyeing her with a hint of fear.

She took a step towards him, getting in his face.

"And just what the fuck's 'playing around with Arnold' supposed to mean?"

Vihaan stood his ground.

"Well, it's true" he said." Today's a prime example. I'm stuck behind a monitor—"

"No, husband. That's *not* what I asked. I asked what you're accusing me of doing when you say, 'playing around' with Arnold? I sincerely hope that's just a poorly thought-out choice of words. Well?"

Vihaan cocked his head to one side, sending her a questioning expression.

"Why so sensitive? Feeling guilty about something? Have something to hide?"

She took two steps toward him, shoved his chest hard, sending him windmilling backward, fighting to keep his balance.

She screamed, "Sleep on the couch, *asshole*. Don't you dare try to open that door. Now out!"

She made a shooing motion.

At 3:55 PM Prisha's iPhone alarm tore her from black, empty, dreamless unconsciousness into the reality of unfinished work to do without enough sleep. Rolling off the queen-size bed, she beelined for the bathroom to splash cold water over her face to help her awake fully.

A few seconds before 4:00 PM she dropped back into her chair at the kitchen table. Only four hours. But the break did help refresh her. She glanced into the living room in time to catch Vihaan slip from the bathroom and turn back into the living room.

Neither one spoke.

She revived the laptop from sleep mode and signed back into the chat room. As she waited for Arnold to log in, she glanced back into the living room where Vihaan now sat rigidly on the couch, staring at his laptop screen, assiduously avoiding her. The acute plummet in room temperature saddened her.

Why was he suddenly accusing her of messing around with their boss? What had she done to warrant such an accusation?

Or was he fishing? But that brought up the most important question: why even *suspect* that type of behavior from her? What had she ever done to plant a seed of suspicion? Or was it nothing more than a manifestation of his own imagination? Having to ask herself these questions intensified her sadness.

Arnold

Armed with a fresh cup of black coffee, Arnold logged into their primary chat room and found the team already back to work. A glance at his watch. He was one minute late.

He greeted them with, "Hey guys, sorry I'm late. Everyone catch a few Zs?"

Being rhetorical, he got right down to business: "I'd like Lopez, Ito, and Vihaan to continue working with Mays on locking down Cor-Pace's network while Prisha and I script tonight's meeting with Bosko." Pause. "Any questions?"

"Yeah," Vihaan immediately replied. "Why's Prisha working with you tonight instead of one of us? Why do we three always end up with the shit assignments?"

Arnold flashed on his conversation with Prisha about her husband's suspicions. Apparently getting rid of the Larkin Standish supervisory role didn't do much to appease him.

Arnold said, "Okay, let's walk through the options. First of all, Brian's in Honolulu, right?" He paused, letting that one sink in. "So, he's not even a consideration. Second, you and Carlos are already intimately familiar with their network. Prisha isn't. It'd be a waste of momentum—something we seriously can't afford right now—to put her on that task this late in the game. Third, we're trying to entice Bosko by dangling Kara in front of him, right? So, it just makes sense— at least it does to me—to pair her with another female. Or does this not make sense to you?"

Arnold realized that Vihaan in general, in addition to his recent complaints in particular, was beginning to really piss him off. Not good for anyone involved. Especially for team morale. He slowly inhaled, hoping to tamp down his brewing tension.

"When you put that way, I guess it does," Vihaan admitted, "but back it up a few steps to when we started this job. Was there ever any doubt from day one that you'd choose Prisha for the best jobs? No. And that seems to be a consistent factor in the way work is distributed within the group."

Palm-wiping his face, Arnold considered how best to deal with this mess. The last thing he wanted was to inflame Vihaan any more than he was already.

And besides, he had no feel for how the others viewed Vihaan's complaint. Did they buy it?

Had Vihaan been grumbling to them behind his back, fomenting discontent?

"Look, Vihaan, I acknowledge what you're saying, and am happy to have the team to discuss this once this job is finished, but I bet we can all agree that this isn't the best time to distract ourselves over the issue. Can we at least agree on this?"

Not hearing a response, Arnold asked, "Vihaan?"

"You're really not giving me a choice, are you?" Vihaan answered, making no attempt to mask his deep-seated irritation.

Uh-oh.

"Look, I'm really sorry you see it that way." Arnold paused briefly, giving Vihaan one more chance to vent.

After several seconds of silence, he continued with, "Okay then, let's get back to work. Prisha, why don't we drop down to Chat Two," referring to their second chat room, "and we'll continue there."

Arnold switched virtual rooms. A moment later Prisha's image popped up.

She said, "Sorry about that."

She glanced away from the webcam toward the living room. Probably checking to see how Vihaan was reacting to the comment.

Arnold said, "I'm sorry that you're having to deal with this, but I suspect this isn't the best time to discuss it. But once this case is finished—regardless of the outcome—we, as a group, we need to discuss his complaint."

"Couldn't agree more. But for now, how do you want to play this thing with Kara?"

"Let's arrange to pick her up at six o'clock, then drive up to

Dick's. We can brief her along the way. Once we're up on Capitol Hill, I'd like you to drop me off on Harvard—the block to the west of the drive-in—oh, maybe around six fifty or so. That'll give me enough time to be at Dick's before you guys drive in. I plan to be at the dining counter before you park in the lot and she's out of the car. That way I can keep an eye on her without appearing suspicious. See any problems with what I just laid out?"

Prisha seemed to think about it before answering.

"Sounds reasonable to me." She checked her watch. "In other words, I should be heading over to your place soon. Does Kara know when we're planning to pick her up?"

"She does. I told her to be waiting outside the Second Avenue doors and we'd pick her up in the bus zone."

"Roger that."

Prisha

Factoring in the traffic at this time of evening, Prisha decided it was time to leave to pick up Arnold. She stood in front of the coffee table and told Vihaan, "I'm leaving now but when this job's over, why don't we take a couple days off and see if we can get a cabin over on the coast for a few nights. Maybe Iron Springs Resort. Whatdaya think?"

Without looking up from the laptop, he shook his head.

"I'm not sure what to think. All I know is you're spending a lot of time with Arnold."

Prisha rolled her eyes and blew a breath.

"Husband, look at me. I married you because I love you. Nothing's changed. Don't create a problem that just isn't there, okay?"

But she knew this was a lie. A lot of things had changed. Both of them were changing. Life dictates change, and so the relationship had migrated to another place along with it. Dramatically.

Vihaan neither looked up nor acknowledged her comment.

He knows it too, she realized. She continued to stare at him a moment longer before deciding to leave it alone. She turned and walked out the front door.

Arnold

As Prisha pulled away from the curb at Arnold's house, she told him, "I worry that this entire fuss Vihaan's making about assignments is just a smokescreen. What's really at the core of his anger is his misguided belief that something's going on between us."

Arnold looked at her. "You're kidding! Between *us*? As in you and me?" Pointing from her to him.

"Right."

Arnold whistled. "As I said, you've got to be kidding, but obviously you're not." Pause. "Man! Any idea how he came up with that?"

"Actually, yes. I've been thinking about it. A lot."

She tapped her turn signal, preparing to jog left onto Aurora once the turn lane light gave her the green arrow.

"I suspect it's because the few times you've been in town it's for our big jobs like the two pen-tests we just did. On those, we worked very closely together. I think those specific cases are what's made him jealous."

She was referring to the pen-tests the team had done for the prestigious law firm, Larkin Standish. Not only were those jobs insanely intense, but they had worked closely together on them. But so had the entire team.

"Yeah, those jobs were, like, super-focused, but that doesn't mean something's going on between us. I still don't get the reason for his concern."

Accelerating into a left-hand turn, she said, "We both realize it's a senseless claim, but he apparently sees it differently."

Arnold sucked an incisor for a moment.

"So, what're you saying?"

She responded with a resigned sigh.

"I'm not saying anything. I'm just telling you what I *think* might be the cause of it. And no, I don't have any bright ideas on what to do about it. Not a damn one."

Arnold sensed she wasn't finished, so he waited for her to continue.

A moment later, she added, "And to be totally honest, I'm not sure I want to even try. Vihaan's just being, well, Vihaan. Sometimes he sees things that far as I'm concerned just aren't there. I don't mean he's hallucinating or anything like that, but he's becoming increasingly insecure about our relationship, and far as I know, I haven't given him a single reason for it. I can't be blamed for something I didn't do and I'm sure as hell not going to change how I do my job just to accommodate his paranoia and fantasies. That'd do nothing but undermine our relationship further."

Pushing his glasses back up his nose, Arnold said, "But this has got to put a mondo strain on your marriage."

"No shit. But what I'm saying is, if our marriage is starting to fail because he's insecure about you and me, then I'm not sure how much effort I want to put into trying to salvage it. Assuming, I even knew what I could do to save it." Pause. "How's that for brutal honesty?"

Arnold whistled. "Pretty freaking honest."

For several seconds they drove in silence as the car nestled into the long line of slow-moving traffic snaking into the city, its flow progressively more choked as arterials continued to merge into State Route 99 on the approach to the Aurora bridge.

Arnold finally broke the long silence with, "As far as how we work together, I can't see us changing. You and I make an incredibly symbiotic team. I don't want to mess with that."

She nodded enthusiastically.

"Totally, dude. And we shouldn't have to, either."

Prisha braked her Toyota at the curb in the middle of a busy bus stop directly in front of the lobby doors to the office building where Kara worked as a paralegal for Cain, Tidwell, Stowell. As she was braking to a stop, Kara came streaking across the sidewalk for the car. Arnold jumped out, leaving the front passenger door open. He scooted into the back seat as Kara tossed her rucksack into the front footwell, then slid into the shotgun position, pulling the door closed just as a bus driver aggressively laid on his horn while edging his bus up against the

Toyota's rear bumper.

Kara said, "Thanks for picking me up."

Prisha began merging back into the hectic flow of downtown traffic, the entire process clogging the busy bus zone took no more than a few seconds.

6:04 PM Wednesday, Arnold noted. A little less than forty-eight hours until the deadline.

Glancing at Kara, Prisha asked in a bemused tone, "Wow, is that your typical business attire?" referring to the tight blue jeans and a lightweight black turtleneck that showcased her killer figure and red hair.

Kara laughed.

"You bet. Especially when taking depositions. No, I changed before I came down to the lobby. My regular clothes are in there."

She nodded at the rucksack.

"What you're wearing now should catch his attention," Arnold added.

With an oinking sound, Prisha shot him an admonishing side-eye, which Arnold pointedly ignored. After all, the goal of this little exercise was exactly that: to capture Bosko's attention. The dude would have to be brain-dead for that not to happen.

"Thought we'd cruise by to check it out before we set up," Prisha told her.

When Kara didn't answer, Arnold asked, "Nervous?"

Kara scoffed. "Not until you mentioned it…"

Arnold: "Don't worry, you'll do fine."

"Leave it," Prisha said, as if addressing Chance. "You're only making matters worse."

As Prisha drove, Arnold walked Kara through their plan.

CHAPTER 20

PRISHA DROVE EAST on Olive Way to Broadway, turned right, and passed two other buildings before making another right into the Dick's Drive-In lot, Arnold scrunching down in the back seat to keep from being spotted should Bosko have elected to arrive early to scope things out.

The mid-century-style building sat centered in a deep rectangular lot dwarfed between two larger multi-story buildings. Jutting from the roof was a large extension to shelter customers standing around the serving windows or scarfing burgers and fries at a stainless-steel dining counter. One-way traffic entered off of Broadway, ran the north side of the lot to the alley, and returned down the south side of the building, with both sides offering diagonal parking slots along their flanks.

Prisha continued slowly past a few parked cars on into the alley, then around the back of the restaurant before coming down the south side of the lot to make another right turn back onto Broadway.

Once back into the flow of traffic she told Arnold, "Didn't see him hanging around outside, but he could be in a car."

After sitting back up, Arnold checked the time. Fifteen minutes until the designated meeting. Prisha turned onto Harvard Avenue and then, halfway down the block, curbed the Toyota in a passenger loading zone.

Arnold climbed out onto the sidewalk, leaned down and said, "See you guys in a few." He closed the door and started moving towards East Olive Way.

After following the same route to the drive-in that Prisha had just driven, Arnold sauntered up to one of two service windows, purchased a bag of fries, a tub of catsup, and a Diet Coke, then scooted into a spot at the stand-up stainless-steel dining counter under the portico. Getting into character, he nibbled his first fry. Three other diners were also standing at the metal counter, while several other people were scattered in clumps, chatting. He didn't see Bosko. The evening was pleasant enough, in the high sixties. At precisely 7:00 he saw Prisha's white Toyota roll into the lot, nose slowly down the north side of the building, and disappear. A moment later her car crept along the opposite side, then turned into an angled parking space just three stalls from the exit back onto Broadway.

Kara stepped out of the car and came walking toward him into the serving/dining area. She stopped to glance around as if searching for someone but as agreed upon, made no eye contact with Arnold.

Arnold popped another fry into his mouth, then washed it down with a sip of Diet Coke. A moment later Kara approached the dining area, turned and leaned her back against the counter, directly opposite him, to face the parking area.

A moment later Bosko seemed to suddenly materialize at her side, putting them directly across the rectangular stainless-steel table from Arnold.

He heard Bosko ask, "Are you Sharon?"

Turning to face him, she answered, "And you appear to be Alfred."

Arnold could hear their words clearly.

"I am," Bosko said, eyeing her with a hollow, empty expression that gave Arnold a serious case of the willies and set his antennas to humming. Bosko's chilling tone and demeanor were a distant cry from the hot-to-trot messages of last night. Now, his hard black eyes gave him a cold predatory look.

After a visual once over, Kara smiled and said, "You're better-looking in person than your picture."

Completely poker-faced, Bosko hesitated before asking, "Who'd you say gave you my name?"

Arnold already had his cellphone out, casually dialing the phone number they'd found embedded in the Cor-Pace device. Putting the phone to his ear, he listened to the call click over to a recorded message saying that the number dialed was presently not in service. Well, did he really expect Bosko to be walking around with that phone? No, not really, but hey, they had to at least try. Stranger things have happened.

Kara's expression suddenly dropped from an alluring smile to stone-cold serious.

"What's with the third degree, bro?"

Eyeing her again, he answered, "Why shouldn't I be super-curious when a hot chick comes on to me straight out of nowhere?"

Bosko's voice had a whiny nasal quality to it that Arnold found off-putting. Then again, he freely admitted that he was strongly biased against the guy.

Kara crossed her arms and straightened her posture.

"Oh, is that what I'm doing? *Coming on* to you?"

By now Arnold was thinking, *no no no, we can't let this opportunity slip away.* Yet in watching the encounter unfold, it was obvious that their one chance to snag a grip on this asshole was rapidly self-destructing and there was nothing he could do to salvage the mess. More importantly though, Bosko was radiating a serious scary-dude vibe. A dude he didn't want Kara to be close to.

Then Prisha was out of the car, heading straight for Kara, calling, "Yo, Sharon, getting late girl, we gotta bump."

"Who's she?" Bosko asked, flashing a perplexed expression.

Not budging, Kara locked eyes with him.

"Hey, I told you yesterday I have another engagement tonight. I'm with her at the moment."

When Bosko didn't respond, Kara said, "You going to give me your phone number so we can text, or you want to simply chalk this up to a bad experience? Your call, bro."

Bosko frowned, asked, "What's with the interest in my phone?"

Kara took a step toward Prisha, then stopped to turn back to him. "What's with the paranoia? You know texting is much quicker than email."

Bosko backed away a step while glancing from Kara to Prisha, then back to Kara.

"No, something's not right about this whole thing. You're pushing too hard."

He turned and started walking toward Broadway.

Prisha shot Arnold a quick raised-eyebrow look, as if to ask, *What now, coach?*

Arnold picked up a fry and just before popping it into his mouth, said, "Stick with the plan."

Watching the two women return to their car, he put the straw to his lips for another sip of Diet Coke before wiping his fingers with a thin, nonabsorbent paper napkin. He wadded it up, then tossed it and the fries in the nearby gray plastic garbage bin, having just lost his appetite. Keeping the Diet Coke with him, he turned and began trudging the reverse route back to their designated meeting spot.

As Arnold scrambled into the back seat of the Toyota, Prisha was saying, "Well, that sure went sideways in a hurry."

"Sure did," Arnold agreed, pulling the door closed. "Damn. We put a lot of effort into this, too."

"I can't help but think I did something wrong," Kara said, "something that totally freaked him."

Pulling away from the curb, Prisha said, "Not as far as I could see. That guy's just a basket case of paranoia is all. Arnold? Whatdaya say? You were standing right there."

Prisha stopped the car in the middle of the road, turned to Kara to ask, "Remind me. Am I taking you back to the office or home?"

Still frowning Kara replied, "Hopefully you're taking me home. And you didn't forget because I don't think we ever discussed it."

"Got it," Prisha said, accelerating toward the intersection ahead.

Fumbling with mating his seatbelt into the latch, Arnold waited until it clicked securely in place before answering Kara. "Naw, you did nothing wrong. I could hear the entire exchange. I agree with Prisha. You did exactly as planned. Prisha's right: dude's just paranoid as hell, is all. Far as I can tell, there's nothing you could've said or done that would've changed the outcome. But it was definitely worth a shot."

No one said a word.

Burying his face in his hands, Arnold groaned, "Aw man, it's already Wednesday evening and we're no closer to finding our guy than we were on Sunday."

"That's not entirely true," Prisha said. "We have a very likely person of interest, we've shut down at least two of his portals into Cor-Pace's network, we've hacked our suspect's network, and we have the FBI shadowing our investigation. I'd have to say that's a very reasonable amount of solid progress in a very limited time."

"Yes, but," Arnold snapped, "we don't have one solid piece of evidence to directly implicate Bosko as our hacker."

Arnold's phone started in. Fisher.

With hopes soaring, he said, "Hold on, it's Agent Fisher. Maybe he's got some word on the phone number." He answered the call on speakerphone. "Agent Fisher, what do you have for me? Oh, and you're on speakerphone."

"What I don't have for you is good news, Gold. The number you're so interested in is a TracFone on the Verizon network."

"Why's that bad news?"

"Because even if I had a magistrate-approved warrant in my hand right now and was able to serve it tonight, Verizon wouldn't get around to handing over the name on the account for perhaps a week to ten days. And there's no way to jump the priority line on this one. Sorry."

"Ah, man…" Finger combing his hair, Arnold could feel the odds of nailing Hacker slipping. "Well, thanks for trying, Mr. Fisher. I really appreciate you looking into it."

"We're not finished with this conversation yet, so don't hang up. As long as we're having this little *tête-à-tête*, have you found anything of value on your target's computer?"

Arnold realized that he'd been so focused on this Kara thing that he'd completely forgotten about that lead. He'd check with Lopez soon as this call wrapped up.

"To tell you the truth, I've been too busy working another angle, so I haven't had time for an update on that. We've got two other team members on it, so I'll check with them soon as I can. I'll let you know the moment anything turns up."

"Good. Keep me informed. Good night."

And with that he was gone.

"Don't look so down, girl," Prisha was telling Kara. "It was a long shot. We all knew that."

"And we did learn something from the encounter," Arnold said in an attempt to buoy her spirits.

"What?" Kara asked.

Arnold didn't have an answer for her, so opted to go for a distraction by saying, "Hold that thought while I call Lopez to see what's up."

Again, on speakerphone, he dialed.

Lopez answered by asking, "You guys get anything?"

"Not what we wanted. Dude got all paranoid and suspected we were trying to pull something on him—which we were—so just walked away from the meeting. That's why I'm checking in with you guys. Come up with anything yet?"

"What a coincidence. At the moment we have a good news/bad news thing going on. The bad news is that Bosko found the malware we embedded with the Zero-Font trick and removed it. That might explain his hyper-paranoia." He paused. "The good news is we were able to sneak in another trap door that he hasn't found yet. We're just about to give it a try. Want to hold while we do that?"

"Hell yes," Prisha called from the front seat.

Prisha found a spot to pull over so they could listen.

A moment later, Lopez was back with, "Shit. The bastard found that one too."

Oh perfect! Just freaking perfect.

Arnold told him, "Nice try though."

"I'm not sure about that. Later."

Lopez disconnected.

"Ah, *shit!*" Arnold muttered.

"What?" Prisha asked, shooting him a quick glance from the front seat.

Shaking his head, Arnold answered, "Lopez's right. He damn well knows we're onto him. That's why he bolted at Dick's."

Prisha said to Kara, "See? You didn't mess up. He'd found our malware, so knew he was targeted and being set up. Not only that, but I'm willing to bet you're his only recent encounter. So why wouldn't he be hyper-suspicious about you? Damn! We tripped ourselves up on this one." Then, addressing Arnold: "Which means, of course, we're now totally fucked."

But Arnold was staring blankly at his phone, depression enveloping him. They'd messed up. The entire team was now aware that they were going to lose this one and there was no way to salvage that trajectory.

After several seconds of silence, Arnold muttered, "There's got to be a way to nail this bastard. We can't let this asshole get away with killing another patient."

Kara said, "You seem to be taking this case awfully personally. Why?"

"No, not really," he answered defensively.

"Oh, you bet he is," Prisha contradicted.

Kara continued with, "I can't say I buy it. When I listen to you talk about this job, it almost sounds like you're in a personal jousting match with whoever the hacker is. To me, it looks like you've been forced to take on an impossible case with the expectation of coming up with a miracle. If you can't determine who this whack job is before something awful happens, it's not your fault."

"But if he kills a patient Friday, it'll be on me," he responded with a tinge of anger at her for not seeing the obvious.

Kara shot back, "I don't see it that way at all. And I can't believe anyone else does. The way I see it, if this whack-job offs a patient, that's on Harris for not contacting the FBI after that first call on Sunday. Harris is the one putting patients' lives at risk. Not you. You can't be held responsible for his lack of reasonable judgment. Prisha, what's your take on it?"

Nodding vigorously, she answered, "She's absolutely right, boss. Bosko offs someone, it's not on any of us. We didn't spark his fuse. We're the ones racing for a fire extinguisher, and we may or may not find one in time."

There was no sense in arguing with them.

Instead, he suggested to Prisha, "We need to do some serious brainstorming after dropping Kara off. There's got to be a way to catch this asshole."

Although he wasn't convinced he believed it.

But he couldn't just roll over and give up.

"You want some help?" Kara offered.

"Naw," he replied. "You've got your job to focus on. And besides, we'll probably work straight through the night on this one."

Prisha asked, "Whatdaya think about pulling Vihaan off Cor-Pace to help us?"

Hmmm...What was their key priority at this point: plugging a hole in Cor-Pace's network or finding a trail to Bosko?

Put in those terms, the answer was obvious.

"Oh man, I should've thought of that," he muttered as he dialed Vihaan's number.

When Prisha's husband picked up, Arnold said, "Why don't you tell Mays we need you on Bosko's machine." It really wasn't a question.

A long moment of silence was punctuated with: "Why now?"

"What do you mean, why now? We need you helping Lopez and Ito."

"Why the sudden shift in assignment?"

Arnold wasn't sure what point Vihaan was trying to make, but from the underlying confrontational tone, he sensed an argument brewing.

"Aw Jesus, Vihaan, can we postpone the drama for another time? Here's our status. The meeting with Bosko ended up a freaking disaster. We came away with zip. At this point I think our best strategy is to focus all of our resources on gathering any evidence we can on him. In the meantime, Mays can continue working on shoring up their network. Okay?"

"What will you and Prisha be doing?"

Aw man!

"At the moment we're taking Kara home. After that we plan to brainstorm a way to stop Bosko from killing someone, okay? Or do you have an issue with this too?"

Arnold fought a losing battle to keep his voice as neutral as possible and there was no way Vihaan wasn't picking up on it. Which probably wasn't helping things.

Silence.

Shaking his head, Arnold glanced between the front seats at the rear-view mirror where Prisha was eyeing him with raised brows; an expression, he decided, that could be interpreted several ways.

"So, will you do it, Vihaan?" he finally asked.

"Oh, all right," Vihaan answered in a snot-nose petulant-adolescent tone.

"Thank you," Arnold replied through gritted teeth. Shaking his head, Arnold disconnected the call and leaned back in the seat to close his eyes for a moment.

"That's the kind of shit I have to deal with day-to-day now," Prisha said, making no attempt to mask her annoyance.

Kara, the consummate diplomat, appeared to be silently studying the tacky sights along Aurora Avenue just north of the bridge as if totally unaware of the little drama playing out.

"I'm sorry" was all Arnold could muster.

What else was there to say?

Once again, the car settled into the monotonous hum of road noise. Arnold scoured his brain for another way to worm into Bosko's machines despite knowing that the effort was nothing more than spinning his creative wheels. Especially now that Bosko knew someone had made it past his firewall once. By now, if Bosko really was the hacker, the computer or flash drive containing the serial numbers was probably securely locked-up in a Swiss bank vault.

So, what was the use of even trying?

Prisha turned to Kara with, "Next block?"

"Yep. Second building on the right."

A moment later, Prisha curbed the car in a passenger loading zone in front of a newish-looking non-descript apartment building.

Kara stepped to the curb, crouched down to look at both of them, said, "Thanks. It was worth trying to pull off despite it not working. Yeah, it was definitely worth the try. Good luck." Then she turned to Arnold, "I meant it when I said you shouldn't take this so personally. If this goes south, it's not on you. Goodnight you two."

She started to close the door.

Opening the back door, Arnold said, "Hold it. I'm going to move to the front."

After closing the back door, Arnold approached Kara, wrapped her in his arms and hugged, saying, "Thanks again for all your help."

He held her closer and tighter than a simple goodnight hug. When he finally released her, Kara gave him a questioning yet approving smile. Causing Arnold's face to start in on the space-heater imitation.

He said, "Good night," before returning to the car, to slip into the front seat, and then pull the door shut.

Prisha and Arnold watched until Kara was safely inside the lobby with the door securely shut before saying a word.

Prisha engaged the left turn signal and checked the driver side-mirror for traffic before pulling into the street.

She said, "I thought we've been over this."

"Been over what?" he answered. All Mr. Innocence.

"Don't pull that whatdaya-mean shit on me. You know exactly what I'm talking about."

After a moment. "There's nothing going on, if that's what you're referring to."

"Oh bullshit. I saw you hugging her. Looks to me like nothing's changed. You were probably drawing wood with that hug." Pause. "We've been over this, boss. Getting close to her isn't in your or our best interests. There. Enough said."

Silence.

What could he say?

She was right. But he couldn't ignore his visceral-level desire for Kara. Worse yet was the suspicion that she might be similarly attracted to him. As improbable as that seemed.

He changed subjects by saying, "We need to find a way to drive a stake through that bastard's heart before Friday evening."

"Why Friday evening? Why not Friday morning? Now that I think about it, I don't remember hearing any specific deadline time, did you?"

Perfect. He'd distracted her from the Kara issue. But she did raise an interesting point. Why did he assume the deadline was 6:00 PM? That specific time was never designated, was it? Not that he could think of.

"Why indeed," Arnold finally muttered. "Hold on and I'll call Mr. Harris to clarify that."

Not that a few hours one way or the other would make much difference if Bosko wasn't stopped.

Or…if Bosko wasn't the hacker.

Fuck!

Arnold removed his glasses to palm-wipe his face.

Once he had the Cor-Pace CEO on the line, Arnold asked, "When Hacker demanded you shut down the trial, did he give you a specific time on Friday?"

After several seconds of hesitation, Harris said, "Now that you mention it, no, I don't think so. Or if he did, I don't remember. I just assumed he meant by end of business, which I took to be around five or five thirty. Why? Do you know something about this I don't?"

"No. It was just a point we wanted to clear up."

Arnold wished him good night and ended the call. Again, they rode in silence, closing in on Arnold's home.

Prisha was the first to speak: "Why don't we stop by Flavio's and pick up dinner so we can devote however long it takes to work up a plan?"

He glanced over at her. She appeared totally serious.

"That's a great idea, girl, but don't you think the timing sucks to be working together in person at my place? I mean, given Vihaan's allegations?"

"Oh, no doubt it's the absolute worst. But the fact is we're really up against it, and time *is* running out."

He studied her for a moment longer. Clearly she was pissed. He wasn't happy becoming a pawn to be sacrificed in the Patel family feud. But she seemed to know what she was doing. Say no and she'd be pissed at him too, and if it came to choosing sides, there was no question he'd be with her.

"Fine," Arnold said, pulling out his cell, "if you say it's okay, then I say let's do it. Working in person is always more productive than through a chat room. I assume I should get the usual?"

"Yeah, the sausage one," she said with a note of malice. "Vihaan's the one who insists on vegetarian. And don't forget to order extra olives and mushrooms."

Arnold already had Flavio's number on his screen.

"I'm all over it."

Prisha detoured their route to take them the few extra blocks to the pizzeria, where their luck held: no cars in the designated passenger loading zone. Arnold wanted to interpret this as a good omen for a productive evening, for they certainly needed one, but he didn't want to jinx it.

Standing at the counter, waiting for his order to be pulled from the oven to slide into the waiting box, he thought about Prisha and Vihaan.

How could she not realize that working at his place would inflame her husband?

She wasn't stupid. On the other hand, it was her call, so he'd just see how things played out.

Was she purposely looking to piss him off?

Sure seemed like it. A gnawing feeling kept telling him that the evening wouldn't end well for the couple.

Minutes later, Arnold flicked on his kitchen lights, then deposited the pizza box and kale Caeser salad container on the table, along with paper plates and the roll of white paper towels in its free-standing dispenser. As usual, Flavio had thrown in a handful of parmesan cheese and hot pepper packets.

For a moment, Arnold stood staring at the pizza on the table, thinking.

"I suspect I know your answer, but I'll ask anyway. Shall we have beer with dinner? I'll put on a fresh pot of coffee for afterwards, but the idea of drinking coffee with pizza seems, well, god-awful."

She pursed her lips a beat.

"You definitely have a point. But we'll be working." Then, seeming to reconsider her statement, she amended it with, "What the hell. A beer might just free up our creativity, which God knows needs some liberation. Go for it."

"Good. I have a perfect one too."

Arnold removed two cans of Bodhizafa from the fridge, passed one to her before dropping into his usual spot. He levered open the tab with a hiss of escaping carbonation.

Prisha sat down and eyed the pizza.

"Before we get started lemme call husband to tell him I'll be working from here this evening."

Was that a twinkle in her eye?

As she dialed, Arnold opened the pizza box and served them each a slice.

With the speakerphone on, Arnold could clearly hear the connection ring, then Vihaan answer with, "Where are you?"

Confrontational was the word that immediately flashed through Arnold's consciousness.

"I'm at Arnold's," she said with a sugary innocent tone. "Since we got absolutely zip from using Kara as a honeytrap we're going to brainstorm another way to get something the FBI can use for securing a search warrant. Which brings me to my next point: have you guys found anything of value in his machine?"

Vihaan didn't answer immediately, and when he did, he clearly wasn't happy.

"Why're you over there instead of back here?"

Prisha shot Arnold an I-told-you-so look before answering, "Because, husband, we have better synergy working in person than working via chat room."

"I bet you do!"

Prisha stood, eyes hard as moissanite.

"And what's is that supposed to mean?"

"Don't try to pretend you don't know what I'm saying. You know exactly what I'm talking about."

"No, husband, I don't. If you have something to say to me, go ahead and say it directly rather than through innuendo."

The anger in her voice reaching a crescendo.

"Okay, since you asked for it, I'll spell it out. As Arnold's exalted second-in-command, you're over at his place fooling around while the rest of us are busting our asses doing *your* work. There! It's been said."

"Fooling around? *Fooling around?*" she repeated, voice growing to just below a shout as her free hand balled into a tight fist. "What the fuck's that supposed to mean?"

"Oh, come on, Prisha. It's not as if there's any great mystery to this. The whole team knows what's going on between you two."

With eyes turning to thunderbolts now, Prisha stared at the phone in hand.

After a moment of silence, she began to moan, saying, "Oh yes! Right there! Ohhh…right there, that's it, oh, oh yes, yes…don't stop, I'm almost there…oh, yes yes." Then she screamed, "I'm coming!"

Silence.

"Did that get you off, husband?" Prisha asked in an ice-cube voice. "Did that satisfy your sicko cuckold fantasy?"

Vihaan didn't say a word.

After several seconds Prisha asked, "Answer me! Because I'm beginning to think that's exactly what you want to believe."

Arnold decided that it'd be prudent to simply stand clear of the blast zone, sip beer, and wait to see how this awkward, embarrassing situation played out. For a nanosecond, he felt a twinge of sorrow for the poor bastard for being humiliated like this. Then again, he realized that every intimate relationship is tempered and molded by the personalities involved. In truth, he knew nothing of the behind-closed-doors workings and needs of the Patel partnership. Although, from what he'd observed, Prisha was the stronger. And now that he thought about it, was that another contributing factor to Vihaan's jealousy?

"Vihaan," she said, finally breaking the ensuing silence, "if you seriously believe that something's *going on* over here, then grab your laptop and Uber over. But make up your mind right now because we all have a ton of work to still ahead of us." Pause. "Well?"

More silence.

Arnold suddenly realized that he hadn't breathed for almost a minute. As he inhaled, several pragmatic questions popped into focus.

Foremost being: *just how bad were things between the two?*

And just how destructive would this war of the Patels be on the team in the hours and days ahead?

Aw Jesus. Just one more thing to worry about.

Prisha: "Make up your damn mind, husband, because this call needs to end so I can get back to work."

"I'll be over."

"Fine. See you when you get here."

She disconnected, paused, gazed off into space, then shook her head.

"I'm at a loss on how to deal with him."

"Sorry. Can't help you with this one."

She shook her head again.

"Naw, I wasn't really asking for advice. I was just making an observation." She blew a breath. "Okay, where were we?"

CHAPTER 21

TWENTY MINUTES LATER the doorbell rang. When Arnold opened the front door, Vihaan was standing with a well-worn black North Face rucksack slung over his left shoulder in a pathetic pose that seemed intended to portray nonchalance. Instead, his obvious embarrassment made him look pathetic and humiliated.

Arnold struggled for casual words to ease Vihaan's obvious discomfort but for a strange reason the situation triggered memories of the emotional stew he'd been dropped into when he realized that Rachael had moved out while he was here working a case—making him feel awkward and at a complete loss for words.

He simply stepped back from the doorway and asked, "Had dinner yet?" in attempt to make some sort of amends.

For what exactly, he wasn't sure.

Just felt very sorry for the poor bastard.

"Had a PBJ about an hour ago," Vihaan replied, slipping off his rucksack and dropping it on the black leather living-room couch.

Which was about as noncommittal as you could get.

"Well, if you're hungry we have a couple pieces of pizza left, but they're sausage," he explained, knowing Vihaan was vegetarian.

Vihaan's face brightened.

"You don't have any left-over kale salad, do you?" Knowing that

that was Arnold's go-to order at Flavio's.

"Yep, but not much. You're welcome to it." Arnold pointed to the living-room couch and coffee table and said, "You can set up out here. We're in the kitchen," and headed back to where they were working.

Being an open floor plan, the living room flowed into the TV area and kitchen. The only separation being the freestanding stairways; one to the second floor with the one to the basement directly below it.

Vihaan tailgated Arnold into the kitchen.

Handing him the plastic container of salad and a white plastic fork, Arnold said, "Just brewed a fresh pot of coffee, if you're interested."

He'd disposed of the beer cans in the recycle bin shortly after Vihaan announced his imminent arrival. Figured it would just look more professional this way. He didn't want to fuel hubby's jealous suspicions more than they already were. As it was, the room temperature was teetering just above zero degrees. Or at least that's how it felt to Arnold, what with Prisha glaring at Vihaan, who was doing his best Mr. Nonchalant impersonation: back propped against the counter, forking Caeser salad into his mouth as if nothing at all had happened.

"So, Arnold said," tucking back into his usual chair, still at a loss on how best to roll with this increasingly awkward and land-mined situation. "What's the latest on Bosko's computer?"

Vihaan finished chewing, then shook his head.

"So far, we haven't been able to reestablish a link."

Silence.

Unable to stand the tension any longer, Arnold looked from Prisha to Vihaan, said, "Know what? Not only is this situation intensely uncomfortable but it's obviously destroying any productivity from three-fifths of the team." Then to Vihaan: "I suggest we all do our best to focus on the job at hand. Time's running out. Got it?"

Vihaan shuffled from one foot to the other for an awkward moment before stating, "I'll be in the other room."

He turned and left the kitchen.

Arnold called after him, "Fantastic idea. Thank you."

As Vihaan disappeared into the living room, Arnold said to Prisha, "It disturbs me that there's no evidence of the serial numbers or other incriminating evidence on his computer."

He didn't elaborate.

After a moment, she nodded.

"I agree. But I'm not surprised."

"Which leads us to believe—"

"That he's using another computer for the hack," Prisha finished for him. "Which is what we've assumed all along."

"So," said Arnold, "the only way we stand any chance of getting our hands on that evidence, is to come up with a way to locate that computer. At the moment, I'm drawing a complete blank."

After stifling a yawn, Prisha said, "I'm not doing much better."

From the front room, Vihaan called, "Hey, can you guys keep it down out there? I can't concentrate with that noise going on."

Turning his direction, Prisha yelled back, "That's what you get for insisting on rushing over here to chaperon me, husband dear. You knew damn well we were working. So, either live with it or ask Arnold if he has some cotton to stuff in your ears."

That does it!

Arnold was up from his chair, moving to a point halfway between the living room and kitchen, arms out from his sides like a football referee breaking up a pile.

"Hey, kids, enough of this shit. I think it's time for you two to go home and hash out whatever's going on in your marriage because right now you're destroying what remains of the team's productivity. And besides, I've got enough on my shoulders that I can't devote another freaking minute to dealing with your incessant bickering."

"But we need to figure a way to trap Bosko," Prisha insisted, also standing now.

"No shit. But your personal issues are destroying any ability to work this case. Not only that, but your escalating squabbling is dragging me down." Pause. "I'm stone serious, Prisha. You and Vihaan need to go home and find a way to move forward so that you can either remain viable members of this team or not. And if not, then one of

189

you—or maybe both of you—will have to go." This said with a finger-pointing at the door. "I'm dead serious about this too. Things just can't continue as they are."

Hands on her hips, Prisha set her stance, drilling Arnold with hard eyes.

"It's not my fault, dude."

Arnold pressed both palms against his temples and said, "Either you're not listening, or you simply don't get it, Prisha. Whose fault it is, is not my problem at the moment. Right now, my biggest concern is trying to keep Bosko from knocking off some poor unsuspecting mensch because you two can't get your shit together."

By now Vihaan was drifting back into the kitchen with a smug see-it's-your-fault expression. Arnold caught it in his peripheral vision, spun around and leveled a finger at him.

"Knock that shit off right now, goddamnit. That kind of crap isn't helping anyone. It's only making the problem worse." Then to Prisha, who now had her car keys out: "Take your little *War of The Roses* home so I can actually get some work done."

She began to open her mouth, but Arnold cut her off with, "No. I don't want to hear another word from either of you until you've worked things out. At the moment, that's what's best for the team. That's final."

She sent Arnold a questioning look.

His answer was to point a finger at her and say, "Not a freaking word."

She turned to glare at Vihaan a moment before storming out the door with him trailing her.

Soon as Arnold closed the front door, he beelined to the kitchen to jump on the main chat room to talk with Lopez and Ito before The Bickerers could make it home and log in. He told them about what had just gone down. Rather than assign blame to either Patel, he simply wanted his team to understand the issue in play so they could mentally prepare for two very likely possibilities. First, it was pretty much assured that they weren't going to neutralize Bosko before the Friday deadline, and he didn't want either of them to feel guilty or bad about it when it happened. This particular job had, after all, been a long shot from the moment Mr. Cain crammed it down their throats. Second: they needed to know about the impending nuclear melt-down in the Patel marriage. He wasn't sure what effect their resolution, however it turned out, would have on the team. But the present situation was clearly increasingly volatile with no clear path toward de-escalation. At least, that's the way it appeared to him.

Lopez said, "I'm really sorry about coming up empty on the computer thing, but all of us pretty much came into this believing he used a completely different phone and computer for the hack."

"Yeah, that's why I felt it was a complete waste of time trying to break into his network," Arnold said with a weighty mixture resignation and annoyance at Harris for insisting on it.

As they stared into their respective webcams, Arnold realized they were waiting for him to continue, so added, "Okay, back to the reason for this conversation: we need to make contingency plans should one or both of them decide to leave the team. Obviously, if both decide to take a powder, we'll be in deep shit. On the other hand, I don't think we can tolerate the present situation much longer. But one way or the other, I anticipate things are soon going to change drastically."

A long silence ensued.

Finally, Lopez offered, "If we have to lose one, I'd be a lot happier if it was Vihaan."

"Yeah? Why's that?" Ito asked with a note of interest, as if he'd been thinking the same thing.

"Because in a side-by-side comparison, she's way more productive and creative than him. Not only that, but that guy's a real downer most the time."

Arnold said, "Ah, man, I sure hope..." and realized he wasn't sure how to finish the sentence.

Ito replied, "This is the type of situation that makes me glad you're the boss. I'd hate to be caught in their crossfire."

Arnold began scratching the crown of his head, debating what to do next.

Any hope of solving this case had gone right down the sewer, so putting any more effort into it seemed to be a waste of time.

Right now, his highest priority was trying to salvage team morale. Especially now that the loss of at least one Patel looked like it would be inevitable. Meaning that for the moment and the near future, the remaining team members needed to be in the best shape possible.

After a deep sigh of resignation, he proposed, "At this point I don't see any reason to continue pushing ourselves on this. Go ahead and crash and we'll pick it up again in the morning. We could all use some serious sleep."

If the team was going to crash and burn on this job, they might as well be rested when the deadline blew past.

CHAPTER 22

Prisha

AFTER BUCKLING HER seatbelt, Prisha slammed the car door harder than necessary. She fired up the engine as Vihaan settled into the passenger seat. Once his door was shut, she pulled away from the curb without waiting for him to buckle up, eyes straight ahead, face a portrait of anger on the cusp of exploding.

They sat like rigid mannequins, eyes not wavering from the road directly ahead, Prisha's hands were balls of white knuckles squeezing the steering wheel at ten and two o'clock. The only sound inside the Toyota was the soft hum of road noise.

After several blocks, Vihaan said, "Are you going to just sit there throwing a silent hissy fit or do you want to discuss this like adults?"

"Discuss this like adults? *Now* you want to discuss this like an adult? What's to discuss, when you come off acting like a jealous paranoid teenager instead of the grown man I thought I married. You owe me a big-ass apology, husband."

He turned to her.

"*Apology*? Seriously?" He returned to stare straight out the windshield, hands clasped in his lap, radiating a self-righteousness prissiness. "After that crap you pulled on the phone with all those…those lewd sounds. You embarrassed me."

Prisha scoffed.

"Embarrassed you? What do you think you did when you accused me of sleeping with our boss? Huh? Just exactly how did you expect me to react to that shit?"

"Certainly not carrying on as if he was making you come."

Shaking her head, she said, "I can't be blamed for playing out your fantasies in lurid terms."

"No, they're not," he said like a petulant child.

She glanced at him in slack-jawed shock.

"Oh, give me a fucking break. Then what in hell were you saying when you tossed out that explicit accusation?"

He continued to stare straight ahead. Mr. Prim and Proper.

"I wasn't accusing you of anything."

She wanted to strangle that smug sanctimonious expression right off his face.

"Oh bullshit. Sure you were. Furthermore, I'm not going to tolerate that kind of shit."

"To quote Shakespeare, 'The lady doth protest too much, methinks'."

"See? There you go again with the accusation. Tell you what, shove your Shakespearean quote straight up your butt, dude."

She warned herself not to let him push her buttons any further. He was egging her on. For what reason she wasn't sure, but she wasn't going to play his stupid game.

Another block of nothing but road noise.

Vihaan broke the silence with, "I want you to stop working for him."

That did it! She exercised massive restraint to not slam on the brakes right there in the center of the busy street. Instead, she spotted a free COMMERCIAL PARKING ONLY section of curb and pulled in, shifted into Park, turned to lock eyes with him.

"Did I just hear you order me to stop working for *our* company?"

"News flash, Prisha. It's not our company. It's his company. We all know it. Reality check: the name is *Gold* and Associates. We're a profit-sharing partnership. Period."

"Well, here's a news flash for you, dipshit. I was his first hire and first full associate and I'm second-in-command, so if either of us needs to leave, it's *you*."

"Yeah, but—"

"But what?" she interrupted, eyes boring into him now, as pressure built between her ears and chest to fist-clenching rage. "Because you're my *husband*? That's what you were about to say, wasn't it."

Not a question.

"Well, forget that shit. It just ain't happening."

After three long silent seconds, Vihaan said, "Look what this job's doing to us?"

After a long groan of frustration, she propped herself between the door and seat and worked on corralling her anger by concentrating on her meditation breathing exercises: deep breath in through her nose and out through her mouth.

Vihaan waited silently.

Finally calm enough to speak in a civil tone, she said, "Okay, sure, at this moment this particular job is sleep-depriving and stressing us maximally. I get that. But that doesn't explain your insulting and baseless jealousy. I mean, think about it. Except for when we're involved in a hands-on case like this, Arnold's living in Honolulu. How can you possibly claim we're playing around?"

She encased the last words in finger quotes.

"I see the way you two are when you're together. I'm not blind."

"Yeah? And how's that?"

"You act like an old married couple the way you seem able to read each other's minds. You even finish each other's sentences sometimes."

"Oh, for christsakes." She paused for another deep breath. "Well, you're right about one thing; we *do* think alike. We're both insanely pragmatic, so we often jump to the same conclusion. That doesn't mean we're romantically involved."

Continuing to stare straight ahead, he crossed his arms. Now, Mr. Huffy.

"Your denial doesn't change a thing. I demand you quit working for him."

Prisha recoiled in shock. He actually looked serious. She couldn't believe it. But he was.

"Or what?" she finally asked, challenging him.

That apparently seemed to give him pause. She saw a flicker of self-doubt flash through his eyes.

She continued to wait for his answer.

The silence in the car interior grew more intense and ominous.

He licked his lips, hesitated, then said, "Or I'll move back to Long Island."

"To your parents' place?" she asked, with a note of incredulity accentuated with raised eyebrows. "Because I know you can't afford to rent a place on your own. Unless of course you've got another job all lined up."

"Regardless, that's what I'll do," he said with enough halting finality to convince her it was a bluff.

She now faced a pivotal decision: call his bluff and embarrass him further or…or what? There wasn't any other *or*. He dug the hole. Now let him deal with the consequences. Although she did feel a tinge of sorrow for him. But only a tinge.

With a laugh, she scooted back into the driving position, ready to restart the car.

"Well, good luck with that because I ain't quitting my job, and that's non-negotiable."

When he didn't reply, she pulled her cell from her jeans.

"Who you calling?"

"Arnold. I'm going to tell him we're taking the rest of the night off to get some sleep. I know I need it."

She gave him a quick side-eye. He remained perfectly still, hands clasped in his lap, staring out the front window. For a moment, another pang of compassion stabbed her heart. He'd leveled an ultimatum, been called on it, and was now facing the enormous decision of whether to follow through or eat crow. Then again, he'd brought this on himself.

When Arnold answered, she said, "Hey boss, it's me. Look, we're like maximally stressed and suffering from some serious sleep deprivation. So, when I get home, I'm shutting off all my devices and climbing into bed and sleeping until I wake up. Sorry. I know this puts additional stress on the team, but we simply can't win them all. At the moment, Vihaan and I are running on empty."

"Yeah, I totally get it." He gave a sarcastic laugh, said, "Well at least one of us has a plan. Go ahead and get some rest and I'll hear from you when I hear from you. Ciao."

She purposely made no mention of the pickle that Vihaan had put himself in. And besides, she wasn't sure what he would actually do once he was able to sleep on the ultimatum.

CHAPTER 23

Arnold

ARNOLD BEGAN DOING what he always did when confronted with a sticky situation like this one: he paced. He couldn't tolerate the idea of Bosko skating on this. There had to be a way to nail his ass.

He drank a cup of black coffee. Then paced some more.

Glanced at the clock. 1:30 AM

Tapped out, mind still blank, he decided to follow Prisha's lead by paying back some of his Z-debt. He trudged upstairs, fell atop the bed fully clothed, curled up on his side and dropped into a deep dreamless sleep.

At 5:15, he sat bolt upright.

Before his plan could vanish from consciousness—as dreams tend to do—he dictated the bare essentials into his iPhone. Then ran it through his reality center in the light of full consciousness. Amazingly, it still made sense.

Totally amped, he stripped naked, stepped under the refreshing (and much needed) shower, and while lathering up, rehashed the plan once more. Even on this third pass, it seemed reasonable and forehead-thumping obvious. Why didn't he think of it before now?

Run it by Prisha?

Naw. Not while she was doing exactly what he'd asked by sorting out her personal issues. He would wait for her call. In the meantime, however, he wanted an objective reality check from a trustworthy friend.

Kara?

Naw, scratch that.

Okay then, how about Fisher?

Jesus, another forehead-thumper. Of course. He was, after all, involved anyway.

Downstairs, he poured a cup of stale coffee, put it in the microwave to heat, emptied and washed out the carafe, then started brewing a fresh pot. He dialed the FBI agent.

Fisher said, "Sounds like a solid plan to me, Gold. However, I just hope you realize the entire success of this operation hinges on just one thing, and one thing only: that Bosko is our hacker. Have you seriously considered the risk you face if your suspicion turns out dead wrong?"

Arnold was pacing again, phone to ear.

"Of course I have. But what exactly is your point?"

"My point is that I'm not only putting my ass on the line if I back you on this, but I'm also putting the Bureau's in the jaws of the woodchipper. If you're wrong, we're all going to look like fools when we're put on the stand to testify under oath. Because if our search turns out to be nonproductive, we'll all be facing a very nasty civil suit. You *do* realize this, don't you?"

Jesus.

Arnold dried the palm of his free hand on his jeans.

"Of course I do."

"I certainly hope so, because you can bet your ass that's exactly what'll happen if you're wrong." Fisher paused briefly. "Having said that, let me ask you one more time. Do you want us to move ahead with your plan?"

Arnold inhaled deeply and weighed his answer.

What actual proof did he have to connect Bosko to the hack?

In truth, other than knowing that his father died during the initial phase of the clinical trials, he had no tangible evidence. Well, there was that malware attached to the returned Quality of Life questionnaire, but that didn't prove that he was responsible for Elijah Brown's near-fatal arrhythmia. And since he was being truthful about what he did know, the death of Bosko Sr. provided only a possible motive. He finger-combed his hair.

Several seconds ticked by.

"I'm waiting."

Arnold swallowed.

"Yeah, I'm sure."

"You're sure of what?" Fisher pushed.

Arnold closed his eyes, said a silent prayer.

"I'm sure that Bosko's our hacker."

"Okay." Pause. "I'm hoping to hell you're right. I'll set things up on my end. Do the same on yours. Let me know when it's time for us to move."

CHAPTER 24

Prisha

PRISHA AWOKE TO the realization she was, as usual, curled up on her side of the queen-size bed, facing the edge. Without bothering to roll over to look, she knew Vihaan wasn't beside her. Still, she groped blindly to where he'd normally be. Nope, not there. This saddened her.

Eyes still shut, she let out a heavy sigh but remained still.

How did they end up at such a contentious point in their marriage? Where did it start? What was driving it now?

Her fault or his? Or was this a logical evolution, a hold-harmless byproduct of their individual development? After all, they'd married as twenty-year-old NYU students, neither of them having been out on their own, both still at home with their parents in Queens. Vihaan was always the conservative one whereas Prisha was the risk-taker. She was the one to walk over sidewalk grates instead of around them as he did.

Reflecting back on their eight years of marriage, it was these subtle trifling differences that had grown more pronounced as their relationship aged. To the point of even seeping into their love life, which, now that she thought about it objectively, seemed to contribute to their growing divide.

How had that happened?

A wise older woman once told her that, "If a couple isn't fucking, they're fighting."

Was that part of it?

Vihaan's conservatism had certainly been a drag these past couple years in the bedroom. He was so damn unimaginative, so locked into the boring and unsatisfying missionary position that she preferred to get herself off. Although clueless, he wasn't stupid. Surely he must realize that this aspect of their marriage was also failing. If so, did this affect his conventionally constrained image of himself as a man? Was this one more driver for his baseless allegations about her relationship with Arnold? Well, it certainly seemed worthwhile to consider. But, at that moment, her bladder took priority.

Before entering the bathroom, she glanced into the living room. As suspected, Vihaan was asleep on the couch.

Why there instead of in their bed?

Because he didn't want to wake her? Or was this his way of making a statement? She suspected the latter.

Under the refreshing stream of shower water, she reflected on how they'd ended up together. It wasn't a particularly interesting or unique story. And, in fact, not that atypical for a lot of immigrants. The chain of events could be traced back to when her Hindu grandparents emigrated from India to Queens to establish a better life. There, they bought a struggling Indian restaurant and successfully turned it around. Enough so that they were able to put their only child, son Aadel, through an electrical engineering degree program at NYU. While there, Aadel met Ziana, a second-year medical student at the same university. Two years later they married.

As an only child, Prisha idolized her father. Which was probably the reason she chose to study electrical engineering. But unlike her father, who ended up designing printed circuits, she became intrigued with coding. Perhaps it was her canny pragmatism that made her excellent at writing concise, efficient software.

She met Vihaan at NYU during a chance encounter at the Bobst

Library Computer Center. He was having an issue with his laptop that she took care of. To repay her, he treated her to a latté at a nearby Starbucks. They began to date. Nothing serious at first, but her parents approved of him instantly and began to encourage the relationship. It probably didn't hurt that he too was a career-driven electrical engineer of Indian descent and Hindu religion. She married him for all the wrong reasons. And way too young. Retrospect: always so unblemished. In self-defense though, he was different then; less cautious and certainly less paranoid.

Before graduation they were both courted by Google and slated to be hired upon graduation. Which was a great deal, because they would both be working in the New York office. Six months later Vihaan was offered a promotion contingent on a transfer to Seattle. He eagerly accepted the new position as a way of getting ahead in the massive company. Unfortunately, Google wasn't able to offer Prisha a job at that office and she and Vihaan didn't want to attempt a coast-to-coast relationship, so she began scratching around the Seattle job market for employment.

She ended up being hired by a local start-up biotech company, Camano Biopharma. It turned out to be ultra-cool working for a grass-roots start-up. There was a thrill at being an integral part of a company of twenty employees instead of just a badge number plodding along in a cubicle for a behemoth boasting of a gazillion offices worldwide. That was, until Camano Bio got torpedoed by a hacker who released a bogus report from the company's media-relations department. The false report sent their IPO straight down the toilet, along with the company's viability. Hence, Prisha rejoined the continuously waxing and waning ranks of unemployed Seattle techies.

Then the car accident drastically monkey-wrenched their lives.

Vihaan was cruising through a busy intersection when a drunk driver blew the stoplight, T-boning the Toyota on the driver side, sending Vihaan straight to the OR followed by intensive care. His physical injuries eventually healed, but his emotional injuries now seemed to be superglued to his personality.

Especially after the number the ambulance-chaser personal injury lawyer did on him. Yes, it was an excellent settlement, but Prisha couldn't help but blame that shark for stoking the flames of Vihaan's emotional sequelae. She believed that his pre-injury positive personality was gone forever. He was no longer the man she'd vowed to love and cherish through sickness and health. Lately, those vows were becoming progressively more difficult to honor.

Just one more thing to be sad over.

Weeks before the accident, he'd begun dropping hints about how much he wanted a son.

In retrospect, having children was a critical topic they should've discussed seriously prior to considering marriage vows. But they never did. He wanted children. She didn't. And this became a huge issue that was also not discussed. Not surprisingly, it became just one more major fault line that was now breaking apart the marriage. Now he was tossing alleged infidelity into the mix. Was he trying to drive her away? Certainly felt like it.

From the other side of the shower curtain, she heard the toilet flush. There was a time in their marriage when he would've joined her under the spray.

Was that type of love between them irrevocably gone?

Seemed to be. This realization weighed down her sadness. But life is always in constant flux, for life is by nature, changing. Constantly. Forcing you to either adapt and move forward or become mired in the quicksand of the past.

Turning the water off, she stood very still, listening to a few residual drops splash against the white shower tiles. If he made good on his ultimatum and returned to Queens, what would she do?

Not go with him. That much she did know.

But she *would* miss him. For she still felt an obligation to him.

Obligation?

He thought about that word for a moment. Obligation: a one-word summation of the glue still binding their tenuous relationship together. She cared for him as a person, but that caring was not the same love she'd originally felt. Or thought she'd felt.

Somewhere along their path, this job began to shoulder aside that love. The job per se didn't directly damage the relationship, but did the job's importance to her grow *because* of a failing marriage? Now *that* was a question worthy of future reflection.

In the immediate aftermath of the Camano Biopharma disaster, when the start-up was being liquidated to pay investors pennies on their dollars, the CFO held a fire sale for what few tangible assets were left smoldering in the ashes. Although she wasn't sure why—other than it seemed like a smart investment—Prisha bought their computers for a pittance. Then stored them in their rented storage locker. Somehow—she was a little vague at remembering the exact details—Arnold Gold had learned of their existence and offered to buy them from her.

At the time, Arnold was putting the final touches on his newly rebuilt Green Lake home and was in the market for computers. Again, thinking back on the sale, she still had no idea what he'd wanted them for. Because Vihaan's personal-injury settlement was still in negotiations and neither of them were bringing in any money other than unemployment insurance, they needed the cash. She sold them to him. Turned out, Arnold also needed a sidekick to help with a case he was working on for his lawyer. *Voilà.* She went from receiving unemployment insurance to receiving a full-time paycheck. Vihaan, on the other hand, never did regain employment until Arnold ended up hiring him as an employee instead of an associate.

She and Arnold ended up nailing the hacker who'd torpedoed Camano's stock price.

Poetic justice or karmic retribution?

She didn't care. It just felt super-cool to catch that sonofabitch.

From the start, she and Arnold resonated. When the case wrapped up, Arnold offered her a partnership position with Gold and Associates. She accepted. And, by so doing, legitimized the company's heretofore grandiose name. She loved the job. It became integral to her identity. Perhaps that was part of the problem.

Bottom line: if Vihaan ran back home to Queens, she'd stay. And be comfortable with the decision. It'd be an adjustment for sure, but one she could easily make.

After toweling off, she brushed her teeth, then combed her luxurious black hair, all of which made her feel halfway human again. But she still wanted to catch up on a ton of sleep once this job wrapped up.

Now wanting a cup of strong black coffee, she caught a glimpse of Vihaan in the living room on her way to the kitchen. He was sitting on the couch, laptop on the coffee table. She didn't say a word to him, nor did he turn from the screen. Although she knew he knew she'd just passed by.

Hands on her hips, she frowned at the carafe on the burner of the coffee maker. A thin slick of overcooked coffee coated the bottom. Enough to justify not starting a new pot? Not in her opinion. But for sure he'd argue that.

Passive-aggressive turkey. Typical.

She knew better but couldn't help herself.

"Nice, Vihaan. Very thoughtful."

"What?" he asked in his most innocent tone.

Asshole.

"Don't give me that shit. You know exactly what I'm talking about," she said, tossing the burnt-smelling dregs down the drain, then carefully adding just enough tap water to cool the Pyrex without cracking it before thoroughly rinsing it out to start a new cycle.

As the coffee brewed, she leaned against the doorway to the living room to watch him assiduously avoid acknowledging her.

Say something? Yeah? Like what?

"Talk to me, husband."

Eyes still fixed on the laptop, he answered, "About what?"

Rolling her eyes, she said, "Take a wild-ass guess. About *us*. About your plans."

"What about us?"

"Oh, for christsakes, Vihaan, you know exactly what I'm talking about. This hole we've dug ourselves into. But if you need me to spell it out, how about we start with your ultimatum."

"What ultimatum?"

She sighed and dropped into the leather armchair facing the couch so he couldn't avoid her without turning away. Evenly as possible, she said, "That if I don't quit working for the team, you're gonna move back to Queens. I need to know if you're serious."

After several seconds, he glanced up from the laptop and met her stare a second before glancing away. A moment later he returned to her.

"Of course I'm serious," he said, then dropped his gaze again. Tick, tick, tick. "Why do you ask?"

"Because you should know my answer. I wouldn't dream of quitting, especially in response to some chauvinistically driven jealousy-inspired ultimatum." She took a deep breath. "Either reconsider your demand or let me know when you're moving out so I can start making appropriate plans."

The moment the words flew from her mouth, she knew she'd boxed him into a corner by not giving him a face-saving exit.

"Or," she quickly added, hoping to salvage a bad situation, "we can discuss this rationally like the adults I assume we are."

Whew! At least she'd made an honest attempt to toss him a life preserver. Now, if he chose to ignore it...

"What's to discuss, Prisha?" he said, sitting back on the couch now, arms crossed, eyes hard as blood diamonds. "I think you're involved with Arnold on more than just a business relationship."

Head cocked to the side, she studied his eyes, picked up a flicker of doubt. But his baseless accusation stung too much to consider tossing him a parachute. He was on his own now. Shaking her head, she stood.

"Then do what you need to do, husband. But I'm not moving."

She returned to the kitchen to pour a cup of fresh coffee.

"I just made fresh coffee if you're interested," she called out before sitting down to enjoy her first aromatic sip, always the best of the day, especially when this fresh. In a few minutes she'd enjoy a slice of peanut butter toast. But for now, she was content to savor the freshly brewed coffee and ruminate over why their marriage went sideways.

Or were they a prime example of two people who never should've married?
She suspected the latter.

CHAPTER 25

Arnold

ONCE ARNOLD HAD Mr. Harris and Mr. Cain together on a phone call, he said, "Mr. Harris, I want to meet with both of you in-person in one of your conference rooms at four o'clock this afternoon. It's urgent. I also need Michelle Mays and Doctor Bradford there too. Can you please arrange that?"

Already Thursday approached noon and Arnold felt time was like mercury slipping through his fingers no matter how hard he tried to contain it.

"What's this about?" Harris asked. "Did you discover who our perpetrator is?"

"I think so."

"You *think* so," Harris said with a note of condemnation. "That doesn't sound very convincing."

"I want you to hear me out before making a judgment on this. Will you set up the meeting or not? I need your answer now."

He regretted being short with the totally stressed CEO, but no one was feeling good about the situation.

Well, except maybe the hacker.

"John, I advise you to hear him out," Cain added.

Call finished, Arnold reconvened the team—including Prisha and Vihaan—in the chat room to explain his plan and ask for suggestions on how to improve it. When no one offered a suggestion, their total silence sent waves of anxiety reverberating through his gut. Did they see a miscalculation that he didn't and were trying to not ruffle the boss's feathers? If so, that wasn't the critical thinking he wanted from them. Especially now. He desperately needed to know if he was missing an obvious flaw. Everyone's ass was on the line if his plan failed.

"Come on, guys, think. There must be *some*thing. No plan is flawless."

Vihaan finally spoke up with, "You're taking a huge risk on this, but I suspect you know that."

That's not very helpful, Vihaan.

But what did he expect from Mr. Negativity?

"Of course I do," Arnold admitted, "but I don't see any way around it at the moment. That's why I want all of us to critically look at it."

Prisha said, with a hopeful note to her voice.

"Well, you're absolutely right about one thing: time *is* running out on this. So, I have to agree we have no option but to try it. In other words, it's worth the risk." Brief pause. "Want me to be there with you?"

"Naw, it's going to be pretty straightforward from this point on. I just need to get things set up and ready to go. Thanks for offering."

Because of her calming influence in stressful situations like this, he would've loved to have her help him with this. But considering their current marital issues, it would be best to go it alone. He didn't want to feel any responsibility for a flare-up. For the moment, he'd leave them alone to work out their issues.

If that was even possible.

CHAPTER 26

ARNOLD SAT AT the kitchen table, listening to the sawing noise coming from the base of the limb on which he perched.

Try to ignore it?

Nope. Impossible. What he needed was a distraction: something to do other than stare at that freaking laptop and listen to the loud mental stopwatch tick relentlessly toward the deadline.

He gazed out the French doors at the backyard and sky. Looked pretty nice out there, the temperature close to seventy degrees with a high cloud cover. Just about perfect for Chance to have the back porch and yard to himself until he came home from the meeting.

A moment later, he was throwing together the pooch's afternoon meal of kibble and diced chicken, then set the platform feeder with Chance's water and food bowls on the back porch, along with the bed that usually sat just inside the French doors.

He took the Belgian Malinois out to the deck, squatted on his haunches and gave him a healthy dose of choobers, saying, "Daddy goes. Chance stays. Daddy will be back." The three phrases he always said to Chance before leaving.

Chance wagged his tail and planted a doggie kiss on his cheek.

Arnold hoofed it over to the nearby southbound RapidRide bus stop on Aurora Avenue with five minutes to spare before the E-Line's scheduled arrival. Luckily, when he boarded there was an empty seat. He settled in for the ride downtown. Glancing around at the other riders, a feeling of wonder flooded him: they were all part of the drama that would play out in the next forty-eight hours, albeit in very different dissociated roles.

Stop it.

Leaving early to finish this one task before the meeting was supposed to be a distraction, but it wasn't turning out that way because something always seemed to trigger his apprehension again. He closed his eyes. But it didn't make a difference: the worry-worm slithered right back into consciousness.

Jesus!

He pulled out his phone and opened the *New York Times* app to read an article but realized that although his eyes were moving from word to word, his mind wasn't taking in their meaning. He stuffed the phone back into his pocket.

Gazing back out the window, he watched the three red-and-white six-hundred-foot communication towers atop Queen Anne Hill grow larger until they passed to his right.

At the 7th and Thomas bus stop, he dismounted and moved away from another departing passenger, stood still, then slowly took a quick 360-degree look around. It'd been over two years since he last visited this neighborhood, so it was startling to see just how much it changed. Same story for other parts of the city. There were, of course, the familiar anchor landmarks such as the Space Needle, just a few blocks to the west. But new buildings and different traffic patterns gave the area a disorienting unfamiliar vibe. As if he knew this city yet didn't. Which, for his "hometown," felt a bit bewildering. But most cities were always in a state of flux.

Was he losing this one?

He didn't want that.

Seattle was the place he'd identified as home for most of his twenty-nine years: where he'd gone to school, learned to ride a bike, become fascinated with computers, and started Gold and Associates.

Was it still home? Or had his allegiance moved to Honolulu when he'd been forced to flee?

Huh.

He remained standing there, soaking in the surrounding streets and buildings... weighing his emotions. Suddenly a revelation hit, one eerily similar to the renewed familiarity of retrieving a favorite summer coat from the back of the closet now that the long, dark, cold days of winter were beginning to yield to warmer, lighter mornings and the Super Bowl becomes a dimming memory; that "ah, yes, this is how I remember it" emotion of reuniting with an old friend. Yes, he still loved this quirky and at times frustrating city. Without question.

The traffic light changed. Crossing the intersection, walking east toward Westlake now, his thoughts drifted to Noriko and their relationship. She was his first foray into his socially stunted dating scene since Rachael moonwalked out his front door months ago. Mercifully, Noriko had put up with his lack of social *savoir faire*. Which helped him rehab his confidence. For this he felt thankful, but was this love?

Well, see, that's the problem: where was the threshold between affection and love?

Or does one even exist? Especially for a novice like himself. Or was the dividing line similar to distinguishing art from porn? You knew it when you encountered it. Yes, she was physically attractive. Plus, they shared several passions such as their dedication to their respective businesses. But his feelings for her weren't even close to the-moon-and-back kind of love that made you want to commit to something more than...what? Something more than a steady date with fringe benefits? Well, that was certainly a nice situation to be in, but how long was that sustainable? And wasn't that a tad bit self-serving? Yeah, probably. But what if she was getting exactly quid pro quo from the relationship? In that case no harm, no foul, right?

Yeah, probably.

At Westlake he began to trudge north again, taking his time, the fatigue of the past several days of totally blown-up biorhythms and topsy-turvy routines making him feel like a drained battery. Not only that, but the exhaustion made him worry about the acuity of his decision-making abilities. Especially for this winner-take-all gambit.

Minutes later he was staring through a sheet of plate glass at a white Tesla Model 3. He'd memorized the various options available from paint color to all-wheel drive, to battery range, and wheel type, etc. But he'd never set his butt in the driver's seat of one. Do it now?

Well hell, why not?

Taking a serious look at the actual car was, after all, his only reason for making this out-of-the-way side-trip before the meeting, right?

Partly right. It was also supposed to be a distraction.

"Would you like to take one for a test drive?" the salesperson asked, tearing Arnold's attention from the ultra-simplified dashboard and black leather upholstery. He was standing at the open driver-side door, left hand on the top of the door, right hand on the car roof, checking out the interior, his mind grappling with the many sobering ramifications of actually buying the vehicle rather than simply romancing the idea. For if he bought one, it would mean he was also making the decision to move back here full-time. Which he hadn't. Was he ready to commit to a choice of that magnitude, especially under the present circumstances of stress and sleep deprivation? Probably not the wisest move he could make today.

Arnold turned toward the voice and was staring into the large brown eyes of an attractive woman with black hair in what he vaguely identified as a pageboy cut. He opened his mouth to answer.

CHAPTER 27

"MAYBE ANOTHER TIME," he told the pretty salesperson. Then added, "I'm already running late for an appointment. But thank you."

Back on the sidewalk, he moved south along Westlake. A quick check of his watch suggested that at this rate he should arrive right on time for the meeting. He smiled. The distraction had been just what he needed to cleanse his mind and polish his pitch. The go-for-broke gamble of the job. And any future relationship he may or may not have with Special Agent Fisher and the Bureau.

As Arnold entered the building for the Cor-Pace office, he remembered that floor access required a key card.

Mr. Harris answered his phone with, "Are you downstairs in the lobby?"

"Yes sir, I am."

"Excellent. I'll be right there."

A few minutes later one of the four elevator doors parted, and a very haggard-appearing John Harris called, "This one," while holding open the door with one hand and waving him in with the other.

Facing the elevator doors for what seemed like an interminable ride up only four floors, Arnold remained silent but was acutely aware of the anxious anticipation radiating from the CEO. Everyone was aware of the seconds ticking down to the deadline, increasing the pressure to do something to stop Hacker before another innocent patient ended up in much worse condition than Elijah Brown, who owed his life to his son's excellent CPR skills.

The cage finally decelerated to a smooth stop. The doors parted. As they approached the locked door to Cor-Pace Arnold fought a surprisingly strong urge to turn a one-eighty and leave the building. But knew he couldn't. Not now. If it hadn't been for his indebted relationship with Mr. Cain, they never would've touched this quagmire. But he and Prisha had allowed this catastrophe to be crammed down their throats, so now they had to see it through. Good or bad. And the odds were looking like it'd be bad.

After fobbing open the front door, Harris led Arnold through the small reception area into the cubicle farm ringed by small offices.

Harris said, "We're in the conference room across from my office," and extended a hand in that direction. "The rest of the group is already assembled and waiting."

Entering the conference room, Arnold scanned the other attendees seated at the table, all appearing as haggard and stressed as their boss. The only person Arnold hadn't met previously was Kevin Bradford, the medical director.

Once Arnold was seated at the rectangular table, Harris said, "It's your meeting, Mr. Gold. We're all anxious to hear what you have to say."

Arnold felt anticipatory eyes lock onto him. He glanced around for a pitcher of water to wet his mouth and throat, but saw none, so dry-swallowed.

He started by saying to Mr. Harris, "It's my understanding that you're expecting a call from the hacker sometime this afternoon or evening, right?"

Harris nodded, "That's my expectation, yes."

"And the point of that call is for you to update him on your progress in closing enrollment in the Everest trial, right?"

A nod. "Correct again."

"Okay then, here's where things stand with us. We *suspect* we know the identity of your hacker but haven't been able to dig up enough proof to convince the FBI to do a search and seizure of his digital devices."

With an incriminating edge to his voice, the CEO replied, "But I thought you were intending to break into his computer to search for that."

As if this would miraculously resolve this awful mess.

"That's right. And we did. But the machine he uses for routine work doesn't contain one bit of incriminating evidence. No serial numbers, no evidence of your device firmware. Nothing."

Harris's hopeful expression quickly segued into barefaced irritation.

"In that case, why are we having this emergency meeting? I thought the purpose of the meeting was to give us some good news. So far, I haven't heard any."

Christ!

Arnold raised a just-a-minute finger.

"Hang on and give me a chance to finish my proposal. Okay?"

Harris shut his mouth, crossed his arms, and went stone-faced. Still clearly pissed.

Arnold inhaled a deep breath to calm his own frayed nerves before continuing.

"From what we've learned about our suspect, his personality is characterized by three traits. He's extremely bright." Arnold skipped a beat. "Second—which has been a real problem for us—he's crazy paranoid. Finally, the dude's highly skilled at computer security."

He paused to let these points sink in.

"Like any good hacker, he's bound to have several computers. Given this presumption in addition to knowing that he's security-conscious, it's a safe bet that the one we're looking for isn't even turned on unless he's using it against you. And if he's as smart as we believe, this means it won't be found if his place is searched, leaving us with no case." Arnold paused briefly. "You with me on this?"

"Yes, Mr. Gold, I'm following you," Harris answered, obviously irritated at the banality of the question.

"Sorry if that came across as condescending, but to stand any chance at all of catching this slippery bastard, I really need you to work with me. Like, one hundred percent."

Harris made a rotatory get-on-with-it hand motion.

"We also suspect he uses more than one phone and that he calls you on a burner instead of his personal cell."

Which was a bit of a stretch. They weren't convinced about anything. Yet.

"The bottom line is we need to create a situation in which the FBI has a good chance at seizing both the computer *and* phone before he can destroy or dump them. If we can do that, we'll not only prove he's our guy, but we'll also eliminate any future threat to your company and the clinical trial."

Harris appeared to weigh Arnold's words before responding.

"I'm still listening."

"Good," Arnold said, relieved to finally have Harris calm enough to hear him out.

"So, when he calls, I want you to emphasize that you're working hard to convince the board to terminate the trial, but you have two holdouts who believe that the threat is nothing but an elaborate prank."

Harris scrunched up his face.

"What earthly reason would they have to think that?"

Luckily he'd anticipated this question and had a plausible answer ready.

"Tell him that they believe that your alleged hacker is nothing more than an opportunist who is trying to leverage Mr. Brown's severe heart condition into a scam."

Harris reared back in mock shock.

"That sounds even more ridiculous. It doesn't make any sense at all. How would an *opportunist* even know about Mr. Brown's arrhythmia or the Everest trial?"

Arnold raised both hands and said, "Hold on. Please just let me finish and I think you'll understand." He paused to get back on track. "I'm not saying the story needs to make any sense to you or me, but to a paranoid person under a ton of pressure, it doesn't have to make sense. All you want is to *sound* like you're stalling. Which you are."

Obviously frustrated, Harris shook his head.

"Now I'm completely lost. Why won't that just give him more motivation to move ahead?"

Arnold glanced at the floor and fought to keep from expressing his own frustration. After a calming moment, he looked back at Harris.

"Please just bear with me and let me run through the entire plan. Okay?"

After a lip-flapping exhale, Harris said with obvious reluctance, "Go on."

Jesus, you pompous bastard, I would if you'd give me a chance.

"I want you to give him that story and then plead for more time to wind down the study."

"How much time?"

Waving away the question, Arnold throttled his frustration over the constant interruptions.

"I don't know," he said. "Just ask for more. A day. Two. The actual amount of time is irrelevant because I suspect that just asking will make him dig in his heels and stick to the original demand."

Harris looked away, shaking his head some more in silent irritation.

Arnold plowed ahead with, "If things go as I suspect they will, he'll refuse to budge. At that point you ask him to clarify what time the absolute deadline is and what'll happen if it isn't met."

"What the hell will that accomplish?"

"Two things. The FBI will be listening to the conversation. If you can get him to answer those questions, it'll establish that an actual threat is being made and the phone he's calling with. Since Mr. Fisher's entry team has our suspect under continuous surveillance, we'll know his exact location. If we're correct and he *is* the hacker, he'll be calling on the burner and will have his computer with him. The moment the Friday call comes in, the FBI will execute a search and seizure. This is the only way we're likely to get our hands on both devices. You with me now?"

Harris seemed to think hard about what Arnold just proposed.

"It seems to me that you're putting all your eggs in one basket. What happens if you're wrong about this Bosko person?"

In that case, I'm toast.

Arnold said, "In that case, the plan's a total bust."

What else was there to say?

"And some innocent person may die as a result of this…this gamble."

"You don't think I know that?"

Harris stared back at him, poker-faced.

"Then at least we tried, Mr. Harris. This is the best I can do. Take it or leave it."

Again, the CEO appeared to consider Arnold's proposition. Briefly.

Harris: "Let's assume your prime suspect actually is the hacker. Doesn't Agent Fisher need to serve papers before they can execute a search and seizure? My point is, what's to prevent Bosko from triggering a fatal arrhythmia or disabling a device in a patient before the Feds can neutralize him?"

"Ah, that's the next part of the plan. Is there a way to monitor all your implanted devices for an externally issued command?"

Harris turned to his medical director.

"Kevin? Could you answer that one for me?"

Frowning, the medical director asked Arnold, "Just to be clear, you're asking if we can monitor *all* our devices presently in service? In real time?"

"Yeah, exactly," Arnold answered.

Dr. Bradford's brow furrowed. "No one's ever questioned that before. I don't know if we have the bandwidth." Then, to Harris: "Kent's the one to answer that."

Harris said, "Then get him in here."

Once Kent Sheffield, their lead engineer, joined the group, the CEO posed the question.

Sheffield appeared to roll it around for a couple seconds before answering.

"Interesting question. I can't give you a definitive answer because we've never field-tested that specific scenario before. But since we can monitor any device singularly, it's theoretically possible to monitor them all." Then, glancing at Mays, the sysadmin, he asked, "Do you see any problem from the bandwidth standpoint?"

After a moment, she slowly shook her head and said, "Not offhand, but I'll continue to work on it."

"Is that a yes?" Arnold pushed.

Eyes closed, pinching the bridge of her nose, Mays said, "Oh man…" and then to Dr. Bradford, "How many devices do we presently have in use?"

The medical director fingered his lower lip as he quickly calculated the answer.

"Between all trials…we have, I believe, a total of thirty?" Pause. "Yes, I believe thirty is the correct number…plus or minus one or two."

"We'd be monitoring thirty devices in real time?" Harris pressed for clarification.

Dr. Bradford said, "In theory, yes, but if you think about it, we don't have to actively monitor them simultaneously. We just need to be on standby to react to an *error* message from one device. That simplifies the task enormously."

"Are you telling us it can be done?" Harris pressed with a clear tinge of hope.

Nodding slowly, Dr. Bradford said with more confidence now, "I don't see why not."

All eyes were now fixed on the CEO.

Harris glanced at the ceiling, then back to the medical director.

"Let's assume a worst-case scenario: he triggers a fatal arrhythmia in one of those thirty patients while simultaneously disabling the device's AI self-diagnosis and treatment capability. Do you believe we have the ability to gain control again and remotely reverse the arrhythmia in time?"

Dr. Bradford acknowledged the question with a soft grunt before responding.

"The answer's not as simple and straightforward as it sounds. There are numerous factors out of our control." Obviously not finished, he paused for a deep breath. "From my perspective, Mr. Gold's plan gives us the obvious advantage of focusing the majority of the risk into a relatively short time period. This means that we'll be prepared to react as quickly as possible to whatever problem might arise. In my opinion this makes the overall risk more acceptable than if we were to do nothing at all. Put another way, I believe it's worth the gamble."

Clasping and unclasping his hands, Harris stood at the window, staring across the street toward the five-story brick apartment building. After several seconds, he returned his intense gray eyes to Arnold.

"How certain are you that the person you've identified is, in fact, our hacker? I want a percentage estimate."

Arnold began nervously finger-combing his hair, searching for an acceptable answer. Fact: he lacked concrete evidence to implicate Bosko. Certainly, not beyond any doubt. Yet his gut insisted that the circumstantial evidence pointed directly at him and no one else. Bosko clearly knew about the trial and had sufficient motive.

Well, the motive was pure conjecture. But still...

What if he was dead wrong about Bosko?

If so, this desperate Hail Mary plan would be a total waste of time and would risk a patient's life.

Could he live with a failure of that magnitude?

"Well?" Harris asked.

"A percentage estimate?" Arnold asked, stalling for another second or two. Too high of a number might give Harris a false sense of security. Too low a number might cause Harris to back away from the plan.

Okay, so what was the sweet-spot figure that would green-light the gambit?

Everyone was looking at him now, waiting.

He wanted to say eighty percent. But based on what exactly? No way was he *that* convinced.

But seventy percent? That instinctively sounded too low...the odds got sort of dicey at seventy percent.

On the other hand, if they went for it and Bosko turned out to not be the hacker, he would know that at least they'd given it their best shot.

Assuming, of course, Mr. Harris bought into his plan.

Jesus.

"Arnold?" Noah Cain asked impatiently.

"Eighty percent," Arnold blurted, knowing that that figure was way too high.

All eyes turned to John Harris now who was be gazing vaguely at some distant object, drumming his fingers on the tabletop, repeating, "Eighty percent..."

CHAPTER 28

WITH A NOD, Harris finally said, "Okay, let's go with your plan. What do you want us to do now?"

After quickly checking his watch, Arnold said, "It's four thirty-three. He could call at any moment now, so I guess all we can do is wait." Then, to Mays: "How buttoned down do you think your network is now?"

"No way to know for sure, but I'm feeling pretty confident about things. We changed all the encryption codes, so that helps. But the thing is, he's already got everything he needs to keep the threat up. The only way I see to fully protect our patients is to make a major protocol change and we simply don't have time for that."

"Why not?" Arnold asked.

Harris answered for her.

"Once a protocol's been approved by the various institutional oversight committees and the FDA, any revision is time-consuming. Too time-consuming for what we're up against. Believe me."

Pushing up from his chair, Noah Cain asked Arnold, "Will you be needing me for anything additional at this point? If not, I still have a great deal of neglected work awaiting my attention at the office. As always, I'm available on my mobile."

"Naw. At the moment it's just a waiting game," Arnold assured him with false confidence with his gut churning like crazy.

Mays was already drifting toward the door; Kent Sheffield had faded from the conference room moments before.

Arnold told Mr. Harris, "I'll be in the hall making a call. If you need me, just signal."

After moving into the hallway, Arnold phoned Agent Fisher to tell him that Cor-Pace had just bought into the plan.

"Outstanding, because our team is on Bosko now. Where are you?"

"At Cor-Pace. I plan to stay put until our hacker calls."

"Good. Just remember, if and when he calls, note the exact time the call came in and the number he's calling from. Although we have the number he used previously, it'd be good to know whether he's using the same phone."

Arnold underlined his mental note to do as instructed. At this point he couldn't afford a mistake.

"Got it. Anything else?"

After a brief hesitation.

"Not at the moment. Just hope your big hunch is on target, Gold."

"You and me both!"

Next, Arnold linked Ito and Lopez into a conference call to let them know the plan was now in play and in the meantime to resume catching up on their routine work orders if possible. The team was now officially seriously backlogged. In addition to being seriously whipped.

"What about Vihaan and Prisha?" Lopez asked.

"No idea," Arnold replied. "All I know is they have a few marital issues to work out before they stand any chance of working effectively as team members again, so I think it's best to just let them get back to us when the time's right."

Calls finished, Arnold glanced around. To his left was a floor-to-ceiling glass wall of a conference room. Inside a group of six Cor-Pace employees huddled around a conference table in what looked to be a spirited discussion, the whiteboard on the far wall covered with words and equations.

Engineers, perhaps?

Arnold meandered back to John Harris's office, where he and Dr. Bradford were now seated at the small conference table, rehashing the plan. As he entered, Harris trailed off to glance up at him with questioning eyes.

"I'm done with my calls," Arnold said. "Mind if I wait with you so I can be here when he calls?"

Harris motioned for him to take one of two chairs facing his desk.

"Help yourself, but we're rehashing the plan, so if our conversation becomes an issue, help yourself to an empty cubicle to camp out in and I'll come find you when I need to. I think we both know what you want us to do when he calls."

Just then Harris's cell began blasting the marimba tune. He picked up the phone, looked at the screen, and announced, "Bingo. An unidentified number with a 206-area code. This could be him."

"Read me the number," Arnold asked.

After doing that, Harris turned on a small Sony recorder on his desk, set his phone next to it and answered the call on speakerphone.

"John Harris," he said.

Arnold texted Mr. Fisher the time and phone number.

An electronically distorted voice said, "It's me and I want to know the status of the Everest trial."

Harris gave Arnold a confirmatory nod, at which point Arnold stepped back into the hall to call Agent Fisher, Fisher picking up after only one ring.

"He's talking to Harris now," Arnold whispered, then cut the call so he could return to the office.

"...I understand that," Harris was explaining, "but I still have two hardliners—heavyweight investors—who refuse to believe that someone would willfully commit murder in order to shut down the study. At the moment, they're refusing to close the study, and—"

"Close it anyway," Hacker demanded before Harris could finish his thought.

"If I could, I would, but you have to understand that I need a hundred percent approval before I can execute an action of that nature.

225

You'll be happy to know that one of the holdouts is close to agreeing that the threat is valid, but I need more time to bring the other around. All I'm asking for is a slight deadline extension…Monday afternoon. Or even Sunday, if Monday isn't acceptable."

He looked at Arnold with eyes seeking approval.

Approval of what, exactly? His story?

Or that Arnold would have an additional trick up his sleeve if Hacker miraculously agreed to the extension? Assuming, of course, that Bosko really was their hacker. No, they needed to resolve this situation now. Arnold shook his head, mouthed *Stick with tomorrow*.

"You expect me to believe a bullshit story like the one you're trying to hand me?" Hacker asked. "You're just trying to stall. In fact, I suspect you've got someone trying to track this call. No! No extensions. You either terminate the study by tomorrow or I'll terminate every last fucking patient until the Feds close the study for you."

"Believe me, I'm trying," Harris pleaded with Academy Award sincerity. "But as I said, winding down a clinical trial isn't as easy as throwing a light switch."

"I'm done with this bullshit. Tomorrow. That's final."

"Wait, wait," Harris said, waving his free hand. "How do I contact you if I find a way to stop recruitment?"

He glanced at Arnold to confirm that he was catching all this.

"You can't. You'll just have to wait for me to call. And be prepared to answer with a simple yes or no. No more bullshit and absolutely no extensions. Period."

"Wait, wait. What time will you call?"

"Why do you want to know? You trying to set up some kind of trap?"

"No. I just want to know exactly how much time I have left to work on this. All I'm asking is to be given until the close of business. Which would be six o'clock."

"We'll see."

The line went dead.

Harris studied his phone a beat before placing it gently on the desk as if it might explode on impact.

"Now what?" he asked Arnold.

Good question.

With a resigned sigh, Arnold simply shook his head.

"There's nothing we can do now but sit on our hands and wait." He glanced at his watch. For all the good that would do. "We should have a resolution to this...ah, situation in about twenty-four hours."

Harris nodded solemnly before turning to gaze out the window. The portrait of a troubled man.

Arnold stood and announced, "See you tomorrow."

"What time," Harris asked without turning from the window.

Without giving it a thought, Arnold replied, "Four o'clock."

Yeah, that sounded about right.

CHAPTER 29

CHANCE'S NOSE WAS flat against a pane in the French door, tail swishing back and forth as Arnold slouched into the kitchen. The moment Arnold headed toward the doors, the pooch started his happy dance. His plan was to kill two birds by walking Chance over to PCC market. This way Chance could get in a walk while Arnold foraged through the deli section for dinner. For some reason, the thought of leftover pizza just didn't cut it tonight. In fact, at the moment, not much in the way of food appealed to him, what with his stomach churning from the anxiety tornado twisting through it.

At the market, he ordered three thighs and three drumsticks of fried chicken, and a tub of potato salad. He'd already picked up a bottle of Sauvignon Blanc from the wine section, figuring that one with fewer tannins than his usual cabernet would sit better with him at the moment.

On the stroll back home, he decided to cut through Green Lake Park so Chance could enjoy some quality nose time at the shrubs to help him assuage his guilt for spending less time with the pooch over the past few days.

As Chance sniffed, Arnold tried to distract himself from worrying about whether Bosko was their hacker, but the harder he tried, the more the question consumed his consciousness.

Fucking Bosko.

"Arnold!"

He froze at the instantly recognizable voice, turned, and there she was.

He'd known that this moment would come. One of these days. The law of probability was stacked in its favor, and he'd been dreading it.

In a partial crouch, Rachael stretched her arms out as Chance tugged on the leash. Arnold let go of the leash and Chance sprinted to her dragging it, poo bags and all. She started in by giving him a rousing dose of choobers as he gave her a couple of doggie kisses.

Arnold ambled over to them and muttered, "Oh, hi..." while reaching down for the lead.

With Chance officially back on-leash, Rachael stood and gave him a visual once-over before saying, "You're looking good, Arnie. You back for a job?"

Arnie? She'd only used his nickname when they first began dating. Why did she use it now? *Did it matter?* No.

Shrugging the rucksack into a more comfortable position, he said, "Yeah," and then, after an awkward pause, added, "Where are you working these days?"

She was an RN, so he simply assumed that she'd easily picked up a job within days of moving back here. Maybe even had one lined up before she left Honolulu.

"Oh, just over at Swedish." Ms. Nonchalant.

"Ahh," he responded automatically. Then started frantically scratching for something cool to say but coming up empty.

Suddenly *Three Hearts in a Tangle* rescued him from his mental Sahara. Awkwardly, he began to dig the phone from his front pocket. Saw Prisha's name on the screen.

Thank you, Jesus.

He glanced at Rachael. "Sorry, have to take this."

"No problem, I've got to be going anyway. Well, good to see you."

With a nod, he said, "Bye," and tapped ACCEPT. Raising the phone to his ear, he watched her continue in the direction she was heading when their paths intersected. Well, that's over. The encounter was bound to happen, and it wasn't so bad. Right?

Right.

"Yo girl, what up?"

"Can I drop by? I need to talk to a friend and you're the designated listener."

Uh-oh. Didn't sound good.

"You bet," he replied, unable to remember hearing her sound so stressed.

He flashed on the food in his rucksack.

Enough for two?

Probably.

For sure the bottle of wine should cover the conversation.

"Had dinner yet? I just picked up some fried chicken and potato salad at PCC and am on my way home. I should be back before you arrive if you plan on leaving right away."

Which, from her tone of voice, seemed to be a reasonable assumption.

"Actually, I'm in my car only a few blocks from your place."

Arnold tugged the leash to get Chance moving again.

"Roger that. Got Chance with me, so you'll undoubtedly get there before I do."

She did.

When the house finally came into sight, he saw Prisha's white Camry parked at the curb with her leaning against the front fender, arms folded across her chest. Chance began to pull the leash, eager to run to her, so Arnold let go of it. Chance took off, bounding up the hill dragging the leash again. And just as Rachael had done, Prisha dropped into a crouch to greet him with a dose of choobers. Chance seemed to have quite a following.

Soon they were in the kitchen, a French door partially open so Chance could wander in and out to the back porch ad lib. As Arnold unpacked his groceries it dawned on him that she hadn't answered his question about dinner so asked again.

"Had dinner? There's enough for two."

Originally, he'd planned on buying enough for dinner tonight and lunch tomorrow but had no problem hitting PCC again if necessary.

She appeared to debate her answer.

"Yeah, sounds good, actually."

"I brought a bottle of Sauvignon Blanc but also have a few cans of Bodhizafa in the fridge. You choose."

"Fried chicken and potato salad? That screams beer to me."

Arnold pulled two orange cans from the Gaggenau, handed her one, and set the other at his place at the table. From a drawer he came away with a couple of paper plates and forks which he also set on the table, then transferred the paper-towel dispenser from the counter to the table too. Almost reverently, he pulled dinner from his rucksack to set out, then dumped the empty pack at the end of the counter to schlep to the front closet later.

He tucked into the table, saying, "Okay, what's going on?"

Prisha said, "Take a guess," as she levered the tab on her beer then took a pull.

"Given the circumstances and your tone of voice, I'd have to say it's Vihaan."

A nod. "And you'd be correct."

At this point Arnold chose to just sit back and let her run with it.

Prisha spent a moment studying the condensation coating her beer can.

Then, "I'm not sure what to do, boss. I was hoping some sleep would help smooth things over, but it didn't. In fact, the situation just got worse. He gave me an ultimatum." She paused briefly. "Either I quit working for you, or he'll move back to Queens. Can you believe that?"

Arnold instantly realized how much he relied on her leadership, technical knowledge, and the simple comfort of knowing that when it really came down to it, they had each other's backs. Although he could probably keep the team together without her, it'd take a massive realignment, and maintaining customer satisfaction with lagging turnaround time would be iffy. He swallowed hard, knowing that nothing he could say or do could influence the outcome of this potential catastrophe. It would just have to play out. He wasn't on the Patel Marriage Committee. This drama was solely between husband and wife. Instead of saying anything, he snapped open his IPA and took a sip.

She studied him, as if waiting for him to say something.

Well, okay.

"Jesus, Prisha, I don't know what to tell you other than Gold and Associates can't function without you."

Her eyes brightened.

"Do you really mean that? I mean, like, seriously?"

"What? You think I'm blowing smoke up your ass? Of course I mean it."

She paused for another sip of beer, her eyes taking on a far-off distant look. She remained like this for a moment before returning to him.

"What'll we do if he actually makes good on the ultimatum?"

A rush of relief hit. Her question implied that she wasn't about to leave the team. He pursed his lips, taking a moment to carefully craft his answer.

"Good question. How serious is he?"

Head cocked, giving him a quizzical look, she said, "He wouldn't joke about something this serious."

He nodded. "No, I guess not."

Her expression transformed from questioning to sadness.

"That's the problem. He's dug himself a hole when he handed me that...that..."

She gave a sad headshake while looking at her hands.

"He should know damn well I hate ultimatums, almost more than I hate the idea that I should follow my husband's dictums simply because he's my husband. What makes it worse is I suspect he realizes he's way out of line." Pause. "Essentially, I told him that if he really meant what he said, then to let me know so I can start looking for a roommate to share expenses with. Now the hard-core reality is probably beginning to sink in and he either has to back down—which I know will be, like, overwhelmingly difficult for him to do—or move back in with his parents. Which would be, like, admitting…I dunno…that I just cut off his balls. Basically, if you think about it, he's royally screwed no matter what he does. But, know what? He's got only himself to blame."

After a moment of silence, she added, "If I weren't so pissed about the ultimatum, I'd feel sorry for him, but man, that's just too much to ask in my present state of mind."

Arnold began to massage the back of his neck, looking up at the ceiling, parsing the situation. If Vihaan made good on his threat and resigned from the team, hey, no problem. But if he backed down and stayed…that'd be a gonzo issue because no way could he trust him again. Not after the allegations he'd made about his job assignments and wife's faithfulness. Meaning. Arnold would be faced with the tricky task of coming up with a way to get rid of him without actually firing him. Ideally, make it Vihaan's choice.

Prisha seemed to be waiting for him to answer.

"I agree," he finally said, "he's boxed himself into a corner. What're the odds he'll make good on his ultimatum?"

Shaking her head again, she said, "Honestly? I dunno."

"But if forced to guess."

She took a deep breath. "Knowing how proud he is, he'll have a very difficult time backing away now." Then, putting a shrug in her voice: "But with what's a stake, I could be wrong."

"I don't want to sound like I'm ignoring the emotional blowback it's going to have on you, but I need to consider the repercussions it'll have on the team. If he leaves, it's going to strain an already maxed workload."

He paused, choosing his next words with extreme care.

"I know Lopez, Ito, and I are ready to pick up the slack." Then, he gave her an apologetic eye: "The other day when all this turmoil started bubbling up, I presented this very possibility to them. I apologize if this seems like a breach of confidence, but I thought as team members they should be made aware that an issue was brewing with him."

"Yeah, I totally get it," she said with a touch of resignation. "And, in a way, I'm relieved that you were worried this might happen." Giving a woeful headshake, she bemoaned, "Nothing's been the same since that goddamned car accident! That asshole."

Arnold assumed she was referring to the other driver, so took another sip of beer and waited for her to continue.

What more could he say?

She was saddled with a supremely shitty situation. He wished for some words of comfort to say but he knew that at this point nothing would help her face this existential struggle. Most likely, just being here to listen and support her was enough. He hoped so.

She opened the container of chicken, pulled out a drumstick, and set it on her plate. A moment later, she looked up at him.

"What? What's going on?"

Damn, she could read him too well.

Of all the times to broach the subject, this was absolutely the worst. But there was no way to avoid it now. His turn to give a resigned sigh.

"For the past year, I've been tossing around the idea of designating this as my primary residence. If I end up doing that, it's just going to throw gasoline on the fire."

"Look, Arnold, that's your own personal decision. It's not relevant to the soap opera playing out between Husband and me."

With that, she bit into the drumstick and nodded as if to say *So there!*

Arnold's custom ringtone started in. He glanced at the screen. His eyes widened.

"Jesus, it's Vihaan!"

She dropped the drumstick on the plate and locked eyes with him.

"Are you shitting me?"

Turning the phone so she could see, he said, "See." Then, "I'm putting it on speakerphone."

"Yo Vihaan, what up?"

He set the phone on the table next to him.

"Is Prisha there?"

Eyebrows raised questioningly Arnold looked at her. She shook her head.

"Uh no. Why?"

"You seem unsure," Vihaan said with a distinct *edge*.

"Yeah, guess that's how it might've sounded. So, let me rephrase that. Yes, I'm sure she's not here," he said adamantly. And immediately felt scuzzy about lying. But to correct the statement now would come across as even more suspicious. "The thing I'm not sure about is, why even suggest I'm lying? Is it just one more accusation to add to all the others? I don't get it. Where's this shit coming from?"

"That's because I have eyes, bro. I can see what's going on."

"I don't know what to tell you, *bro*, other than you're wrong and you caught me in the middle of dinner, and I don't like the tone of this conversation, so I'm going to say good night and hope the two of you work out your issues."

He tapped the red disconnect circle.

"I better get going," Prisha said pushing back her chair.

Arnold waved for her to sit down.

"Go ahead, finish your chicken. I doubt he's going to Uber straight over."

"But if he does?"

Arnold considered that.

"At least take the drumstick and a couple paper towels with you."

He walked her to the door, where she gave him a quick hug.

"Thanks."

"For what?" He opened the door for her.

"What you said about Gold and Associates. Means a lot to me."

"Good luck."

CHAPTER 30

BACK AT THE table, Arnold pulled a thigh from the container, bit off a hunk, and began to ruminate about Gold and Associates. Sure sounded like Vihaan had mired himself in an extremely sticky situation, seeing as how Prisha wasn't about to quit the team to satisfy him. Meaning he was either going to lose face by backing down or leaving. If he left town, they could deal with it. For a while.

But permanently?

That'd be iffy given their current flow of work orders. And there was no indication that those were about to lighten up. Which meant either scouting around for a replacement or cutting a few clients. Neither option carried much appeal, but the issue needed to be resolved as soon as the dust settled. Clearly Gold and Associates was facing a major pain in the ass.

So, the mondo question, the one he needed to resolve now was what to do if Vihaan stayed?

No doubt his passive-aggressive personality would drive a huge wedge through the morale of the team. Especially now that he was becoming more paranoid. If Arnold had had any doubts about this before now, they were gone. How to get rid of him?

Hmmm....

After washing down the chicken with a pull of IPA, he decided that a distraction might juice his creativity. What?

Call Noriko?

Naw...that'd be a mistake. Didn't want to poke that sleeping bear until he knew how things shook out with Bosko.

Okay, so how about rehashing his encounter with Rachael?

Given that they lived within a couple blocks of each other, he anticipated this would happen eventually. He'd been dreading it. Now he was shocked at what a non-event it actually was. It was like...totally non-impactful. Other than he came across as a total nerd.

Yeah? So what?

That's who he was.

He was grateful and relieved that that hurdle was officially in the rear-view mirror. It was time to move on.

The rich dark meat spurred his appetite, so he dished a scoop of potato salad onto the plate to nibble on but lost his appetite after finishing only the thigh and the scoop of salad. He stored the remainder of the food in the fridge.

Instead of sitting back down, he paced, focusing on tomorrow, about the fate of his hand-picked team, about which residence to declare as his primary, about how to inspire Vihaan to move on.

At the French doors, he paused to look at Chance stretched out on the deck, snout between paws, snoozing. The clear advantage of this house was that deck and backyard. The clear advantage of the Honolulu home was close proximity to parks where Chance could wander off-leash. Here, there was no place close by where that was allowed. But Seattle had distinct seasons...

Back at the table, he woke up the laptop and once again browsed the Tesla website. He pulled up the page for designing a Model 3 and began to sort through the options one more time. If he were to purchase a car for here, it'd be best—considering the hills around town—to opt for the all-wheel drive. Thirty-five K for that one. Okay, that was doable. He added a center console and then went to paint color. Stealth gray? Meh...White? Naw, too plain. Passed on the black because it showed dirt too easily. Blue or red? Hmmm, how about Quicksilver? He decided to look at a few on the road when he was out to see how the colors struck him before making any decision. The interior? White leather would be nice. Especially during the drab dark winter days. But with Chance riding shotgun, he worried about dirt showing. Self-driving capability? Naw, didn't trust it, especially considering that most of his driving was here in the city.

So, there it was: a Model 3 for thirty-five K. But once you added a nice paint color, tax and delivery, etc., the bottom line would be closer to $51K. But then there was a rebate...

Hmmm.... The Model 3 wasn't as nice as Mr. Davidson's Model S, but it would serve him well in the city.

His finger hovered over the purchase link.

CHAPTER 31

Friday 5:30 AM

ARNOLD AWOKE HAVING benefited from a well-deserved restorative sleep: several blessed hours of reprieve from the unrelenting anxiety ratcheting up as the deadline grew closer.

Was Bosko really the hacker? Or were all his eggs in the wrong basket?

Approximately twelve hours from now, he'd know the answer. He also knew that as the pivotal hour approached, time would slow. Einstein was correct about that: time was a relative phenomenon rather than a constant.

A quick shower and shave with his Norelco, then down the stairs he went to let Chance into the back yard. As Chance ran outside, he flipped the red power switch to his coffee maker. One of his last chores each night, before climbing the stairs to the bedroom, was to routinely prepare the Braun to brew a fresh pot in the morning.

Then he was standing at the kitchen table, looking at the awakened laptop screen, the Tesla order still there, waiting for him to either press the purchase button or abandon the website.

A mondo decision. For it wasn't really whether or not to buy the car. What made it massive was deciding whether to claim this house as his primary residence. Living here full-time was the only valid reason to buy the Model 3. Especially considering the Mini parked in the Honolulu carport.

Well, how about shipping the Mini here, and then renting a car when in Honolulu on vacation?

He palm-wiped the lower half of his face. Jesus, talk about first-world problems... Then there was the question of Noriko.

Did she factor into the equation?

Or, stated a bit differently: if so, how?

While ruminating about these issues, he put together a breakfast of Muesli with blueberries from the freezer (thawed in the microwave) and a handful of hazelnuts, topped off with milk. He ate his breakfast standing, butt up against the stainless-steel counter, wrestling with the questions, struggling for clarity.

There was also the massive Vihaan issue hovering overhead.

He inverted the washed cereal bowl on the drain board, poured a cup of black Kona coffee, and tucked back into the table to stare at the silver Tesla. On another page of his browser, he opened his brokerage account to check the status of his stocks. SAM—his AI neural network—had executed several profitable trades since he last checked. Making that fifty-K seem like less of a stretch. And if he turned around and sold the Mini to, say, Carvana, he could pile those proceeds into the payment.

Well, it was something to think about, right?

He was into the *New York Times,* scanning the morning headlines, when his phone rang.

"I was just thinking about you, Noriko," Arnold said, leaning back in the chair, phone to ear.

"I realize I'm not supposed to call but wanted to check up on how the case is going. Today *is* a deadline for something, isn't it?"

"Ah, yes," he admitted with a bit of hesitation, preferring not to box himself in.

Box myself in? Into what?

He paused to listen to himself.

"Does that mean you'll be flying back soon, like maybe

tomorrow?" she asked.

It wasn't her choice of words, exactly. Nor was it her tone either. Rather, her question left a residue of disconcerting uneasiness in its wake. He opted to answer with silence, fearing that anything he might say could be held against him.

After a moment, she pressed the issue.

"Well?"

Forcing him to answer with intentional vagueness.

"I'm not sure. I still have a few things I need to wrap up."

The moment those words came out, a memory bobbed to the surface: an eerily similar interaction perhaps a year ago with Rachael. At that time—like now—he was putting the final touches on a job here in town but needed a few extra days to tie up several loose ends before jetting back to the island. In retrospect, Rachael's icy response to his extension had perhaps been a harbinger of something amiss between them. Back then, the significance blew right past him.

This time, however…

"Like?" she persisted.

He debated where to take his answer.

Nothing wrong with being honest, was there?

True. But there could always be repercussions if the answer didn't suit the recipient.

After a deep breath, he replied, "Well one thing is that I'm debating if I should buy a Tesla for here."

Absolutely true. Just not the entire story.

He could practically hear her brain cranking that one through the grinder.

"What does that mean, buying a Tesla for there?"

Was that a note of accusation in her voice?

Or was he just being overly sensitive as a sequela of Rachael?

Did it matter?

"It means exactly what I said. I'm considering buying a car for when I'm here."

She gave a sigh of frustration before saying, "Don't use that I-don't-know-what-you're-talking-about tone on me, Arnold Gold.

You know exactly what I'm getting at. Does that mean you plan to spend more time there?"

Well, how did he expect her to respond?

Shrieks of glee while doing cartwheels down the hall? He felt sorry for doling out such obtuse answers but couldn't be more concrete until he felt comfortable with a decision. Whatever it might be.

"Look, I'm being truthful with you when I say I don't know. All I can tell you is I'm *thinking* about it."

"Just answer my question, Arnold. What does that mean for us?"

And there it was: The Question. The one he wasn't prepared to answer.

Because?

Well, see, the problem was, their relationship was only one of many issues factoring into his decision. He liked her a lot. She was smart, attractive, and totally easy to hang with. But more than that? Was she enough to keep him living full-time in Honolulu? Especially considering that all their big jobs were here?

He didn't have an immediate straightforward answer to that either. Then it struck him: perhaps not being able to answer was in itself an answer. On the other hand, she was pushing for a binary yes-or-no answer. He crafted his response to be as neutral, objective, and truthful as it could be under the circumstances.

"This decision isn't about us or our relationship, Noriko. It's about the best way to run my business. My job's here in Seattle. This is where I work the hands-on difficult jobs."

"It's Rachael, isn't it," she said, making a statement.

"What? No." Pause. "Look, Noriko, I don't know how to say this any clearer. Rachael and I are done with. She doesn't factor into this decision at all. Haven't we been over this?" *Too many times.* "Look, this is really a bad time to be having this discussion. Can we please put it off for another time, say, tomorrow?"

"Just tell me if it's Rachael."

"I just did. *No*, it's not Rachael. You're wrong about that. Seriously. Now, goodbye."

CHAPTER 32

NOAH CAIN MET Arnold and Prisha in the lobby of the office building to escort them up to Cor-Pace.

As the elevator began ascending, Cain said, "The team has everything set up and ready to go in the conference room where hopefully we can react quickly and appropriately."

Yeah, hopefully.

Hopefully was the operative word for what was about to take place.

Arnold noticed the lawyer wringing his hands and resisted the urge to do likewise. What he really wanted was a Tums.

Jesus.

Arnold said, "I checked with Agent Fisher on the drive over here. His entry team's in place and ready to move the moment I give the word."

As the three of them entered the conference room, Sheffield and Mays were on opposite sides of the rectangular table, each with two monitors in front of them and a desktop computer by their feet where heavy-duty extension cords snaked across the floor to separate wall outlets. Dr. Bradford paced behind Sheffield, awkwardly biting at the corner of his right thumbnail.

Nervousness or a hangnail?

Jesus, all it would take was a building-wide power outage or someone tripping on one of those cords, pulling it from the outlet, and this whole caper would go right down the sewer.

Arnold flashed on the CrowdStrike outage not so long ago that brought down entire computer systems in airports, hospitals, and office buildings worldwide.

Stop it. You're just getting worked up for no reason.

Which he knew was a lie. There *was* a very good reason for his skyrocketing anxiety: this entire plan could be victimized by a simple unanticipated adverse event. A glitch. No way could they protect against every possibility.

Was there an obvious monkey wrench lurking about that he wasn't taking into account?

Prisha elbowed him, and whispered, "Keep it together, boss. We're on stage."

A moment later Arnold's iPhone dinged. Mr. Fisher, texting to say that he was in the lobby.

"Mr. Cain," Arnold said, "Agent Fisher's downstairs. May I use your keycard to bring him up?"

Cain, looking as nervous as Arnold felt, nodded.

"I'll go with you."

On the elevator ride back to the lobby, Cain shook his head.

"I don't know, Arnold, although this plan seems straightforward, Mr. Murphy was right: there are a great many things that can go wrong. There always are. And they're usually the most straightforward glitches, the ones we should anticipate. For the sake of everyone involved, I hope this gambit works as planned." And then, almost under his breath: "This has been one of the most stressful cases of my career. I suspect yours too."

With a woeful headshake, Arnold said, "Got that right."

Everyone knew each other from working on the Cain, Tidwell, Stowell law firm ransomware case, so Fisher, Cain, and Arnold simply exchanged solemn hellos while shaking hands, then rode the elevator back up to Cor-Pace in anxious silence, Arnold wanting to break the tension but suffering from an acute loss of words.

In the conference room now, Noah Cain introduced Fisher to those he had yet to meet.

Introductions over, Fisher told the group, "I want to make sure we're all operating with the same set of instructions. The Bureau needs you"—he nodded to John Harris—"to answer the hacker's call on speakerphone so we can record it as evidence of the threat. This obviously means that the rest of you need to remain absolutely silent with your phones set to not ring. I'll be on a direct comm link with the leader of our entrance team. Once the verbal threat is made, I'll give the order to execute the search and seizure."

It was 5:45 PM. The room was mortuary silent except for the soft tap-tap-tap of Sheffield's right heel as he sat bouncing it nervously off the floor with his leg pumping up and down like a piston.

Fisher pulled his push-to-talk phone from his pocket, raised it to his mouth, asked, "Our target still home?"

"Roger that," came the reply.

Fisher nodded and sidled up to Arnold, and whispered, "Just hope you're right about this, Gold."

Arnold swallowed and glanced at Prisha.

Deadpan as usual in such situations, she turned to stare out the window toward the apartment building across the street. Ms. Nerves-of-Steel.

Arnold tried to focus on the apartment building too, but the steady tattoo of Sheffield's bouncing heel kept fueling the iron fist squeezing his gut.

What if I'm wrong?

This phrase kept reverberating through his mind like an earworm song he didn't want to hear but couldn't stop hearing.

Checked his watch again. Five fifty-five. Five more minutes until straight-up six o'clock.

Assuming Hacker would call at six.

Interestingly, he'd just thought of him as Hacker instead of Bosko.

Arnold started to pace, finger-combing his hair, feeling the weight of everyone's eyes on him, probably wrestling with the same questions.

Well, the situation was officially out of his control. Either he was right or dead wrong, but there was nothing he could do at this point to nudge the odds one way or the other.

All he could do was wait helplessly for this ordeal to play out.

Jesus.

Arnold glanced up, caught Mr. Fisher studying him with disconcertingly incriminating eyes.

Suddenly the marimba ringtone started.

All eyes locked on Harris.

Harris looked at Kent Sheffield and asked, "Ready?"

The phone rang again.

His lead engineer answered, "As ready as I'll ever be. Just don't forget, we haven't field-tested this part before."

He shrugged as if to say, *No guarantees.*

"Got it." Then to Mays: "And you?"

Another ring.

Alright already. Just answer the freaking call.

Mays's eyes locked in on her monitor.

"Roger that."

Fisher asked, "Is that the number?"

Harris checked the phone again, nodded affirmation.

"It is."

He accepted the call with "Harris here."

A brief pause, followed by, "Are you on speakerphone?"

There was a tinge of annoyance in his voice despite the electronic distortion.

Arnold realized his head was cocked to the right, listening with his preferred ear, searching for any hint that the distorted phone voice was the same as he'd heard in the Dick's parking lot.

Listening for what exactly?

That whiny nasal quality, he realized.

Harris: "Yes, I am. Why?"

Hacker: "I don't like that."

Arnold glanced at Fisher with questioning eyes.

Why didn't he give the order to seize the phone?

Fisher ignored him.

Frantically, Arnold focused on Harris who seemed to be scrambling for an answer.

Harris licked his lips.

"Remember me telling you about a board member who isn't convinced you're serious? Well, he's here with me, and I hope that by hearing you he'll be convinced we need to comply with your order."

"You've stalled long enough. I want an answer. Yes or no?"

"Please, just give us until Monday. I give you my word I'll terminate enrollment then. But with the caveat that we'll need to continue supporting our patients with the Cor-Rate II."

Arnold realized he was fidgeting like crazy. The longer the entry team held off, the higher the risk that an innocent patient might end up dead because of some psycho's personal vendetta.

"You've drawn this out too long. You're not going to keep playing me like this."

"Wait! Hear me—"

The line went dead.

All eyes were riveted on Agent Fisher now as he remained standing behind Sheffield, arms crossed, eyes locked onto Arnold.

Fisher said, "Don't give me that look, Gold. He didn't explicitly threaten anything."

"Yes, but I know that's him."

Fisher's eyes were boring into him now.

"How can you be so sure? The voice was distorted."

Fuck!

All attention was now focused on him, weighing him down. He kept replaying the Dick's Drive-In encounter, comparing the whiny nasal voice of that person with the electronically altered tones from the phone's tiny low-fidelity speaker. There was no way he could be certain they were the same person. He had nothing but circumstantial evidence...

A hand touched his shoulder. Prisha whispered to him, "You're okay."

"Gold, I need an answer."

The weight of the decision increased.

He nodded at Fisher, said, "I'm pretty sure it's him."

"*Pretty* sure?" Fisher said. "Cut the wishy-washy. I need a definitive answer. Was that him? Yes or no?"

Arnold swallowed hard.

"Yes, it's him."

"You're absolutely sure."

A hybrid statement if there ever was one: equal parts question and declaration.

Clenching his fists, eyes shut, Arnold nodded, said, "Yes, absolutely."

And immediately realized that he'd just taken one of the riskiest gambles of his gambling career.

Putting the push-to-talk phone to his mouth, Fisher said, "Go!"

"We just got an override command!" Sheffield yelled to the group, never taking his eyes from the monitor in front of him.

"Show me the tracing," Dr. Bradford, the cardiologist demanded, shouldering his way into a straight-on view of the screen.

Sheffield's fingers blurred above the keyboard, typing in commands. A moment later a scrambled EKG tracing—at least it looked scrambled to Arnold—flashed across the screen.

Dr. Bradford bent down to study the tracing.

"Damnit! He's in VF and the logic circuit can't resolve it."

Arnold knew enough to realize that Bradford had just referred to ventricular fibrillation, a lethal arrhythmia, but he didn't know anything more than that.

Dr. Bradford said, "Get me into the override mode."

Sheffield started typing again, muttering, "Here's the part we haven't field-tested yet."

"Yeah, yeah, yeah, I'm well aware of that," Dr. Bradford said, clearly intent on gaining remote access to the device before the arrhythmia could be fatal. "But this is our only possible chance to stop it."

"Here you go," Sheffield said, vacating the seat.

Dr. Bradford slipped into the chair, typed a command, hit enter, then studied the screen.

"Goddamnit!"

He typed another command, watched, shook his head.

"Come on, come on…"

He typed again, punched enter, and stared intently at the screen. Silence.

The cardiologist continued to study the screen.

Outside, a car honked. Another car answered with a more prolonged honk.

"Well?" Harris asked his chief medical officer.

CHAPTER 33

DR. BRADFORD CONTINUED staring at the screen, then finally exclaimed, "Okay!" and slumped back in the chair with drops of perspiration glistening on his forehead.

"What?" Harris asked.

"He's in normal sinus rhythm again."

A collective sigh of relief rippled through the group. Although Arnold didn't know what had just taken place, he figured it had to be good news.

Just to be certain, he asked Mr. Cain, "That's good news, right?"

"Yes, indeed."

Out of the corner of his eye, he saw Fisher drift over to the window to look down at the street, face etched with concern.

Sidling up to him, Arnold asked, "Any word from the entry team?"

He sensed Prisha standing on his left side, listening too.

"Not yet. I expect to hear any moment now."

Soon the rest of the group was clotted around them, all anxiously awaiting a call from the entry team, the group tasked with the tricky high-risk job of securing the targeted digital devices before they could have case-making sensitive content destroyed. Especially when dealing with a paranoiac as crafty as Bosko. All it would take for Bosko to wipe the hard disk and destroy critical evidence would be a simple command or, say, a programmed self-destruct dead-man's switch triggered by something as innocent as merely closing a laptop.

"Is John on the team?" Arnold asked, referring to John Chang, a Special Agent working as a CART agent. The Computer Analysis Response Team: specialized forensic FBI agents trained and equipped to copy the contents of digital devices (computers, phones, cameras, etc.) in a way that allows them to be inspected for evidence while still preserving the critical chain of evidence required to successfully prosecute a case. Arnold had worked with John on the infamous Noah Cain ransomware case, so knew the agent's competence firsthand. Knowing that John was on the team comforted Arnold. Some. But that would only be relevant if Bosko turned out to be the hacker.

Arnold heard the words, "Hey, Gary," from Mr. Fisher's phone.

Fisher raised the push-to-talk cellular to his ear.

"Go."

Arnold moved closer to him hoping to hear if the caller was John.

"Be advised one TracFone, two desktops, and one laptop are now secured. Also be advised that we have one extremely pissed-off suspect."

With a wry smile, Fisher responded with, "Roger that. Nice work."

Lowering his radio, he announced to the group, "We have the target's phone and computers in our possession. At this point we—meaning those of you in this room—play the waiting game." After a glance at his watch, he added, "I don't know about the rest of you, but I'm exhausted and in need of dinner and a Scotch. Don't expect any additional reports tonight. We'll probably know something by late morning. Good night, people."

With that, he started for the elevators in his brisk man-on-a-mission stride.

Arnold caught up with him as he was pressing the elevator call button.

"Will you call me soon as you know anything?"

"You look worried, Gold. I thought you were positive that was

Bosko on the call."

Prisha joined them just as Arnold shrugged and said, "Are you kidding? With the voice distorted like that?"

An elevator arrived. Arnold stepped into the cage along with Fisher and Prisha. He turned to Prisha: "You down for dinner or you want to get back home?"

"Don't fuck with me, Gold," Fisher said, following him in. "How certain are you?"

Arnold thumbed the button for the lobby.

"Pretty sure."

He then raised questioning eyebrows at Prisha as if to say, *I'm waiting for your answer.*

She nodded. "I'm in no rush to deal with husband at the moment, so dinner sounds like a great idea. I can't remember the last time I ate, so now that I think about it, I'm famished! What'd ya have in mind?"

"Answer me, Gold."

Arnold asked Prisha, "Does Vietnamese sound good?"

She grinned.

"I never turn down Vietnamese. What are you thinking?"

To Fisher, Arnold said, "Pretty sure." Then to Prisha. "Ever eaten over at Monsoon? The place up on Capitol Hill?"

She gave an emphatic headshake. "Nope."

They were lucky enough to score a table without a reservation. Even luckier to be seated in the bar area where, for some reason, the acoustics allowed for easy conversation without having to shout like they would have at some of the other restaurants Arnold liked.

"How about a cocktail?" Arnold asked, completely out of character for the wine dude.

But the relief of having hit the end of the road with this case seemed to call for a celebration. Even if they had no idea what evidence might or might not be found on Bosko's laptop. Now, one way or another, they were finished with this hot potato.

Prisha seemed to debate the answer for a couple beats before saying, "Sure, why the hell not?"

A moment later a server materialized and asked, "May I get you folks started with something to drink?"

Arnold nodded for Prisha to order.

Flashing her signature white-teeth smile, she said, "I'll have a Verspetine." A gussied-up martini made with botanist gin, cardamon, and Chinese green tea-infused vodka, Norden's aquavit, letterpress limoncello, and dolce bordeau blanc.

Sounded like it would fit the bill for him too, sooo…

"Make that two," Arnold said, handing the waitress their cocktail menus.

"Would you like me to get a food order started now or wait?"

With a heavy note of weariness in her voice, Prisha said to Arnold, "Since you've eaten here, why not just order what you like."

"Not a problem. That makes it easy." Handing both menus to the waitress, he said, "We'll have the green papaya salad and drunken chicken. But let us enjoy our drinks for a moment before you put in the order."

"Any rice?"

Arnold raised his eyebrows at Prisha.

"Not for me," she replied. "I'm laying off carbs for now."

"No rice," he confirmed to the waitress.

Arnold floated in a relaxed comfortable silence, feeling no urgency to make conversation at the moment. Yet he worried about what Prisha must be going through with Vihaan. If she needed to talk about it, fine, but he wouldn't ask.

Then again, he should at least let her know he was open to discussing it if she wanted.

"I'm sorry about your domestic problems. If you feel like talking about it, I'm here to listen."

"No, not really, and that bothers me." Pause. "Bothers me a lot, in fact. I mean, what does that say about me? That I'm giving up on our marriage?" She shook her head. "I can't believe he actually gave me an ultimatum. Does he really expect me to walk away from a job I love, especially under these circumstances?"

Since the questions sounded suspiciously rhetorical, Arnold

didn't answer.

Their drinks arrived, so any pressure he felt to respond was overshadowed by the need to take their first sip.

Prisha immediately exclaimed, "My, my, my, pretty damn good. I better watch it, or it'll go down in a blink and then I'll want another, and I'm driving."

Carefully setting his drink back on the table, Arnold smacked his lips.

"Wowzah! Totally agree."

"Long as we're talking relationships," Prisha said, "how're things between you and Noriko?"

Arnold blew a long sigh before answering.

"Good question. One I've been wrestling with since I began to seriously consider declaring this as my primary residence again. She's the only real glitch in an otherwise easy decision."

Prisha seemed to roll his answer around for a moment before saying, "Know what? That sounds totally wishy-washy." She appeared to reappraise her words, then amended them with, "Which is a major point. If you know what I mean."

Bingo.

"Oh man, you just verbalized a thought that I've sort of known but haven't admitted to myself."

After another moment of silence she asked, "What's the issue? After that last pen-test, when we were over there, you guys seemed to be totally into each other."

After another sip of his cocktail, Arnold nodded.

"We were. Then."

"But?"

"Man, that's a tough one." He held up an index finger. "Give me a moment."

He struggled with how to verbalize a vaporous feeling.

"The best way to describe it," he said, "is she's getting too clingy."

"Clingy..." Prisha repeated, letting the word die under its own weight. A moment later: "And you're not comfortable with that?"

"When it interferes with my work, I'm not."

He went on to describe the numerous disruptive phone calls this past week after asking her not to call.

When he wrapped up, she took a moment before commenting, "Looks like we each have problematic relationships to grapple with." Pause. "Any idea which way you're leaning? I mean about making this home base?"

Just then their green papaya salad arrived.

CHAPTER 34

BACK PROPPED AGAINST the kitchen counter, tumbler of wine in hand, Arnold considered the weighty decisions he was being forced to confront. Declare this home as his primary residence? Shell out the coin for a Tesla 3? What would John Chang find on Bosko's devices? What to do about Noriko? How to get Vihaan to leave the team if he decided to not run back to Long Island? Which, in view of tonight's dinner conversation, seemed increasingly likely. Continuing to lurk in the background of all this mental noise was his unrelenting attraction to Kara. The Forbidden Fruit.

Chance trotted in from the back yard to stand next to him. Arnold set his wine glass on the stainless-steel counter and crouched down to give him a dose of choobers. The thing about a pooch was their unconditional love. Ultimatum? What's an ultimatum? Doggies don't hand out ultimatums.

Scratching Chance behind the ears, he said, "Good boy. Chance is a good boy."

Chance responded with vigorous tail-wagging.

With a sigh, Arnold locked the French door, then asked Alexa to turn off the kitchen lights in a minute. Wine tumbler in hand, he headed up to the second floor with the intent of enjoying his nightcap while reading the new Michael Connelly novel. Perhaps the wine and mental distraction would suffocate his anxiety over whether Boskso and Hacker were the same person.

James Brown woke Arnold a few minutes after eight. Squinting at the phone, he saw John Chang's name.

He swung his legs over the edge of the bed to take the call sitting up. Then, after clearing his throat, swiped ACCEPT.

"Hey dude, what do you have for me?" he asked with a strange brew of dread and excitement. But regardless of however the report came back, good or bad, he was already massively relieved to have this job from hell end. Now he could move on to other work. Especially with so many other issues in play.

"You really put all your money on one horse to win, didn't you," Chang stated flatly.

Uh-oh…he didn't like Chang's tone.

When Arnold didn't answer, Chang said, "Well, guess what?"

Again, without a hint of what was coming.

"What?"

"No, I asked you to guess. That didn't sound like a guess to me. That sounded like another question."

"Come on, dude. Don't mess with me on this one."

He heard Chang blow a resigned breath. His heart sank.

After clearing his throat, FBI Special Agent John Chang said, with a distinct note of regret, "It's not good news, bro…"

Arnold's heart sank further.

"…for dear old Alfred, that is." Chang chortled. "It's all there: the serial numbers, patient names, everything. We got him dead to rights."

Arnold exhaled a massive sigh of relief.

"Jesus, John, you almost gave me a freaking heart attack."

"Hold on, I have someone here who wants to add a few words."

Arnold heard the phone being handled, then Agent Fisher's familiar voice saying, "You got very lucky, Gold. Extremely lucky indeed. That was a brass-balls move of yours, being so sure when you had so little real evidence to back you up."

Allen Wyler

"Have you told Mr. Harris the good news yet?"

"Not yet. We wanted you to be the first to know. Since it was your ass hanging out in that freezing-cold breeze."

Although he hadn't come close to paying off his sleep deficit, nodding off again would be impossible. Still perched on the edge of the bed, he tapped his phone against his other palm.

Call Prisha with the good news?

Naw, let her sleep. She needs it.

Instead, he took a refreshing shower, then wandered down to the kitchen to let Chance into the backyard to sample the neighborhood scents and take care of business while he started a fresh pot of coffee brewing.

He dropped into the chair in front of the laptop, brought up the Tesla site again, and scrolled through the various Model 3 options one by one. By the time he finished, his coffee was ready.

Hmmm, what to have for breakfast? Peanut-butter toast?

Yeah, that'd work. After putting a slice of Ezekiel bread into the toaster oven, he went back to the computer to scan the headlines of the *New York Times*.

Toast and coffee consumed, he decided it was late enough to call Prisha with the good news.

She picked up with, "Any word yet?"

"Yep. John Chang called earlier with good news. All the evidence was on Bosko's laptop. Serial numbers, everything. We were right. Bosko was our hacker."

"Holy shit! Congratulations. We need to celebrate."

Arnold flashed on the plan he'd been working on. The perfect opportunity.

"Great idea. Let me see if I can nail down a reservation at Maximilien for tonight. What do you think? It that place okay for a celebration?"

Without hesitation: "Wow, what a fantastic idea."

"Good. Check with Vihaan, see if he'll come too At least he won't be able to complain that this is one of those shit jobs he's always assigned."

"Just a second, I'll ask."

He heard her call to Vihaan but couldn't hear his answer. A moment later she was back with, "Yeah, he's in."

"Cool. I check on the reservations and then see if Lopez and Kara can join us."

"Uh, Kara? Why Kara?"

Took Arnold a moment to drum up a sellable excuse.

"Well, because she's sort of an honorary member of the team by now, seeing how she helped us out with identifying Bosko." Then added, "And the pen-test before that." Just to buttress his case.

"Dunno dude, sounds like a bit of a stretch. But hell, whatever." Then, after a brief pause, "Want us to pick you up?"

"Naw. Thanks, but I'm going to work on getting more familiar with the bus routes around here."

At least for the trip downtown. If Kara drove to work, he intended to ask her for a ride home. And if she didn't have her car, he planned to offer to share his Uber since her place was pretty much *en route* from downtown to his home.

Call finished, Arnold jumped on the restaurant website and made a reservation for five, then poured another cup of black coffee.

Back at the computer, he started to revise the Gold and Associates website. Just as he was putting the final additions on it, James Brown started in.

Noriko.

Picking up the phone, he looked at her name for a long moment. *Oh, man...*

Inhaling deeply, he steeled himself for the ensuing conversation, then, "Hey there. Good morning."

"Good morning, Arnold."

Arnold? Since their first dinner months ago at Taormina, she'd seldom used his given name.

"What up?" he asked innocently, despite having a fairly good idea what the impending subject matter was about.

"How did it go yesterday?"

"Do you mean, did we fulfill our objective?" he asked, remaining super-careful to not disclose anything even remotely confidential about Cor-Pace or the case. Yeah, sure, she had no connection with the medical device company, but he made a point of diligently keeping confidential business confidential. That's why it was called confidential. Besides, Gold and Associates had a reputation to maintain.

"Arnold, what I'm asking is, is the job now finished?"

Yeah, I knew that. Why continue to dodge the inevitable?

"We're still wrapping up a few loose ends, but yes, essentially we're done."

Oh bullshit. You finished last night.

"Okay, so when will you be coming back?"

And there it was.

In the next instant he was no longer sitting on the fence. His decision was made.

"I have no idea, Noriko. I have a ton of things I'm working on."

There! It was said.

Well, sort of. Not all of it. She deserved to know.

"Like what?" she asked with a hint of defiance. As if still paranoid about Rachael.

The tone of her question cemented the clarity he'd been seeking; giving him the certitude that "they" were ended. The realization saddened him. Deeply. He still cared about her, but...

"Well, for starters, I just ordered a Tesla 3 for this place." He cringed at the lie. But pushing the purchase button on the Tesla site would be the first thing he would do after wrapping up this call. Or would he? "So I need to wait for it to arrive from the factory."

Well, that last part was a lie since he was still undecided about the car. But he was truthful about where he would live full-time now.

"And then what?"

And that did it. He couldn't bob and weave any longer. It was time to step up and be truthful. As painful as that would be.

He took a deep breath, then said, "Look, Noriko, I've told you before, Seattle is where our big jobs happen."

"What's that mean exactly?" she asked in a voice that was growing smaller. As if she knew what was coming but didn't want to actually hear it.

"That means I'll be living here for the foreseeable future." Then added, "But I plan on coming back to the island now and then."

He winced at how lame that sounded.

The ensuing silence saddened him even more. Noriko was a very warm intelligent person of high integrity. In some ways, even sweet. Of all the personality traits people can have, he valued integrity the most. But in truth, their relationship was tapped out. There was no denying that. Still, the most salient factor that dominated the decision was that Seattle was home to Gold and Associates. It only made sense for this to be his primary residence.

"But what about *us*?"

"Look, Noriko, I really like you. I like being with you. But I have a company to manage and we're facing some serious internal problems that I can't possibly deal with from Honolulu. Don't forget, I have a home there too, so I will be back now and then."

A meaningless statement, he realized, given the present circumstances.

"You're a small business owner," he added, "so you should understand this. If presented with the same conundrum, I think you'd make the same decision."

In fact, according to her, the reason for breaking her engagement was exactly that. She'd chosen her real-estate career over marriage.

"In other words, you're dumping me."

CHAPTER 35

THAT AFTERNOON ARNOLD decided to continue relearning the Metro bus routes because even after he'd shipped his Mini here from Honolulu, he would use the bus for most commutes to and from downtown.

After all, not only were downtown parking lots becoming an extinct species, but those that were available were growing astronomically expensive. As for on-the-street parking? Forget it. Tonight, for example, he planned to bus into town to go to the restaurant. His method of returning home would depend on how the evening progressed, but certainly it wouldn't include riding a bus.

He spent several minutes on the Metro website planning his trip. Although some other bus routes had stops closer to home, those lines were neither as direct nor as fast as the E-Line RapidRide. The downside, of course, was that the RapidRide stop was further away. That walk was, however, not a problem. Especially in reasonable weather like today.

After taking Chance for a stroll through the neighborhood, he decided that it was nice enough for him to spend the evening in the backyard, so moved his water dish and bed onto the deck on the other side of the French doors. With the pooch taken care of, he made one final check in the mirror before heading out the front door for the walk to the RapidRide stop. He was decked out with a new pair of dark blue jeans, a burnt-orange mock tee, and a black leather jacket. His dress-up celebration clothes.

Arnold stepped off the bus at Third and Pike, just a few blocks from the iconic main entrance to Pike Place Market. After running the ever-present gauntlet of panhandlers, druggies, tourists, and randomly abandoned Lime scooters, he made it into the market to work his way back into the southwest corner where Maximilien's was tucked away at the end of an interestingly angled hall. Although he was early, the maitre'd seated him at a table for four in the main dining room, since there were no tables in the balcony area he'd wanted. Unfortunately, Lopez had to decline the last-minute invitation because of a prior engagement. Kara arrived next, having walked the handful of blocks from work. Looking good as ever in a very professional business suit and signature pixie smile. A few minutes later Vihaan and Prisha trudged in, appearing none too happy with each other.

Once they were all seated and chatting, the waiter appeared at their table.

"May I start anyone off with a drink?"

Before anyone else could respond, Arnold suggested, "Since this is a special celebration, let's share a bottle of champagne. Everyone okay with that?"

"I'm in," Kara said without hesitation.

Prisha said, "Me too."

Shaking his head, Vihaan said, "I'm good with water."

Arnold smiled at the waiter and said, "A bottle of the Piper-Heidsieck, please."

"Excellent selection, monsieur," the waiter said before promptly disappearing from view.

"What are we celebrating?" Kara asked.

Prisha and Arnold exchanged glances, silently agreeing to not divulge anything about the case other than what she already knew.

Arnold spread his napkin over his lap while answering, "We just wrapped up the Bosko thing you helped us on. The team did a great

Allen Wyler

job. Just too bad Lopez and Ito can't be here to help celebrate."

Two waiters materialized tableside, one with four champagne flutes, the other with an ice bucket, the accompanying stand, and the bottle of bubbly. When the three drinkers had glasses of effervescent wine in hand, Arnold announced, "Before we make a toast, there's one more item we need to celebrate. And it's ginormous."

He paused, drawing out the suspense, all eyes on him now.

"This afternoon I made two significant changes to our website that I think you'll want to look at before we toast."

Out came the phones, followed by the flashing of thumbs.

A moment later a wide-eyed Prisha looked up at Arnold.

"For *real*?"

"Not only that, but did you notice I removed any mention of a Honolulu office? I ran it by Ito and he's actually ultra-chill with it. Even sounded a bit relieved."

"Thank you!"

Prisha pushed out of her chair and rushed over to give Arnold a big hug.

Smiling at her phone, Kara said, "Congratulations, Prisha! My, my, Gold, Patel, and Associates. I love the new name."

Without a word, Vihaan pushed back his chair, stood, and stormed from the restaurant.

ACKNOWLEDGEMENTS

JT Gaietto, CISSP, ISCFE, TPN. Principal, Chief of Staff

Jonathan Butts, Ph.D. Co-Founder of QED Secure Solutions

www.ingramcontent.com/pod-product-compliance
Lightning Source LLC
LaVergne TN
LVHW091951270625
814890LV00002B/483